Inch Levels

NEIL HEGARTY was born in Derry and studied English at Trinity College Dublin, receiving his PhD in 1998. He is the author of the authorized biography of David Frost and of *The Story of Ireland*. This is his first novel.

Inch Levels

NEIL HEGARTY

HEAD
of ZEUS

First published in the UK in 2016 by Head of Zeus Ltd

This paperback edition first published in the UK in 2017
by Head of Zeus Ltd

975312468

A CIP catalogue record for this book is available
from the British Library.

ISBN (PB): 9781784975807
ISBN (E): 9781784975777

Printed and bound by CPI Group (UK) Ltd,
Croydon, CR0 4YYH

Head of Zeus Ltd
First Floor East
5–8 Hardwick Street
London EC1R 4RG

WWW.HEADOFZEUS.COM

Inch Levels

For my mother and father,
and for John

1983

TIME TO KILL

September, and the Donegal countryside had already turned to autumn. The summer just past had been warm and wet, and the hedgerows and verges had become heavy with growth. But the grasses were fading and bleaching with the season: and now, late in the afternoon, they were bowed, soaked and dripping with a day's rain. In the ditch, a stream gurgled on its way downhill towards the lough. The rain, though, had lately stopped and the sky was clearing from the west: a pale, clean blue and the air cool and fresh.

And there was Christine Casey, aged eight, cycling home slowly from school.

There was no hurry this evening. Dinner would be a little later than usual: her mum had a meeting to go to in town. So Christine was cycling slowly.

Patrick Jackson saw all this. He watched the scene unfold from behind closed eyelids. Today, a weakening autumn sun was shining through the window onto his bed, onto the sky-blue counterpane, onto hard, white walls, onto his loose skin and prominent cheekbones. It shone onto the translucent skin on his eyelids, and turned his vision into a screen, a wash of dusty pink. But in his mind the scene was harshly lit and immediate: and he was following the girl along the lane that was dim and dripping and shaggy with a summer's growth.

As if he was tracking her, snuffling along in her wake. He had done it so many times by now: following her track, the lane, the soaking hedges and gurgling ditches, aware of the fragrant air, the sinking sun, the gradually diminishing light.

Patrick watched. He knew the way this would turn out. There was only one way.

He kept his eyelids closed tightly, as the autumn sunlight tracked slowly along the walls.

He knew that the child's bicycle was found minutes after she was taken – there, in the wet ditch in the shadow of the hawthorn hedge. Not by her mother, or by her father, but by the farmer who worked the fields on either side of the lane, the farmer who hadn't been doing his job properly on the hedging and ditching front. The farmer who saw her bicycle as he passed along slowly, saw its front wheel gleaming, prominent in the midst of the grasses, in that dusky lane.

This farmer stopped to look around the ditch, filled with a summer of growth and with detritus, with litter and aluminium cans, with water flowing. He looked around. The hawthorn, with its thorns and heavy bundles of red berries, caught and tangled in his hair and lifted the tweed cap off his head. He looked, and an instinct bawled at him to leave this place and get to a telephone: he snatched his cap and ran.

2

His words were reported faithfully the following day, by the newspapers eager to seize on anything that passed for news. Later, Patrick – in the newspaper archives at the Central Library – read these reports and brought them terribly to life. He committed them to memory.

Additional details.

They missed at first a number of other items. They didn't find her schoolbag, for example, until later that same evening. Quite late – after ten o'clock, when the autumn darkness had long since settled in the lane. But a gibbous moon was sailing in the frosty sky and casting a slick of white light on the waters of the lough: and it was just about bright enough for her father, her uncles, a few local men to fan out, to keep looking, to check the fields. The women – the mother and her two older daughters; the house filling slowly as news spread – waited at home. The lane had been scoured earlier in the evening – but her father took it into his head to look again, to really search. It grew darker as he walked along slowly: at points, the hawthorn hedges almost met, creating a rustling ceiling of twigs and branches.

The man had a switch in his hand – an old walking stick that had once belonged to his father-in-law, smooth, long, polished – and he stabbed and swished at the hedgerow and the wet grass as he went. In this way he found his daughter's schoolbag: she had not, it seemed, fastened the buckles, because a mathematics textbook was lying in the hedgerow, a furry-paged yellow jotter, a biro, a long pencil, its end chewed and bitten.

Of Christine herself, of course, no sign.

3

The police arrived and the lane was sealed. Early the following morning, specially trained officers arrived – but in fact there was little or nothing by way of evidence to be gleaned: no trampled greenery, no broken twigs, no indications or clues at all. No footprints, no tyre marks. Neither did the abundance of lemonade bottles, crisp packets and plastic bags lodged in the hawthorn hedges hold clues: this rubbish had evidently been there for some time. There was nothing at all, in fact, to indicate how the girl had been snatched.

Snatched? That she was snatched seemed more and more evident. The police knew from experience that this child was most likely dead already; soon, everyone knew it. Such crimes: they hardly ever happened; they were all about opportunity when they did. Now the parents must be told that there was a very good chance the girl, or her body, would never be found. They were told to brace themselves.

All this Patrick knew. All this had been in the papers: voluminous accounts, details, lists and facts. Every last detail shivered in his mind.

Later, after five days, another thing happened. A pair of dog walkers took their favourite walk – the walk they took when they had a little time, as they did on this Saturday morning. They parked in the car park in the middle of Inch Levels, where a footpath set off east and west in the shadow of the sea wall, straight across the flat fields.

And Patrick could picture this scene too. He had visited, treading in the footsteps of these walkers: the season had moved to winter by the time of his visit, but he could imagine the

September colours they had experienced, the falling leaves, the berries and the light. They had turned west, these walkers, towards the shore of Lough Swilly, a mile or so distant, towards Inch Island and the gaunt silhouette of the castle on its spit of dry land above the water. There were mute swans lying here on the sea, and white-fronted geese in the fields, digging into the black soil and ripping the grass out by the roots: hundreds, thousands of the creatures; and more would arrive as winter came on. It was a sight to behold.

Now, at the end of September, the hedges and overgrown slopes of the sea wall were dense with sloes and glossy rosehips and the last of the blackberries. These walkers had anticipated this: they had brought a plastic carton, to fill with berries on the way back. Now they walked, an energetic couple, and their portly old golden Labrador nosing and sniffing and waving her tail a few steps ahead of them; and the path stretched ribbon-straight under their feet and the causeway marched to their right. This was reclaimed land, but saturated with water after this wet summer, threaded with brimming ditches and little rivers flowing towards the lough.

And there was the brick-built pumping station, surrounded by young birch and ash and humming to itself.

'Listen to it! – and winter not even here yet. Imagine if it failed,' the husband said to his wife. She laughed.

'It won't fail while we're here.'

They walked on.

'What did you see?' the papers asked them later.

They saw the blue hills to west and east and south; and

the smoothly rounded summit of Inch Island to the north. At length the lough spreading out before them and the end of their path, a few picnic tables and the low wall of the causeway across to the island; a gravelled access road, flat, green fields and shining water on which swans floated. They might have walked further: the path along the causeway to the island and the castle and back: another couple of hours, all told. But the Labrador was fat and lazy: and instead of walking further, they intended to drink their tea and eat their sandwiches here at the edge of the lough, before retracing their path back to the car. They shed their anoraks, then, and sat down with a grateful exhalation; what a mild day. The man opened the foil packet of sandwiches and called the dog, intending to feed her bits and scraps, but she was nosing by the water and ignored him.

Eventually he hauled himself up and walked across the gravel to the water.

'What did you see?'

Still clothed, and sodden of course, and simply floating there; bereft, naturally, of much humanity, hardly a shred of it, now.

'That was almost the worst thing,' he said.

That was what they would carry with them, they said, the pity and the pathos of the sight. She was not to be touched: they knew this; they knew the score. And what to do next? To stay, to go? To have one keep watch over this bundle, while the other runs, pants, stumbles back along the straight path to the car, then drives the twenty minutes to Buncrana and bring help? Who should stay and who should go? In the end, the woman stayed, with the Labrador as doubtful support should something go wrong; and the man rushed away on his mission.

Later, the woman described the brief period – this forty-five minutes or so, not very long at all, considering what a lonely spot this was – during which she waited with her dog for the police to arrive. *What do I do?* she thought. *What does someone do under such circumstances?* Keep the dog away from the water's edge, of course: but that was easily managed; she put the beast on the lead. Go to the water's edge herself? No, on balance: she had imagined herself as having a stout constitution, but this was a situation, a sight, quite outside her experience; and the tears were, besides, already pouring down her cheeks. Not much good stepping any closer.

So she stayed put, watched the path anxiously, listening for the sound of a car, of footsteps. Her senses, she said, seemed heightened: the air smelled and tasted of the moist greenness of this landscape, of brackish water; she heard a swan honk and another swan answer, their cries travelling towards her over the surface of the water; in the distance the pumping station hummed ceaselessly, maintaining the delicate balance between land and sea, drawing away the water that would otherwise seep in and drown this place. Out on the lough, she saw another bird: it dived and, after two or three minutes, came to the surface; the water rippled with its activity. She felt – shock, certainly, but also shame at being unable to do anything for the child floating in the lough, unable to assist in scrabbling, clawing back a little dignity and humanity *in extremis*. The woman sat, instead, and listened and gazed out across the water.

The news travelled fast, breaking within minutes against the walls of that neat bungalow on the crest of the hill where a collection of lives already lay in shards. They had found her, in the water at Inch Levels. This family knew, already, that Christine would not be coming back: but such knowledge was neither here nor there, not when – later that day – the pitiless facts were set out.

There was an assumption made, silently, that this was one of those crimes that would never be solved. It seemed highly accomplished or at least flawlessly executed: tracks covered and dust kicked; no traces left at all. Someone might have seen a blue car – but the blue car came to nothing. He – the man, whoever he was – may have done it before, somewhere else; he may have been practiced – these were the thoughts that did the rounds. Besides, the abundance of one kind of crime in this neck of the woods meant that other crimes – normal crimes, the police said to each other, although not to the parents – tended to be overlooked. Little chance – no chance, they said privately – of an arrest.

The chatter faded fast. The colour photograph of the girl that had been circulated to the media was of good quality. Patrick remembered the photograph, remembered how Christine was smiling a beaming smile – but this in the long run made little difference. The family was articulate – but this made little difference too. The case was remembered, talked of – but there were so many others, so many other crimes, so many other examples of depraved human behaviour, of sin and of grief, that this crime became but one on a list. He remembered all this.

What else? Here, facts faded a little and suppositions took their place, though these were easy enough to imagine. Those left behind made an attempt to find their way through it. Some of them knew they could rely on each other; some of them found they could not. For some of them, love and a kind of mutuality would, they were determined, see them through, and so would a will to honour the memory of this girl, this daughter and sister – even if the newspapers had been quick to pull up sticks and move on. Yes: they would make their way through it, some of them. Christine's family could no longer use the lane in which the schoolbag had been found: not ever again, meaning a longer drive, the long way round, into the town; this was one of the facts with which they were obliged to live. Another: the pills shoved in large quantities at various members of the family by well-meaning general practitioners; another was the insomnia. But they made their way through it, some of them. Other families had done so in the past; other families would have to do so in the future. There was nothing else to be done. So they said.

Suppositions, yes – but easily imagined.

Then, on a cold Friday afternoon in late October – the season already definitively over, the town beginning to close down for the approaching winter – Christine's mother made her way down from the crest of the hill, into the town, over the rocks beside the pier and into the water. Nobody was there on hand to see her: nobody loitering on the pier on such an evening, with the light fading and a sharp wind blowing from the north-east and rippling the waves into chill, white crests.

When she was spotted, minutes later, it was already too late:
the ripping circular current that runs offshore here, that sucks
water in from the open Atlantic, through the narrow mouth of
Lough Foyle and out again – it caught her quickly, as she had
known it would and it took her.

Still, they managed to recover her body before night quite
closed in. And that at least, they said – later, at the wake, over
the nips of whiskey and the cups of tea and the ham sandwiches
– that was a blessing.

Probably this kind of thing was said. Patrick had been to
many wakes; he knew the standard patter.

Now he lay stretched flat, in his high hospital bed, under
his blue standard-issue NHS counterpane. Encyclopaedic
knowledge, forensic detail. Yes: because he had made a point of
gathering all the detail he could. The sun had left the room, now,
and the pink screen of his eyelids was replaced by a dull yellow.
Someone had flicked on the overhead light: a few moments
ago, when he was lost in his reverie. And he knew who had
flicked the switch.

He opened his eyes, looked along the length of his body
towards the base of the bed. Not left and not right.

'Hello, Patrick.'

There was Robert, sitting very upright in the dark hospital
armchair to the right of the bed. There he was. Patrick swung
his head a little to the right. There he was.

'Hello. How are you feeling today?'

ONE

Patrick opened his eyes. He was dying, and as if this wasn't enough, now there he was: the unwelcome visitor lounging in the high-backed standard-issue armchair by his bed.

No avoiding such visitors, of course. They were par for the course in this kind of environment, appearing at the door with dreary regularity, slung about with the inevitable grapes and chocolates. He'd said to the nurse, 'Don't people have any imagination?' She smiled, smoothed the blue coverlet on the bed.

Sometimes the grapes came straight from the supermarket shelf, unwashed. He could tell.

And the visitors had not been slow in beating a path to his door. News travelled fast in a city this size, and bad news at the speed of light: and he was hardly through the door, he thought, hardly settled in his baby-blue bed before the faces began appearing, eager noses and avid eyes against the glass.

No avoiding this. And besides, the clock was counting down the days and hours and minutes remaining: people were entitled to feel that they hadn't a moment to waste, were entitled to be on the bustle. In his brighter moments, he could make this concession.

There actually was a digital clock beside the bed, its poison-green numerals flicking the time onwards silently, relentlessly.

'Digital! Imagine: fancy pants,' murmured his sister, Margaret, as she settled him on that first evening. His ward was on the eighth floor, with a sweep of darkening countryside visible outside his window. A book or two, a *Guardian* and his dented old transistor radio, all set out neatly on top of the bedside locker; pungent lilies, all veins and nodding stamens, unwrapped from their clear plastic shroud and plunged into a glass vase on the windowsill.

'Bad taste, if you ask me.' Their mother had contributed the digital clock. Now, Margaret looked again at it, tilted her head to the right, pursed her lips, considered.

'I don't know,' she said. 'Better than one of those egg timer things, what are they called? You know, the sands of time. Imagine if they had one of those, instead, sitting on the window sill, looking at you.' She too smoothed the bedspread. 'You'd be entitled then, to talk about bad taste.'

Patrick closed his eyes. Well, his family had a good line in mordancy, after all. It was their natural terrain.

'I think you can probably go now,' he said after another few minutes. 'I'm settled and besides, I should try and sleep. I mean, if sleep is even possible in a place like this.'

Margaret said, 'Really?' She looked around. She had been there all of ten minutes. Outside, gulls were wheeling and crying; they had been blown inland in the stiffening wind. A visiting family clipped and squeaked along the corridor outside. A child's voice rose, clear and questioning, above the murmuring background noise. He watched Margaret listen, watched her shoulders stiffen and rise a little inside her sensible cardigan.

'Really, yes.' Now he closed his eyes. 'I know you'd like to get up a game of Scrabble among the patients, and that's very kind of you. But you know, this *is* a hospital; and besides, Robert'll be expecting you.'

Sticks and stones may break my bones, but words will never hurt me: well, and how many times had he proved *that* one wrong, over the last few years. He watched her flinch, as though struck, watched her retreat.

And it paid her back for the egg timer, too.

Margaret paused at the door.

'Ma will hardly come in tonight, will she? Too late now, probably.'

'Let's hope it's too late.'

As Margaret opened the door, he said, 'Thank you for the flowers.'

She paused. 'I should've snipped off the pollen heads,' she said. 'We don't want them staining.'

She left, and he waited a few minutes and then pressed the bell. A nurse appeared.

'Will you take those flowers away, please? Give them to someone else?'

'Someone else?' the nurse said, frowning.

'Not fond of lilies.' He gestured with a fingertip at the vase. 'Please. Let someone else enjoy them.'

The nurse pursed her lips, bore away the glass vase, the lurid flowers.

That had been then. And now, a day or two or three later (for time passed strangely in this place), there was the latest unwelcome visitor. There was Robert himself, all long arms and legs in the armchair.

'No Margaret today?'

'Couldn't come,' Robert said. 'So I said I'd pop in instead.' He was tall, lean; his cheekbones stood out in a gaunt face.

They might have been brothers, the two of them. They might both have been sick.

Patrick looked at those cheekbones, looked at the shadows under the eyes and the skin stretched tight over his brother-in-law's skull. Thinner than ever, now. He thought: which one of us has the cancer? If I wasn't lying here in this bed, you'd hardly know.

'Oh, "pop", is it? Pop in. Good of you,' Patrick said.

After a moment, Robert got up and went to the window, looking out at the view, the broad grounds of the place. The hospital had been built in the 1950s, a hulking block twelve storeys high on the crest of a hill: it faced into every wind that blew, and could be seen twenty miles away. To the west, the city opened up, ridge after ridge, with the Donegal hills a blue backdrop in the furthest distance. A grammar school edged the hospital grounds to the south: Patrick's old school, where he had been a pupil and where he had for several

14

years taught; for too many years his alma mater. This was an unfortunate juxtaposition, everyone agreed. The hospital mortuary edged into the school grounds. It was a pity to have so much death in close proximity to a mass of schoolboys, besides which, the sound of the school bell, tolling regularly, mournfully in the school's handsome copper-topped belfry was much too funereal for some nerves to withstand. Very unfortunate; poor planning, to be sure. Nothing much to be done about it now.

Robert looked out at the view for a while and then said, 'Nice, isn't it?'

Patrick said nothing.

'Very nice.'

Silence fell. At last, Patrick broke it.

'One positive thing, you know, about my situation.'

'What's that?' said Robert, still looking out at the hills, the views.

'It concentrates the mind. You think: "well, at least I don't have to put up with certain things any longer". You know, tick tock, and all that.'

There was a little pause.

'Tick tock,' said Robert. 'Sure.'

'So we don't need to go through certain pleasantries, is my point.'

'Sure,' Robert said again. 'Meaning –'

'Meaning you don't need to come again. If I'm going to be knock knock knocking on Heaven's door, I'd sooner be selective about who sees me off, if you get my drift.'

It seemed that Robert did. Their mutual disregard, their mutual dislike, had been absolute from the moment they met. No, since *before* they had met. And it was oddly liberating: both were aware that they could say just about anything to each other; that little was out of bounds – even now.

Still, Robert felt compelled to make some sort of gimcrack effort. 'I'd have thought –'

'And I'd have thought,' Patrick interrupted, his eyes closed, 'that you'd be content, social niceties not after all being your strong suit.'

That settled it: Robert was soon bundled into his coat.

'I'll tell Margaret to drop in tomorrow,' he said.

'Don't.'

A pause, a turn at the door. A hesitation, Patrick saw, as though his visitor were about to say something else, something unexpected. And then a change of mind: and instead, one last parting shot. 'What about your mother? She'll be in soon, I'm sure.'

Patrick kept his eyes shut tightly. 'Ma will please herself, as she always has done. Off you go now.' He kept his eyes closed until the door had opened and then shut with its thin wheeze. Then he closed his eyes very tightly, as though in sudden pain. In the distance, the bell began to toll.

TWO

Patrick lay, stretched on the bed.

Better, always, to think of the past.

This was one lesson he had learned in this month of steadily increasing pain. Even with all its darkness, the past was better. It was over and done with. It was better than a present that was threaded with pain, with regret and guilt.

He remembered a steep, ocean-facing hillside on the northern coast of Ireland.

Long ago: twenty-five years and more ago. The colours, sights, smells, the wide landscape: all were vivid in his mind. He was clear about what he was doing: this was a time of grace, at least for him. A time when their lives were, or seemed to be, intact.

This landscape was a palette of greens, changing with height into the deeper green-brown of bracken, purple of heather, hard silver glint of scree-strewn slopes. Sheep roamed on the upper slopes; and a few tethered goats grazed the rough grass. The lower fields were terraced, some of them, moulded onto the contours of the land – and the potatoes were already up on the west-facing slopes, line after neat line: the soil was dry, crumbling, after days of sunshine and steady southerly winds. Here and there arable fields shone with the fresh, luminous green of early summer, with a dense carpet of white clover, with spangled buttercups behind hawthorn hedges that still held a remnant of pale blossom. Red cows grazed; and away down there the land fell into a glen, along the bottom of which a peat-black stream rushed towards the sea. A few yellow whin blossoms still clung to the bushes, throwing out their languorous, incongruously tropical coconut scent.

These fields ran to the cliff edge: beyond stretched the Atlantic, calm, smooth, unwrinkled. The coconut scent of whin blossom faded out there on the edge of the land, to be replaced by a clean smell of salt, carried on the mild wind. A haze gathered on the blue horizon – and islands floated in the haze: a few doubtful, faint, domed shapes in the warming air. To the left and right the coast swung away, all black gnarls of rock and white foaming waves, and a scattering of offshore skerries and islets, their tips stained a little with guano. And there were the gulls that take refuge on such places: there on the wind, with black-streaked heads and black legs; and cormorants and fulmars, wheeling silently in the blue sky, or perched on crag and rock, or sitting peaceably on the surface of the sea itself.

Yes: this was better. Patrick felt his thin body relaxing a little under the blue coverlet. This was better, this was a comfort.

And the light. The light was not cool as was customary in such high latitudes, but luminous on this day, radiant, pressing: light welled from the sky and broke from the sea; and started in fine, silver, infinitesimal lines and needles from each individual blade of grass waving and moving in these green fields.

Up here, up on the unfenced cliff edge, the ground fell quite steeply down to the sea. Here also was an unexpected hint of the tropics, for the long slopes of the hill were not bare rock but instead were dense with heavy vegetation: a dark bush landscape, suggestive of warmer climes; and the sand on the curving beach at the foot of the slope was brilliant white in the sunshine, and the sea shallows brilliant too, in a range of turquoises, azures, peacock blues. Offshore, the sea broke against the skerries, against a reef of black basalt rocks, which formed a natural breakwater; within this sketchy lagoon, the sea swelled softly, lazily.

Still early in the day: the sun in the sky suggesting eleven o'clock, perhaps; and only a handful of family parties on the beach. And new arrivals to the scene – five small figures walking there in the distance below, picked out against the white sand. A man and two women: and dressed in a way that suggested subtly, in hems and cuts and cardigans, another time. Their car, tucked in the sandy, rough little car park at the end of the beach, made this manifest: a Triumph, perhaps, or something of that sort, in solid, dark green, all curves and outsized headlights.

And with these adults came a pair of children: a boy, aged five or six, perhaps; a girl a year or two older. They dropped their sandals, they wriggled from clothes, they rushed for the water: the boy made it first, only to be pulled up sharply by – it must be – the frigidity of these northern seas. He waded in more slowly now, the girl behind him, then the boy seemed to take a breath – and went under. And now the girl plunged too, and the two children seemed to vanish for a few seconds. A head popped up, vanished again. Now the man, paddling in the shallows, waded a little further in: more splashing, and the children emerged from the water. Definitively emerged: waving arms, and angry gesticulations; and now a raised voice carried along the beach, floated up the slope, up, up here to the edge of the cliff.

The two women waiting on the sand watched. They sat and faced the sea, the pair of them, watching the dipping, the plunging, the gesticulations. One of them motionless; the other stretching her legs out into the sun, pushing her heels, her hands into the warm sand.

A family in early summer up on the northern fringes of Ireland. Dark figures, white sand, black rocks, silver light, green fields, purple heather and blue ocean.

The starkness of it all, silhouetted against the sea. Impressed on the landscape.

Impressed on his mind. Patrick woke.

The nurse – busy with a chart, with a pen – looked up to the head of the bed. 'Alright there, sweetheart?'

Patrick nodded his head, a very little.

'A dream. I was dreaming.'

'A nice dream, I hope.'

He flinched at her hearty tone. 'Remembering when I was a boy,' he said. 'With my sister. A trip to the beach we made.'

The nurse nodded knowledgeably. This was standard, she knew from her training. The patients tended to go back as the end drew near: to evaluate and shuffle memories, reassessing, considering.

'What beach was it?' she asked. It was always best to encourage them.

'Kinnagoe,' he murmured. 'The summer of –'

'– not all that long ago, then,' the nurse said.

'– 1960 or so, I suppose it was.'

'Kinnagoe: that's a nice spot,' said the nurse and left a pause, as she was trained to do, for him to fill. There was silence. 'And what happened in the dream?' she coaxed. 'Can you remember?'

He murmured, 'We were all there. My sister and me, and my parents and Cassie.'

'Cassie? Is that another sister?'

'No. Just someone who lived with us.'

The nurse waited.

'We were in the water. Diving to touch the sea bed.' He stopped.

'And –'

But – nothing now, suddenly: a slight shake of the head and eyes firmly closed; and after a few disappointed moments, she moved towards the door. A difficult patient, they'd already told her: didn't like to play the game. A squeak of shoes on the rubber floor and the door wheezed: and behind her, in the

21

bed, Patrick opened his eyes again. If it wanted to, it would resume. It was out of his hands.

Impressed on his mind: that was it. Like a tattoo, he thought: impressed on the skin, on his brain. He remembered that plunge into the freezing Atlantic – as if it was yesterday and not twenty-five, twenty-six years ago. His mind was humming along today: sorting, arranging, wrapping up, discarding, making sense of a life.

It was true: he had no say in the matter. The clifftop vantage point was a – what? A useful tool? Lying there in his bed, fogged by pain and medication, Patrick was able nevertheless to admire.

To admire – myself, he thought. This is my mind, he thought, my imagination. This is all my doing. Setting the scene: stretching a canvas. Blank, to begin with, a *tabula rasa* to begin with – but already peopled, already filled in a little: a background, a few colours tested here and there. This is not bad, he thought. I wish she hadn't gone, he thought – the nurse, I wish I hadn't chased her away. I want some tea. I never learn how best to manage these people. I was distracted, my mind running away with itself. With myself. Making stories and shapes inside my head.

Outside, the bell began to toll in the school: the end of another lesson. The sound cut his head.

As in the past.

Until four months ago he had been obliged to listen to it clanging in its belfry just above the classroom, every forty minutes, all day long, day and daily. Only a few years, fewer than ten, really – though like so many of his colleagues, he had spent most of the period willing time forward, too much time calculating how many years remained until retirement. Wishing it would come sooner.

'Be careful,' he told a visitor, 'be careful what you wish for.'

'Oh, Patrick, stop,' the visitor replied. She was a teacher too, a colleague; she tittered uneasily.

'I'm serious,' he said. His mouth tended to be dry these days – a side effect of the medication, so they'd told him – and he ran his tongue along his bottom teeth. 'I'm serious: teachers spend too much time at that lark. Look what happened to me.'

The weight, he meant, that began to fall off his frame, which had been lean to begin with. He was perplexed for a little while and then alarmed and then – and then rapidly other people began to notice; and then a belated visit to the GP, and tests and more tests.

And then whisked to the hospital – and gradually upwards through the wards, settling at last here on the eighth floor. Now he resembled his brother-in-law: now his skin was stretched taut on his skull, now his cheekbones stood out, now his reflection shocked him. Now he saw this shock echoed in the face of each fresh visitor. Now his wish for an early retirement had come true. 'Be careful what you wish for,' he said. 'Don't I know what I'm talking about?'

His life shrunk to this one room: this bed, this locker, this corkboard on the wall, festooned with a card or two, those unlined curtains and that shiny, wipe-clean, yellowish paint on the walls.

23

That was it – and the grating sound of the bells – the sound that had accompanied him all the way through his teaching years. 'Well, my comfort is that I won't have to listen to it for all that much longer. So they tell me.'

The visitor tittered again, uneasily.

And in the meantime, he was a fixture.

'A fixture, Mr Jackson,' they said, cheerily. Presumably a good proportion of their eighth-floor residents didn't last much beyond a day or two. He also noted that the 'Mr Jackson' vanished fairly quickly: soon it was 'Patrick' this and 'Patrick' that. Or 'Pat', the sound of which made him curdle. His name shrinking as he approached the end.

Pat: noun: a potato-digging farmer or similar.

Or 'dear' or 'sweetheart': all of these choice monikers proffered by slips of things five or six or seven years younger than he was.

And the bells.

There was, he thought, probably some comfortable idea doing the rounds they were doing him a favour, installing him in a room with a side view into his old school, his old stamping grounds, complete with green copper belfry, grey stone buildings and hipped roofs and smooth green lawns. Do him good, perhaps they said, slapping themselves on their collective backs, he imagined, in true self-congratulatory style. Poor guy, perhaps they said: struck down much too soon – but now he can remember the good times. What a comfort for him.

Clang, clang.

He had thought of complaining, raising a stink, demanding a new room – and then in the very next moment waving a feeble hand in the air and tell them not to bother, that everything was just fine. This was always part of his knack: to turn from waspish to self-deprecatory in a moment: the better, of course, to keep people feeling ill at ease, confused. Well, he thought, it worked on my students; and it sometimes worked on the adults too.

Oh, Patrick, they'd murmur, *he's a laugh, so he is. A right laugh*. Backing off. Glad to shed him and his moods, glad to leave him behind.

Discomfiting people. He'd a lifetime of practice at it.

*

'At what, Patrick?' said the nurse. She paused, turned towards the bed. He opened his eyes.

'What was that?' A thin, whistling voice: this fella was only thirty-odd, she'd glanced at his notes; but he had an old man's voice.

'Practice, you said.' The nurse – was it another nurse, this time? She was poised to go, but something – a native compassion, perhaps, overriding the time-management skills drummed into her during training – something caused her to pause for a second. She said, 'At what?'

He looked – not at her, but at the flat, white ceiling. He was perfectly aware today, she thought, for a dry smile was curling the corner of his mouth. 'God knows, Nurse,' he said quite clearly. 'God only knows.'

And she left, smiling a little too. He's a character, so he is. His eyes were closed once more: when she turned at the door and glanced back, though, only one eye was closed, and the other peeped for a second in her direction. Then it too closed. He'd probably been a decent-looking man, once. She left the room.

THREE

'Perhaps you could keep a journal,' Margaret said.

Unthinkingly: and he made certain that she regretted rapidly the comment.

'And what would I write?' he said. She opened her mouth to reply, and he said, 'Or should I say, what would I leave out?'

Instead of replying, Margaret stood up abruptly, went to the window. 'And thank goodness for windows,' he pursued, 'to look out of. They fill awkward gaps just wonderfully, I find. I had Robert looking out of the windows the other day too, did he mention?'

This was one of his good days.

'He did, actually.'

'So, come on then. A journal. What would I write in it? What would it be called? *The Unfortunate History of Patrick Jackson, and of his Family*; or, *A Decision Made*?' He eyed her over the blue coverlet. 'But perhaps that's a bit too eighteenth-century, a bit too wordy. What about going for something a bit more pithy? What about, let's see, what about,' he paused,

'*Crossroads*? Or *The Snare*? Or, wait, what about *Judgment Day*?'

'Stop it,' Margaret said in a low voice. She was still looking out of the window.

'I like *Judgment Day*,' he said – but now the fire was leaving his belly; and he sank into his pillows.

And in fact, he had considered beginning a journal of some kind. Just once, when his dreams had cut in once too often and rattled his nerves like the lid on a saucepan. Might his mind, his dreams, be short-circuited in some way? Might he wrestle some control out of this situation? But he had always been reluctant to keep any written record, any account of myself. *Really, Patrick?* – so the conversation had gone once, at Wednesday night history club, the meandering conversation moving around to diaries. *Haven't you a diary, tucked away somewhere? Well now, I'd've thought you'd be just the type. Your books, your papers, your pen flying across the page. That was a missed opportunity, wasn't it?*

Oh, shut up, you gaggle of geese. I've never kept a journal, I said. Can't you just listen? – he had wanted to say.

What had he said instead? He couldn't remember.

There was too much to put down. Or perhaps there was not enough of substance. Perhaps 'not enough' was more like it. Not enough that he would want actually to see the light of day.

Too much, and not enough.

And besides, what would he be writing about? The inside of his head, really – and the inside of his head was just not that attractive a prospect, with its blood vessels pulsating, and grey matter shining a little, its cords and muscles and veins. And some of what these blood vessels and grey matter and cords and muscles and veins had produced over the years was not that attractive.

He stuck instead to his history lessons, sandwiched between the bells. There were enough words there to satisfy anyone.

'They were able to move me yesterday,' he told Margaret now. He could not apologise to her – he never apologised, to anyone – but there were other ways of building bridges. This was the Jackson way of doing things: and she responded now.

'Oh yes?' She swung from the window.

'For a couple of minutes: they got me up and brought me over to the window. One of those carers, or orderlies, or whatever they call themselves.'

'Auxiliaries?'

'Some harsh-looking thing, anyway, with cigarette smoke on her breath. God knows where they find them. She probably had her Benson & Hedges stuck in her pocket. But she was built like a sumo wrestler, which was exactly what I needed.'

Margaret smiled.

'And she kind of hoisted me up and walked me over to the window.'

In fact he made a point of asking the nurses and other staff their names: 'Now,' he said, 'which one are you?' – pretending to care, joshing. They liked a little joshing, the nurses, so long as one didn't cross a line. It was a polite thing to do; and it kept on their good sides.

'I'm Sam,' this one had said. A young – well, a youngish – nurse. Sam? But a country accent, and mild; no chance yet, he supposed, to build up her rhino skin. And hefty, though not at all built like a sumo wrestler: that, he conceded to himself, was a mean thing to say. 'Upsy daisy now, Patrick, and we'll take you over to the window. You like that, they tell me.'

Upsy daisy indeed, Sam, he thought: talking to me as though I was five years old.

'Oh yes, I like that,' he told her. Feigning meekness to Sam, who – sweet or not – could make his (remaining) life difficult if she wanted. He allowed Sam to take him over to the window – shuffle, shuffle, he thought, like an old man – and there was the view: down across the grassy grounds, across the hills and ridges, across to the school. And there, trotting in pairs and feral gangs down the school drive, he saw his former charges themselves, black blazers flapping and ties askew or doffed altogether; and the school, never-changing, with its blasted green copper belfry.

'They tell me,' said Sam, 'you taught over there.' Part of their training, he supposed, to encourage their terminal charges to chatter, to do whatever was necessary to stop their brains and mouths from seizing up. 'Can't have been for very long though.' The age of him: not even forty. Not close. 'How long was it, exactly, now?'

Be quiet, Patrick wanted to say, and take your elbow out of my ribs. Go off and put a protective pad on your elbow and come back, and then I might talk to you. And stop patronising me, my dear country cousin. Get along back to your barn.

30

Though at least Sam didn't say *dear*. Upsy daisy now, dear: roll over a little and if you're finished, I'll give you a wipe.

'Oh, six years or so, Sam,' he said instead. 'Felt like longer, though, sometimes. Sam – now, is that Samantha?'

And in fact he really did want to know. Who was to blame for this crime of nomenclature? Did she have especially wicked parents?

Sam nodded – though she didn't fill him in on her parents. 'That's right,' she said cheerily – how he was coming to hate that ghastly cheeriness – and smiled. 'Though really, I prefer Sam. Samantha is just too much, you know?'

Patrick knew, certainly.

The parents, then: blame the parents. Poor Sam. He nodded and concentrated on the view. If he ignored the green copper belfry, then there was a good deal to take in. The roofs of the school and over the roofs a ridge of hill, and then another one, more blue this time, and blue sky too. The river invisible in its deep valley. Sam tweetled on for a while and Patrick let her take his weight – not much of a weight nowadays, he thought, a sparrow's weight, though a few kilos extra would be no sweat to our Sam – and let the windowsill take his weight too, and just looked out. Blue hills and blue sky: he focused very carefully and the school and the belfry – he vanished it. He saw the skyline and the sky, and that was good enough.

For a few moments. Though, reality always grabbed one's heel, in the end. Grabbed it and gives it a good bite.

*

'How is he today?'

'He seems bright enough, I think. Though too weak to get out of bed.'

The matron shook her head. 'And so young. So young. A shame. And they go downhill so fast.'

'He's a gentleman,' Sam offered, tentatively. She added, dishonestly, 'Always polite and always grateful.' She noted the slicing frown mark appear between the matron's brows: was she, Sam, rejecting democracy? Expressing a preference for one patient over another? This was completely unacceptable. Sam recanted hastily. 'So they tell me.'

The matron appeared to reconsider: the cleft on her forehead was smoothed away. 'So they tell me too,' she conceded. 'I imagine he'll go quietly, when the time comes.' She clipped away along the corridor: Sam peeped again through the glass; she looked for a moment at the figure in the bed and then she bustled away too.

*

'I hear,' Margaret said now, tentatively, 'that you told Robert not to call in again.'

'That's right.' And to close the conversation down, 'and of course you don't blame me.' She hardly could, could she?

She shook her head, turned to the window. 'No, I don't blame you.' A pause, then, 'And what about the girls?'

Patrick managed a laugh at that. 'Hardly,' he said. 'Not

the place for them. And they make too much noise, your two. Though, children these days always make too much noise. I blame the parents,' he said, 'don't you?'

And watched her flinch again.

Yes, he thought as the door closed behind the nurse: yes, blame the parents. He thought of his mother, due to visit later, of his long-dead father. Blame them both, he thought: let the blame take the strain. He thought of the sketchy canvas forming in his mind: the lines, the colours, the shapes of characters roughed, sketched in. He thought: do I even have a starring role in my own life? Or have other characters, with a twitch of their buttocks, shoved me right out of the frame? And what a lot of them there are, now I think about it, what a lot of other people, shuffling and pushing their way upstage. My mother, of course, and my father. Cassie. Margaret and Robert: and their two girls – who, yes, had caused so much noise. A few others knocking around.

And a final vignette appearance, to round things off. He'd done his research, he knew the roles.

That should do the trick.

An ordinary life. He imagined what they might say when they went through his belongings, his papers, his tidy filing cabinet: Sam, possibly, in the first instance, charged with clearing out this very room – and now he imagined Sam tapping her chewed nurse's Biro on her strong white, countrywoman's teeth, taking the chance to discover a secret or two.

Well, Sam: this one's for you.

No, on second thoughts: go away, Sam. There isn't anything for you in my papers, in my will. I'm not telling you about my will, the recipients of my largesse – it won't be you: you came along too late. Go back to work, Sam, he thought. Go back to doing what you're good at: at sticking chilly thermometers into people's bums.

The truth was that he knew what he was doing. His mind was taking stock, it was putting a shape to things, it was working against the clock. What was he doing, then, holding it at arm's length? Absolving himself of responsibility, was that it?

Well – yes: that was exactly it. Absolving himself of responsibility: that was exactly what he was doing. He was a dab hand, after all, at this, was he not? And now he must inch back, he must break this habit of mind. There was so little time left. There was so much at stake.

He was a good teacher. I am a good teacher, he had told himself – many times over the years, as he sought to put some value on this life that he seemed so pointlessly to be living: a damn good teacher of English and history. It was all he had, all he could point to with a glimmering of pride and self-esteem. It was never enough, the credit would never outweigh the debit, but it was something to clutch. And so now his mind worked as any good teacher's mind worked: by adding a little context. Context is all, he used to say to his spotty, high-smelling students, even as he averted his gaze from their oily hair and oily skin and blackhead-pocked noses.

I should go for it, he thought as he lay in his bed. I should go for it, I should grasp at the chance to find shapes in my life. I should not write a journal, but instead create a wonderful hanging: bright, he thought, with coloured thread. And what else? Glittering with rhinestones stitched into the fabric in green and blue and deep and mysterious ruby red: the Bayeux Tapestry *de nos jours*.

Not pretentious, he thought: not at all.

And then to fill in the context. To people this wonderful hanging. He imagined Margaret, excellent in so many ways. Not quite at the centre, though near enough; a backdrop, he thought, of fragrant bay and bright, white lilac.

Lilac turns so quickly, after all: come the end of May and it fades and blackens.

And Robert, shadowed, half-disguised behind the bough or a tree or other piece of artistic greenery. Medieval Robert. Ivy creeps at his feet; it clambers up his leg, parasitic, pregnant with menace, filled with poison.

A ghost hovers at his shoulder – though, he thought, how to portray a ghost?

And now Patrick imagined his mother, shadowing Robert, wrapped in pastel pinks and blues: the perfect disguise. My mother, he thought, who comes calling later today. Who comes calling two or three times a week. Who called two days ago, or three, and crunched grape pips at the end of my bed. Who comes… and perhaps, he thought now, perhaps she too has an eye on my will: I wonder what secret means she thinks I have, as she sits at the end of my bed, eating my grapes and crunching the pips.

'Why don't you buy seedless?' he asked, two days ago, or three.

Sarah shrugged a little. 'Special offer on black ones, in Long's this morning,' she said. 'Do you want one? – I washed them, and everything.'

He shook his head.

'Peel it for you if you like.'

He thought: witty Ma.

He thought: it's like being in Wormwood Scrubs, at such a time. It would be better to wipe these people from the story. To unpick the threads – but unpick, snip just one thread, and history would fall apart. He knew this too. He knew this was impossible: he hadn't the luxury of time.

So little time – to make sense, to create a pattern, to tell some sort of truth. To get, he thought, my ducks in a row.

He thought about Margaret. He fended her off, he looked forward to her visits: this was their relationship, now. His week pivoted on these visits, in spite of himself. Well, and that's about right, he thought: my life had pivoted on that one, single relationship. On choices made and deals done and connections forged and severed – and Margaret near the centre of it all.

'Why him?' he'd said to Margaret – in London, on Hampstead Heath, years ago now: the words floating into his mind now almost visibly, letter by pulsating letter by uncomprehending question, exclamation marks. 'Why him? I mean, look at him!' And Margaret turned and looked at Robert, at his lean frame silhouetted on the ridge of Parliament Hill.

'Why not him?' And after a pause, 'I'm not going to get

anyone else, am I?' And another pause. 'Our dear mother has seen to that, hasn't she?'

That was the context: that was where it all began. Neither Sam nor anyone else – in a few weeks, in a month's time, whenever it was – would find these sentences, these words buried in some corner of his effects.

So: what about the context, the background? – So he would ask these students, from time to time: the more promising, less cloddish students. What about all of that?

'What, sir?' they would say, shaking out their greasy hair, little motes of dandruff and ear scurf catching in the light. 'What do you mean, sir?' Sometimes, if Patrick was in a patient frame of mind, he would give them a little lecture: sometimes, this little lecture would work quite well, paid out evenly, steadily, he discoursing on all those other histories, the ones that never made it into the history books, the silenced, stifled voices whose stories are lost for ever; and they listening – yes, sometimes actually listening, taking it all in until the bell clanged above their heads.

Yes, sometimes it worked out nicely.

Of course, he thought now, such discourses should *always* have worked out nicely. How, in theory, could they fail to work out nicely, such an idea in such a city, in such a country as this, where certain histories see the light of day and some do not? Where history is a sort of football, kicked around from morning to night? This kind of history should be bread and butter to the whole lot of us. It should be devoured with gusto. So Patrick thought.

But there it is: he knew that sometimes students – not only students – were lumpen, cloddish. One might as well save one's breath: so he had said, in conversations innumerable in the staff room over the scant few years of his employment. But now, here was his story: and what an irony it would be if he now set out to press the delete button. Honour the living and the dead, he thought: and the dead most of all.

He knew where it all came from: this interest in the living and the dead. It came from his father – who would turn in his grave if he knew how selectively Patrick had applied it to his own life. It came from his father. Patrick could even pin it down to a time and a place. He could remember the season, the weather, the view, the clothes, the car the family had at the time.

On the beach at Kinnagoe, on a sea- and salt-smelling Donegal day in 1960 or thereabouts, Patrick aged six and Margaret eight, and the sand warm under his bare feet and the ocean green and blue and ice-cold, and a picnic waiting.

As precise as that.

Have your swim first, said his father, and then we'll have our picnic.

Patrick ran into the water: the ice of the Donegal sea, the cold of it; no wonder he remembered that day so well. He swam and then he was towelled dry, his father calming down after his anger, his shock, enveloping his son in their great big red towel. Margaret was second with the towel: it was damp by then – but no complaints from her; she was quiet, abashed, aware that something had happened, that a moment had been witnessed. That something significant had just taken place. Young as they were, they both felt it.

Their mother? – Sarah was sitting on the sand, with her face turned up to the sun; and Cassie was sitting too, fiddling with a sandal, maybe, or simply looking at the waves.

He was first into the water. He beat Margaret to it. She was speechless with rage. Older, two years older, but second, this time. Speechless. Goaded beyond bearing. She might have drowned her little brother that day. Instead, she realised how much she loved him. He saw it all now, with the benefit of hindsight.

*

Patrick waded a little deeper. The sand on this beach shelved steeply, a little too steeply. This was why they seldom came here. His mother and Cassie preferred the beaches on Lough Swilly, with their gentler slopes, their warmer waters, and all twenty minutes from their front door in Derry. Cassie got anxious: she'd been anxious even sitting there in the back of the car, being brought out to this unaccustomed beach; she'd wriggled and shifted in the back seat, her sharp hip bones digging into him.

He waded a little deeper. He knew why it was Kinnagoe, today. His father took a notion. His mother usually made the choices – about beaches, about everything, taking Cassie into account – but today their father chose. A rush of blood to the head – though, what was that? He didn't know, but that's what his mammy had said. 'You've had a rush of blood to the head,' she said, before glancing into the back, checking on him, on Margaret, on Cassie. 'We could've been in Buncrana in fifteen minutes. Why Kinnagoe?' she said. 'Twice as far, three times.'

But his father won: or his mammy didn't care enough this time to win.

'Three times as far.'

She usually won.

He waded a little deeper. What an excitement it was, what a thrill. They hadn't been to Kinnagoe this year and they didn't go last: he didn't even really remember the road here, did he? The steep road up to the crest of the hill, the sudden view of ocean and islands? – he couldn't really remember: just a fuzz of a memory, just a haze. He'd whispered to Margaret, there on the sticky back seat, 'When were we last here?' – but she had just rolled her eyes. 'Last year. You were too young to remember.'

Well, he'd get her for that. Some time. He was nearly the same height now as she is. He'd get her.

And then they had reached the crest of the hill, and his father pulled the car to the side of the road. He got out and Patrick got out and: 'Scotland, son, look!' – and they gazed out across the blue sea to the islands, there in a haze on the horizon. That was Scotland.

They looked, all of them: he and his daddy standing in the sunshine; and his mammy and sister and Cassie sitting in the car, looking too. He peeped in at his mammy sitting, saying nothing. She was in a good mood today, a good-ish mood, a quiet mood. Cassie was looking too: she was settled now in the back seat; she didn't seem now to mind being here. Then he watched Margaret watching him, as he stood there with their daddy's arm on his shoulder. Their daddy thought she wasn't interested in some things, being a girl: things in the past, like battles and wars. He talked to her, but about other things; it made her – yes, wild: and yes, up there on the crest of the hill, she was wild. Patrick watched her expression, he watched her being driven wild, he glowed with satisfaction, with glee, with perfect and delightful happiness.

The sun had glinted on the metal roof of the car, on the clean windows: he could see inside, but only by crinkling up his eyes. There was his mammy sitting quietly. She wasn't looking any more: her eyes were closed. Cassie's eyes were open, they were looking at her fingers; Margaret's eyes were glaring, staring at him. Then they drove on, the road falling steeply now, down to the crescent of sand. No, they hadn't been here for ages: he couldn't remember the road, the beach, though he knew better than to admit this now to anyone. Margaret said she could remember it; she was cleverer than he, he knew this already, but this time she was a big liar, probably.

They ran down onto the beach: he ran ahead, faster than Margaret, though she had longer legs. He picked out their patch and dropped his shoes, the picnic bag, the red towel onto the warm sand – and quickly he jumped out of his shorts and ran down the beach and into the water.

And now here he was, first in.

It was icy, the water, and now he was waist-deep and he gasped a little. Icy, icy water: so cold he could hardly breathe. He gasped and gasped again, he took another breath, another step. He heard Margaret panting a little behind him, gasping as he gasped at the chill slap of the waves. I'll duck first, I'll get wet first, I have to: first in, first down, first always.

He ducked.

He was after drowned treasure. I'll be a hero, he thought: I'll find it first. Margaret will rage.

This was why they came here today: the ship, the shipwreck. The Spanish sailors from the Armada: they were on a great wooden ship driven into the coast and wrecked on the reefs here, off Kinnagoe, off this beach. His father told him. Hundreds and hundreds of years ago this happened: oh, hundreds.

This is why they came here to Kinnagoe.

And where was the wreck? – but his father had shrugged. 'Never found, son. Not yet – but the local people know it's here.'

'How do they know?'

'Ghosts, son, on the beach in stormy weather.'

'Ghosts?'

'Ghosts. They ride the white horses to shore, son, and they come ashore, they come off the ship.'

Patrick's blood ran cold, then, deliciously. Margaret made a disbelieving noise: there was, she said, no such thing as ghosts. Their father laughed, then. 'We'll see,' he said. This was earlier: a day or so earlier, in the hot back garden of their new house in Derry. Planning the trip, selecting the beach.

'We'll see. Make a change, anyway,' he said, 'from Buncrana. We'll go a little bit further afield,' he said to them, privately, 'this time.' Then he went indoors and Patrick and Margaret, focused now on other matters on which could make common cause: there would be chocolate waiting for them tomorrow; there would be ice cream, maybe. They sat in the sun and discussed ice cream, until it was time to come inside for tea.

And now Patrick ducked his head into the icy water and the sea enveloped him. He would be the first to see the shipwreck, the bones, the skeletons of Spanish sailors, the chests of golden treasure. He opened his eyes: green sunlit water, a thick strand of waving, drifting seaweed. He closed his eyes and rose to the surface, emerged with a pop, and another breath and down again – the water less cold now, and bones to be discovered – and now he felt his leg grasped, and he was yanked down, towards the sandy, rocky bottom of the sea.

*

Margaret's throat was tight with rage and frustration. How dare he, how dare they, how dare Patrick and how dare their father? How dare they and how dare they?

'Not out of your depth, Margaret,' her daddy said, behind her, from the shallows: he was wading, his trouser legs turned up neatly. 'Go carefully, please.' He said to her. Not to Patrick, who was younger, but who was allowed to wade into the deep water, who could go out of his depth, who was first to take a breath and plunge his head into the waves.

Who was a boy.

She ignored her daddy; she waded faster. Her daddy didn't want to get his trousers wet: she knew this, she'd trade on it. She moved faster, out of his reach, out of her depth: the sandy bottom fell away, she took a breath and plunged and opened her eyes – all suddenly, suddenly, not a moment to lose, the water green and cold, pressing against her wide eyes – and now she saw her brother's left leg, and she caught at it and pulled.

She'd teach him.

She could feel his panic, there in the green water. He was out of his depth now – well out – and he kicked away, but she yanked again, harder. She'd teach him a lesson, she had the advantage of surprise, she yanked again: she'd show them who was strongest *and* cleverest – and she didn't need her father to say so, besides.

And suddenly now her brother's face appeared, white and ghost-like in the green water: they were face to face and his right leg and his arms were thrashing and his eyes wide with shock and fear – and in a horrified, blurred moment she released her grasp of his other leg.

For another instant they stared, suspended, their eyes wide open in the water – and now she felt herself yanked in her turn and pulled upwards – and she surfaced, streaming water, and there he was, her father, livid and streaming too; and now Patrick popped to the surface of the water beside her. His hands were empty: no treasure, no bones; she knew what he was looking for. And now she was pulled ashore.

'What were you doing? What the hell did you think you were doing?'

'I was swimming, diving.'

'I saw what you were doing. Wait 'til I get you home.' Seawater ran down her father's face. Yes, livid: she'd be thrashed this evening, when they got home. So he said – though he'd cool down, later. He never thrashed. And even now he was cooling: the beach had filled up a little, even in these last few minutes, and there was too much of an audience for him; he was cooling right down. She sensed this, her escape from a promised thrashing – but running alongside this relief she was aware of other sensations. Envy, yes, and a still potent fury at her brother's position, his privilege based on nothing. But something else, too.

'We were just trying to touch the bottom,' said Patrick; and she watched as their father turned and looked from one to the other.

Love, of course.

And – the ache that came with it, born out there in the water of a fear that something might happen to this little boy, with his red towel, with his skinny arms and legs and his white, thin face. Patrick was rubbing his eyes, blindly; then his hands dropped and he looked at her – and she saw this same realisation written in his eyes. Margaret would remember this expression – oh, for the rest of her life. Would do anything for this little boy. For this brother that, not five minutes before, she would gladly have drowned, had she been able to get away with it.

She glanced up the beach, to where her mammy and Cassie sat on towels. Mammy hadn't moved: she looked like a… like that statue, Margaret thought, carved in their church from white stone. Margaret saw her and looked away: no need to have anything or anyone interfere with her newfound knowledge, standing dripping here on the warm white sand, on a sunny afternoon.

*

Martin waded into the water. His son had vanished beneath the waves, but there was no need to worry about Patrick: he'd be fine. But Margaret had vanished too, and she couldn't swim – could she? I don't even know, he thought, and with sudden fear he waded further in, peering into the cold, green water. Where was she?

There she was. There was her shadowy form: her long hair waving above her head in dark tendrils, the sunlight falling in bars across her form. There she was, and he grabbed and lunged and pulled her up, gasping, to the surface, onto the beach.

'What were you doing? What the hell did you think you were doing?'

She coughed up seawater. 'I was looking for treasure.'

Your fault, she was implying, without saying a word: all your fault. You mentioned the Spanish treasure in the first place. Didn't you?

Martin did. He accepted his guilt. He would not thrash her, later.

Cassie watched. The sand was warm. 'Take your sandals off, Cassie,' said Sarah, 'why don't you?' – and she did: she did take her sandals off and now the sand is soft and warm under her bare feet. Lovely and warm, and she reached her hands too into the warm, into the beautiful fine sand. It is never as hot as this: my bones are heating; they are heating up to stay warm when the winter comes. To keep me warm. And there's poor Margaret beside herself. Poor Margaret and poor Patrick. And poor Sarah, wrapped up in herself. Always, always, always wrapped up in herself on a beach. She needs to leave the past in the past, Cassie thought – but this is a thing Sarah has never been able to do. Cassie watched the water, the hauling and shouting, she watched dreamily, now. She closed her eyes. She doesn't have to look too closely. Nobody was about to die. Not this time. Lovely, Cassie thought, and closed her eyes.

*

Twenty-five years ago now, and more, that day: Margaret and me, our relationship sealed by murderous rage.

Sealed, Patrick thought, with a yank.

Twenty-five years ago, that talk about Spanish sailors, coming ashore, with the wind roaring and the waves roaring and lamplight and torchlight waiting for them on the beach. Coming ashore to a new world – for them, at any rate. To discover the future, to explore how it would shape up for them.

That was the thing: his father giving him a certain way of looking at the world, at history, at other people's lives. Those Spanish sailors on the Armada ship: what did they think as they came ashore, or as they drowned in cold Irish seas? Nothing about them in the books, which deal with Spanish kings and English queens and Irish chieftains, jockeying for position. Nothing about the others: about the actual people on the ships. For these stories, we have to use our imaginations.

Patrick lay still. Footsteps squeaked and crunched on rubber floors; a trolley wheeled along the corridor; a vast, humming cleaning machine swept past. This was the lesson he was taught, as a small boy: a lesson he was honour-bound to apply to his own life. He thought of Margaret, and Robert: of the living and the dead, of deeds done and not undone. He hadn't applied the lesson, had he?

No. He had done the opposite. He had erased a story. He had failed to honour the dead.

He had wiped the slate clean.

FOUR

'And how is the patient today?'

Sarah repeated the question – almost immediately. This was a favourite approach: she liked to see the other person's mouth open and then close; the faint expression of shock in the face of this pressing, prodding rudeness. This sweet lady – who turns out to be not so sweet after all. 'How is my son today?'

My son, she thought. My son, my son. My son is dying: and there you stand, so sanctimonious. I've had enough of you, of the lot of you.

No saying any of this, she knew. They'd swoop in. They'd take the opportunity to section me, probably, to cart me off to the nearest loony bin, in two seconds. Serve her right, they'd say; nothing but trouble, that one. How many times had she seen the contempt in their eyes? – many times, was the answer to that: contempt for this doll, causing trouble, asking questions.

Well, she'd set them right on that one. Getting older, she might be. But feeble? – no, and with a tongue like the blade of an axe, if she chose to use it. She was no pushover: and the staff in this place knew it by now.

But there was a flipside. Never show my feelings: that was Sarah's number one rule. She knew how to keep her feelings in check, to keep them pushed down – even with her son lying dying right there, on the other side of the door. It was easily done: it really was very easy. A lifetime of experience in that particular art had made her an expert now in stamping down.

And besides, age had made it easier. Because there was nobody to speak to: not for five, six years now, not since Cassie died. She had forgotten how to do it.

'How is my son today?'

Sarah watched the nurse's mouth open again, she watched her lips move. She watched, as if from miles away, as the girl began to speak.

*

'And how is the patient today?' she said. 'How is my son today?'

And the nurse paused for a moment. Warily, by this stage. Too many stings, by this stage. Fed-up, too, by this stage: for Mrs Jackson, this nice, upright lady in her fleecy wraps and her knitting needles and her fondness for pastel shades had a tongue on her, when she felt like showing it off. They had all felt sorry for her, to begin with: not very nice for the lady to see her son fading away like this, fading day by day: to sit and watch this, in silence for the most part.

It was an inversion of the natural order of things: it called for sensitivity over and above what training demanded. It called for kid gloves.

But a few tongue lashings and – worse, much worse – a few biting sarcasms, put paid to all that. *A bit of a harridan, that one*: so went the talk in the nurses' room. *A tartar*; and *she can stand up for herself, that one*. And so now the nurse paused before selecting the right word. The doctors, she thought, they can deal with the ins and outs of it.

'As well as can be expected,' the nurse said, 'considering.'

The fleecy lady seemed to – yes, to consider for a moment. She considered. The nurse waited. Her duties were stacked up like planes waiting to land, today as on every other day, but she waited. This lady had a quality: the nurse felt as though she was being held by a tightening leash.

'Considering,' Mrs Jackson said at last. 'Considering – everything.'

The nurse nodded.

'Well,' said Mrs Jackson, 'that certainly clarifies matters for me, doesn't it? That answers all the questions, doesn't it?'

The leash was released now, it was snapped. The nurse nodded dumbly.

'Thank you, dear.' The nurse turned and scuttled away down the corridor. The fleecy lady paused for another moment: then she too turned and squared her shoulders. She took a moment: and then she pushed the door, and it swung and she entered the room.

*

Moments came and went: of course she'd had her chances, over the years. Plenty of them. One moment in particular came to mind: when the chance arose to – if not set matters right, then at least to speak of them, to begin to sort through them in her head.

'What is it, mammy?' Margaret asked, long ago: sitting up on her bed, tall now and long of limb and of hair, a teenaged pimple or two. *What do you want?* – is what she meant, though she was too polite to put it in those terms: *what do you want?* She looked at her mother, who was perched there on the edge of her bed: a wet February night, the window streaming with rain.

Margaret had been picking fights with Patrick all day, the pair of them cooped up in the house, winding each other up as the rain fell. Now she looked apprehensive, afraid – reasonably enough – that her mother was here to barge at her, to tell her off. But: 'I just wanted a word,' said Sarah with ceremonious formality, and Margaret's expression changed to puzzlement. Not a telling off, then – but what?

Sarah hardly ever entered her children's rooms. Not to draw curtains, not to open windows, not to pick up laundry from the floor. 'You do your own jobs,' she told them, 'and you bring your own clothes to be washed, or else they stay dirty.' Ditto the air in their bedrooms, which stayed stale unless they bothered to open their windows themselves. She had enough to be doing; and she wouldn't let Cassie shuffle around picking up after them either. (Martin, of course, wouldn't think of it, not for a second.)

And besides which, her children liked their rooms to themselves. They didn't exactly stick Keep Out posters on their bedroom walls; they didn't need to; the signals were unmistakable. They took after her – and yet now here she was, having made a trail through a swamp of clothing and paper and schoolbooks on the floor, here she was perched at the end of the bed in Margaret's bedroom. From the living room, where Martin and Cassie sat at their ease, the murmur of the television.

Margaret said, 'What kind of a word?'

And yes: what kind of a word? A word of absolution?

But when it came to it, Sarah manufactured some question or other: *how was school? – and how was homework? – and I was just checking that everything was coming along well enough, you know, what with O Levels on their way next year.* Margaret looked puzzled, as well she might. 'Everything's fine,' she said, after a considering pause, during which a helicopter could be heard passing overhead, skimming the treetops in the darkness, deafening. She waited for the din to fade, then spoke again. 'You know I don't like Physics, but even that's going along, you know, well enough too.' And then: *good*, Sarah said, *that's good*, and she picked her way back through the clothes and books, and slipped out of the room, leaving something – a confused silence – behind.

She remembered this episode now. Twenty-odd years ago now, she thought, more years than I can stand to think about – she remembered it as she sat on the edge of another bed. Of Patrick's bed, this time, in this hospital, smoothing the sky-blue coverlet until he moved his index finger just enough to give her a sign, to indicate that he didn't like her there, that she was annoying him, that she should sit in the chair by the bed – or get out. She was interfering with the bed's level, with its equilibrium.

'The nurse said you're doing well enough today, considering.'

Patrick opened one eye, and looked. Then closed it again. 'Did she indeed?'

And that was about the height of it.

Of course they'd never had much to say to one another. She'd made sure of that. Had watched the two of them, her son and daughter, playing as children, fighting, tussling and wrestling – and talking. Had felt something like pale satisfaction that they were managing well enough, in spite of her.

That, certainly.

But something else too: a pulse of envy, of anger, that they *could* manage, that they had been able to reach out to each other, even though their own mother had long since given up doing anything of the sort. She had watched them: playing and fighting in the waves on warm days at the beach, until their father waded in to separate them; squabbling and playing in the garden together. Being normal. In spite of everything, being normal; or something that passed for it. A club of two, with Cassie in the wings.

Now, she sat by Patrick's bedside, watching him die. At our age, Sarah liked to say to her cronies, we reach a sort of equilibrium. We reach the top of whatever mountain we've

54

been climbing: and now we're on level ground, and we can look back at the view, and get our breath back. Can't we? – and they would nod agreement.

And now she sat in her chair by Patrick's bedside, watching him die. Equilibrium and balance, in the face of all this. No: in the face of her whole life. It was hardly possible, was it? She pulled her woollen scarf a little closer. She could hear the subdued routine of hospital life continuing beyond the door – low voices, wheeling, a genteel rattle and clink of a trolley; and after a few minutes the bell began to toll in the school across the way.

The next day – the day after she had perched on the end of Margaret's bed – had it been the next day? Yes: and it was chilly but dry and she had the day off; so she loaded the car up with her restless children and with Cassie and set off to Inch Levels for a walk, for some air. Clambered up the leeward side of the sea wall, as she always did, grasping onto handfuls of the long grass that grew there – grey now, at the very end of winter – as she always did. And then she was up on top, on the level surface of the wall, and there was the sea before her and the slob lands, level and fertile behind her. The sound of a church bell drifted across the fields: the Angelus, tolling determinedly.

She never tired of this place. Her mind drifted towards it during dull, irksome moments at work, at home: when she was totting sums and in the midst of paperwork; or chopping onions, browning mince in the pan, pouring off the fat; when she was sweeping, cleaning, ironing: when her mass of duties and jobs began to eat at her, she could step out of that life and into this one, all air and a great sweep of sky. Whatever the weather, there was space here and air to breathe. She stood still on top of the sea wall and looked out across the waters of the lough, grey and silver, the purple height of the island on the further shore, higher blue hills to east and west; and a mass of wintering geese in the fields, of wintering swans on the water. She thought – nothing, for a change; she looked and breathed, that was all.

Below her was the narrow beach of shingle and white sand, built up gradually in the hundred years since the engineers designed this wall and the navvies constructed it: laboriously, as she imagined it, stone upon stone, until the sea was safely held back and they could relax a little. The new fields behind the wall began to drain, then, with rich black earth showing against the green of new grass. She knew all about this place: had read up about its history in the Central Library; had made a point of it. They built a railway line across this flat landscape, once they had secured it, running west and away into Donegal's blue distance, and east towards Derry. The line had been taken up recently: nothing remained now but the level embankment, which was already being colonised by hazel and ash.

Today, no movement. No other walkers, nobody but them to disturb the peace and space. Patrick and Margaret were already down there below, crunching along the narrow beach. 'Bring a ball,' she'd said, earlier, as they donned coats and scarves, 'to kick'. Patrick didn't want to come in the first place:

the suggestion of a ball had gone down badly, very badly. He scowled at her, a scornful, hatefully adolescent look; when did he ever show any interest in a ball, any ball? Never, that's when. He and Margaret went and waited in the car, then – and now there they were, walking slowly along the edge of the lough. Beachcombing, maybe, she thought: for a piece of driftwood, for shells, for something brought ashore by the waters of the lough that might hold some interest for a few moments. The shore was scattered with the quills of feathers, of a mass of swandown like a fall of snow.

It was tremendous here: the big sky and salt air, the shingle shelving away gently into shallow water. 'Why do you *like* it there?' the ladies sometimes asked back in Derry – intrigued, disturbed, for people went to actual beaches, smooth Donegal beaches, for walks in this part of the world. They did not come to this sea wall, to these flat fields. The ladies were easily mollified for the most part: over tea and meringues in a booth at the Dolphin Café, Sarah mentioned the sea air, the blue hills and green fields. And the exercise, she added, walking on the flat. I walk and walk, she said, and she pressed the tines of her fork onto the meringue until it shattered.

She liked its loneliness best – though today, with this unaccustomed company, the loneliness of the place was hustled away. During the drive out here, Patrick had grizzled in the back seat, complaining of boredom. Cassie in the back too, silent. Margaret in the front: silent too, discombobulated – it must be – from the conversation in her bedroom the previous evening. The non-conversation. Leaning her head back, gazing out of the windscreen, playing with the matt-black toggle on her duffle coat, twisting its leather thread around and around. Removed, Sarah thought: looking not onto the worn colours of late winter, onto suburbs and industrial plants slipping past the windows, but at something else entirely.

Her mother's daughter.

And beside her, Sarah drove in silence, her gloved hands gripping the wheel, her shoulders set.

Though: what need for set shoulders, for these familiar defensive feelings? She ought to be capable of leaving the past in the past: at her age, she really should be able to do such a thing. It was a long time ago, she thought as she drove: and I was younger and more foolish too, without a shadow of a doubt; not much of a person, really. Cassie could bear witness to *that*. I was different then, she thought, and I am different now, and I don't have to carry my past around with me like a millstone.

Defensive of what? Nothing, so she thought and thought again: nothing, nothing. Night by night looking up at the flat, modern ceilings of the new suburban house, with Martin asleep and breathing almost silently beside her; day by day keeping her colleagues at bay, or walking on the sea wall here in the slob lands, or making her way from shop to shop in the city, lowering her eyes as she passed gun-toting soldiers in groups of six or eight, smiling mildly as she encountered an acquaintance here or there.

Or, hardly a thing: only a history, a series of episodes foisted upon her; a story left behind like an unwanted parcel.

'No, nothing,' Cassie told her. 'Nothing, nothing, nothing,' shaking her head. Over and over: nothing, nothing, nothing.

Why, then, had she made her way along the landing only last night, with Cassie and Martin parked in front of the television down the hall? Cassie's knitting bag and knitting needles, Martin's *Radio Times*. Why had she tapped gently on Margaret's door and… and then the ridiculous conversation to do with Physics O Level, there in Margaret's untidy bedroom, with a misty rain falling through the yellow light of the street lamp outside?

Because. Because Margaret had just turned fifteen: would be leaving school in a few more years; would take off for somewhere else, for university, please God, grabbing the opportunities Sarah herself had lacked; and home and family would henceforth be for occasional weekends only. Margaret was growing up. She was surely old enough to have a portion of the family past filled in; and Sarah besides was aware of an urge, once more, to unburden herself, to seek a sort of – yes, of absolution.

And now here she was standing atop the sea wall, and her silent son wandering the shingle strand below, and her daughter, silent too – but with a different kind of silence – watching him. And nothing said.

Margaret must have picked up – she was hardly a lump of wood, after all – the distress in the room. But nothing was said. Sarah filled the room with distress, and filled Margaret with it too, likely enough, and then left; went along to the kitchen and made a cup of tea instead. Tea, she thought, would perk her up. It had, too. Now she looked down from the sea wall at her children, still trailing along the water's edge. Patrick ought to be wearing his coat, she thought: there was no more rain for now in that grey sky – but it wasn't warm. She watched her children for a moment: Patrick a lonely figure below on the stones, already long of limb and thin, gangly, awkward; Margaret nearby, standing looking at the sea.

'They're fine,' Cassie said from below: she was shadowing Sarah from the gravel path, she was reading her mind. 'It isn't cold.' Though her own hands were shoved deep into the pockets of her old coat – but now laboriously she too climbed up the grassy slope, hands clutching at the long, damp grass until she too was safely on the level. She took a breath of the air, a glance at the flat sea stretching below – and now they struck out in silence, the two women, leaving the two children behind on the shingle.

It was Sarah's usual walk, her usual beat – passing the humming pumping station and on, a mile or so, until the sea wall gave way to naturally rising ground, the lough on one side and the flat green fields on the other. Once she glanced back: there was Patrick on the edge of the water; there was Margaret on the shingle behind him: bent studying, looking for – for something, for seashells and white feathers.

When Margaret was younger, she had passed through a spontaneous, outspoken phase: bursting in from school filled with the latest lessons, with new knowledge she had not possessed only the day before. Liberated from the humid embrace of her school gang – of Veronica and her group – she became for a short period a tomboy: given, as Martin said dramatically one evening at the kitchen sink, 'to martial word and deed'. At thirteen, her class studied the Elizabethan wars in Ireland, the Battle of Kinsale: she was filled with enthusiasm for stories of doom and strategy, of powerful, clashing personalities, of Hugh O'Neill's desperate march south through a frozen, wintry Ireland to succour the invading Spaniards at Kinsale, with a landscape left undefended behind him.

'Powerful stuff,' Martin said, listening with evident pleasure.

'Then when O'Neill was gone, the English came and burned his lands,' Margaret went on. 'When he came back, everything was burned and broken.'

'Burned and broken,' Patrick repeated, the potatoes cooling on his plate. Cassie listened too, her fork suspended in the air.

'And the crowning stone of the O'Neills smashed to bits by the English.'

'How did they do that?' Patrick asked, staring at her through saucer eyes.

Margaret shrugged. It was unimportant, the *how* of it all. 'Some special tool, I suppose.'

Sarah was surprised by the energy, the glee over such material in a girl; and a little disturbed too, war being something that – as everyone was beginning to realise – could not be left to the pages of the history books. Still, she must encourage the reading, the interest: she knew her duty. She took Margaret to the library, and waited while her daughter browsed and then took her home again. But the girl must have caught something: something disturbed, like a ploughed field. Certainly this period had not lasted very long; she changed, practically in front of the family's eyes, into a cautious, measured teenager; she began to hold her classmates at arm's length; she had fewer friends. She allowed Patrick in, but nobody else.

Became, in effect – yes: not unlike her mother.

Well, thought Sarah, apples and trees. Though she tried to reason with herself: children did change, she said, all children change – it was nothing much to worry about. She was unconvinced, unconvincing. She didn't convince herself and she didn't convince Martin, who had thought he was at last getting in that tomboy Margaret a model of a daughter to whom he could relate. No chance. 'Too much baggage in this family,' he murmured one evening; and she took the point.

What's past is past: this was Sarah's official mantra, even if she herself never had the means of putting it into practice. As an approach, it worked well enough: worked on the surface, worked if nobody asked too many questions. Certainly she never told her children much about her past – and nothing at all of substance. Born in Donegal; little by way of family there; met their father and married him: so much they knew. The barest bird-bones of a life, though enough to withstand a little incurious scrutiny.

She had too the wherewithal, if necessary, to augment this skeleton with a few facts, some telling details: their marriage in Derry and, more or less straight after, a short honeymoon spent touring Ireland, the unpleasant crossing to Holyhead in the teeth of a late-summer storm; the resulting shocking seasickness; and the grime of the train to London. Later, the dismal first marital home in digs off a decaying Camberwell Grove; the dirt suspended in dull London skies. 'The smell of gas in the air,' she told them once, cannily, 'and feeding the meter on cold nights to keep the place warm.' Her children looked at their glowing coal fire, looked back at her, wrinkled their noses in distaste at a life they wanted nothing to do with and asked nothing more.

Later still – by which stage her life was in any case slipping into the realm of the known, the verifiable – the removal from London back to Derry, where Cassie joined her once more. Children did not in any case tend to worry themselves about their parents' previous life: and Sarah knew this too. Hers was a story threaded with illusion and opacity: like most people's stories, it served – so long as nobody poked and dug and queried too much. Much better, she had imagined, to remain in a sort of continuing present tense.

But later, as she watched her children grow – their past and present stretching long shadows into their future, pale sunshine and shadows – she was obliged to recalculate. And now, with Margaret fast approaching adulthood, the pains-takingly created structure of Sarah's own life was beginning minutely to fracture. Could there be repercussions? – for her, other people, for children? She watched her children set off for school in the early morning, their shadows running away from them; she saw them return in their usual state of disintegration, with uniforms and ties askew at the end of a long day. Patrick, she imagined, was fine: he was too young to notice much. But there was Margaret, about to step forward into her future, without having much of a past.

Sarah fretted: her thoughts clung, unreasoning and indelible. And she was tired: the exhaustion and tension that came from the effort to keep part of one's identity hidden permanently, permanently in shadow, like the far side of the moon. She held her children at arm's length for so long now that her very limbs seemed set, like plaster of Paris. Too late, now, to think of flexing, of bending. Too, too late: she realised this as she sat on the end of Margaret's bed. She could speak only to Cassie: and Cassie only shook and shook her head.

They reached the end of the wall. There was the shallow sea, with terns and oystercatchers busy in the rich, muddy water. The slight breeze died away; and they stood still looking out onto the water, listening to the waves, the thin sound of water hissing between stones. On the far side of the water rose ruins, the gaunt outline of the castle. Wordlessly agreeing, they scrambled down the smooth seaward slope of the wall and sat on the beach. The stones were larger here, and smooth and polished: they fell away from their feet towards the water's edge.

'Just a beach,' Cassie said suddenly; she slid a glance.

A pause.

'Yes.' Sarah nodded at last. 'Just a beach today.'

'Just a beach, this time,' Cassie said. The stones were soft and smooth against her hands; the wind was gone. She glanced again at Sarah. All morning in the house, all through the silent drive out here to the slob lands, she had felt Sarah's sadness. That was what it was: this is what it is, Cassie thought: the sadness of it, back again.

It never went away. Not really: only for moments now and again, and then it picked it up once more. Again and again.

Sarah, carrying it around with her all these years. So I must say something, Cassie thought: I have to say something. 'Just a beach,' she said.

'Yes,' Sarah said. 'Just a beach today. The best beaches are the ones with nobody on them, I think.'

Cassie imagined about the children. Out of sight now, scrabbling and crunching on the shingle beach. The ground falling away from under them. And no need for it.

Cassie braced and said: 'Stop thinking about it.' She felt, not for the first time, an impulse to reach for Sarah and embrace her, to clutch her hands and arms. But no: Sarah didn't like to be touched: instead Cassie steadied herself there on the shingle, reaching her fingers into the stones as though to root herself to the ground. Enough to ask the question, to say something.

Which was something they never did.

She remembered the strangeness of the feeling the previous night, lying there in her bed in the darkness, with just a rind of yellow streetlight outlining the curtained window. She had imagined she was standing out there, on the silent suburban street, looking in on Sarah's life unfolding on the other side of the window. It was like being at the cinema. The girl Sarah had been, long ago when Cassie first came to the farm, when she first saw her, with the grief of her mother's loss across her pale face; the fields in which she grew up, the seashore and the white gateposts and long, hedge-lined driveway and smoky, white-washed farmhouse. And all that had come later: all this flicked through her mind in short sections, passing by the window, passing out there on the dark street – as though they were the newsreels, Cassie thought, from the old days in the cinema. Pictures of another life.

Though – no: these stories gradually assumed a life of their own. No, a *sound*: birdsong in the fields drowned by the rasp of a low-flying plane above the waters of the lough, turning and banking in the way that she remembered; the rap of those heavy boots on the long driveway; the dry rattle of a poker raking out the ashes in the farmhouse, in the hearth, long ago; the deep sound of explosions at sea, trembling through the house, through the rocks; and the sound of the other explosion, this one a wall of noise as she crouched on hands and knees behind the rocks, her hands covering her head, her ears ringing. Sarah's life, come alive. Cassie took her courage in her hands and said again, 'Stop thinking and thinking.'

'I don't,' Sarah said.

Which was untrue, of course. Of course, Sarah thought: of course I think about it all every day; about everything, about the unfolding of it. She knew her story was only a tiny element – an obscure one – in a larger story. And she understood that this knowledge did not much matter to her. She stayed centre-stage.

So: yes.

And also no: for hadn't she managed successfully enough to shuffle this body of knowledge into a crevice in her mind? – it hadn't even been all that difficult.

'Plenty of people,' Sarah said, 'saw worse things than I did. They don't talk much about it, but they still carry it all around in their heads.' She looked back along the shingle: there were her children now, moving into view, along the edge of the water. 'I do think about it,' she said. 'But I have, don't I, to try to leave it all behind me? I don't have the energy for all this.'

All this concentration on the past *and* the present, she thought: is what I mean. Yet she was: concentrating on present and past; flooding her life with the past: the seawall crumbling. She could smell the danger of it – for them all, and for her children, most of all – she could smell it in her nostrils.

And yet, there was nothing she could do. She was set fast in her course. 'Come on,' she said, 'we'll go back to them.' She got up from the sand with a little difficulty – feeling her age, feeling her weight – and watched thin Cassie get up too, with a sprightlier air: and they began their tramp again along the shelving shingle, back towards Patrick and Margaret. As they went, Sarah scanned the sand for driftwood to bring home – and she soon found a bleached branch, as beautifully smooth as if it had been lathed. She stooped, picked it up, running her hands the length of the cool white wood.

'Martin will like this.' Cassie nodded. 'Come on – let's be getting back.'

Then Cassie said, 'For the children.'

For their sake, she meant: for the children. Stop thinking about it, if you can. What will become of you all, if you keep thinking about it?

And Sarah had no answer to that.

*

Patrick crouched by the water's edge. The shingle was crisp underfoot, the sea calm and almost motionless, with only tiny waves hissing through the sand and shingle. He suspended his hands in the icy water until he felt them begin to numb, his skin taking on a tint of blue. Then he sat back, stood up suddenly, shook his hands in the cool air until they dried. They were out of sight, almost, Cassie and his mother: they were out on the point, where the sea wall ended, with water in front of them and water to the right, and the island and the ruins of the castle ahead. As he watched, they vanished around the curve of the wall.

'Come too, Patrick,' his mother had said: held out her

gloved hands; and then she took her gloves off and he watched her small white hands, reaching, stretching towards him. 'Come too. Why don't you come too?'

Now he blinked and gazed along the sea wall. No: his mother would never do anything like that. She would never say that – at any rate, not to him. He picked up a smooth stone and skimmed it across the lough, and then another and another.

And in a couple of years Margaret would be leaving home. 'Years yet, Patrick,' she laughed – a little while ago, when he first mentioned it. 'Three years at least. Why are you worried about that now?' But three years would come around soon enough: and there'd be nobody to talk to then. Only his father, who was always sick now; and his mother. His mother, who liked to keep herself to herself, who never took his hand, who kept her gloves on, always.

There was a sudden commotion, out on the water. A swan, splashing and foaming through the water in a clap of wings: and now it took off into the air, its neck stretching ahead, and wheeled over the water and the flat fields and was gone.

*

'Come on, then,' Sarah said. 'Time to head for home.'

Patrick looked up at her, his face a mingled expression of teenage sullenness and something else – a bleakness: she took a breath. Margaret had crunched on ahead, was now rushing, climbing the slope of the sea wall; and now Sarah looked at her son, moved by something, by a sudden concern

– but most of all, by shame. 'Alright there?' she said. 'Are you cold?' But Patrick shook his head: it was too late. She clasped her hands together: he got up with noisy, grinding difficulty, and ignored her as he too crested the sea wall; and as she watched her two children vanished, disappearing over the edge. Cassie was silent. They were remote now, each from the other, the four them alone on a sea of sliding stones.

Catch them up, Sarah thought, and suddenly it seemed to her that there was a choice here, that this was another moment where anything might be possible. A turning point, she thought: I only have to speak – and she took a deep breath of salty air and almost called out. *Stop,* right now: *stop, stop and come back. I need to say something to you.* But her son and daughter were gone: and the moment was gone; and now even Cassie had passed her, reaching the slope of the wall and clambering up to the crest – and now she too vanished.

A turning point. A turning missed: Sarah recognised its familiar shape – and here was the very ground of Inch Levels shifting and trembling there under the soles of her shoes. Easier to say nothing, to keep her silence, her distance. Keep her past stamped back into a shadowy corner. Better for all their futures.

She would do it for them.

FIVE

'Who's your favourite figure in history, sir?'

The memory swam into Patrick's head as he lay under the blue coverlet. Good days and bad days: and today, his body was pounded by pain. There was a refuge of sorts in memory, in the past; greedily he plunged in.

Only last year, he thought: only a year and a bit ago. And yes, this question Patrick actually was asked, by one or other of his callow charges. And for a moment he was stumped for an answer. He rubbed his jaw – the spring of 1985: yes, the spring of last year, a warm afternoon, with summer and the end of his teaching year in sight, and the last class of the day, and the green lawns below the windows manicured and inviting and the heat building up in the little classroom under the eaves: a room filled with people waiting for the bell to ring. A helicopter racketed overhead, and after a few minutes another one: trouble, then, somewhere in town.

The bell was a better sound. Clang, clang. Once every day it was a welcome sound, heralding as it did the end of school.

'My favourite?' Rubbing his jaw. 'A teacher,' he said, playing for time, 'isn't supposed to have favourites, Mr Porter, is he?'

A rumble of reluctant appreciation, then young Porter again. 'Seriously, sir.'

'Ah, Mr Porter, this is too difficult a question on a hot afternoon. Ask me again tomorrow, when I've had time to think.'

Spotty Mr Porter did ask – and Patrick had an answer ready. James Cook, Captain Cook, thricefold circumnavigator of the globe, interested not so much in exotica and cannibals and heathens and what have you, but in people. In what they liked and disliked, in what they ate and what kept them healthy, in what they wore and if they prayed and to whom – or Whom – and why.

In what made people tick. He was a favourite.

'Captain Cook,' Patrick said. And another adolescent rumble around the classroom. Captain Cook was – *English*, wasn't he? A sense of scandal in the air: Mr Jackson didn't have to choose an Irishman – but did he have to choose an *English*man?

Patrick explained. And maybe a few of them got it. Young Porter though, he didn't approve, and he said so straight out. 'Not an Irishman, sir, then? What about –' … but Patrick cut him off there: no way, he thought, am I going to listen to some ream of Great Irish Heroes. Life is too short for that.

'Well, Mr Porter,' Patrick said. 'What can I tell you? There are many figures in history,' he said, 'and amazingly, not all of them are Irish.' Porter pursed his lips at that – a sarcastic teacher being universally disliked – and he kept them pursed as Patrick explained his reasons, his expression making it seem unlikely that he was taking much of this explanation on board.

But yes: Captain Cook it was and Patrick explained why. Explained doggedly, even as he sensed the interest fading in the room. That was just too bad: Mr Porter had raised the issue, and now they would just have to see it through to a conclusion. Collective punishment.

Captain Cook. Because he kept his mind open. Because he was a useful observer of the scene – no matter how bizarre that scene might have appeared. Because he was an explorer. Because he took people as he found them – an amazing feat in the middle of the eighteenth century, and still an amazing one in the twentieth. Patrick was aware of how just amazing it was: after all, he himself hadn't kept his mind all that open, had he? And he himself was not so good at taking people as he found them. But he was still a pretty good observer of the scene – though he had already given up the idea of becoming an explorer.

'An explorer?'

His mother's voice, shriller than was customary, high with disdain.

'Well, we'll see how you get on with that.'

And true: he hadn't done much exploration, even when the opportunities presented themselves. He was a dilettante, when it came right down to it.

'Will you come with me?' Margaret asked – later, weeks and months later, when the business was over and done with. 'I want to see it for myself: I mean, the place.'

He said, despairingly, 'Why?'

'I just want to,' Margaret said, 'but I can't go on my own.'

'I can't.'

She squared up to him. 'You have to,' she said, 'because I can't go on my own.'

They went: quietly in the middle of the Christmas holidays, a raw, chill Wednesday afternoon when they could be fairly certain that there would be nobody else on the path, nobody else on the flat fields of Inch Levels or at the water's edge. They parked the car and set out on the gravel path, crunching west towards the distant shore. To their left, water lay slicked across the landscape; the slope of the sea wall to their right was covered with grasses: dead, but still rippling and bending in the bitter wind; as they walked, the grass gave way to a low growth of leafless hazel. 'This wasn't growing here,' Margaret murmured, 'when we used to come here with the parents, was it? It seems changed.'

Patrick slid a glance at her. 'I'll say it's changed.'

She looked away.

'Did you tell Robert we were coming here?'

She said, 'What do you think?'

They passed the pumping station, they reached the water's edge. Stood, looked, scanned the grey water, and the crumbling outline of the castle which rose on the far shore. There were still bouquets being left here: three or four today, encased in plastic, several rotting, one still fresh. They weren't the only ones, then, to walk out across the fields to this spot.

He expected – what? A burst of tears, a flood of horrified emotion, regret, guilt? He hardly knew. He watched Margaret as she stood by the water's edge and looked out across the lough; as she scanned the shingle at her feet; and as she looked up at the grey sky. Her expression was set.

Then, they walked back to the car and drove home.

And that was that. So much for exploration. Terrain, or the heart: Patrick stayed away from both, after such an experience.

In any case, this ostensibly adventurous thread in his personality was too easily subsumed by daily life: so he told himself. By paperwork, class plans and administration; by rates bills and car tax – and now by cancer; each in its own way a highly efficient means of quelling the spirit of adventure. Any urge he actually did – honestly did – have to be in the thick of things: naturally, life took care of that. He saw where such urges led and he began to recast his dreams, his inclinations.

Now, though, lying under his blue NHS coverlet, with an abundance of time to think, to consider and reconsider, Patrick was coming around to the idea that his spirit of adventure had always been a myth.

'An explorer?' Sarah scoffed – and there it was; perhaps she was right after all. He had always been comfortable with maps, charts, atlases, with pocket encyclopaediae of Flags of the World: more comfortable than actually going to any of these places.

More desiccated, perhaps, that he had allowed: and now in his bed, he closed his eyes tightly.

There was a postcard on the corkboard hanging on the wall to the left of the bed: a lurid affair, a cartoon map of a Greek island portrayed in blues and hot, mustard yellows. 'Which island is that?' he had asked the nurse when it arrived in the post, peering at it (this was one of his bad days) through eyes that were yellow too.

The nurse peered too. 'It's from – Jim, or John, or – I can't really read it. Does a Jim or a John make sense?'

'Which island is it?' he asked again, sharply; and the nurse flashed a glance.

'Zante, it says.'

He knew Zante. He knew all the Greek islands: had set himself to learn them all, long ago: to learn all their names and all their little island capitals. In the same way as he had learned all the capitals of the world, all the flags of the world – long ago, to please his teachers, to please himself.

More dry, yes: more desiccated than he had ever allowed.

'Now where's Zante?' the nurse asked, thawing a little. And he was able to tell her. And later, to tell himself that he was nothing more than a Casaubon, comfortable with his lists and his reams and his charts. More comfortable than he would ever be with real life. He had walked the fields at Inch Levels that day with Margaret: that was all the real life he could stomach. No other examples were needed.

Not an explorer, then. More like one of those pond-skating insects that stars, from time to time, in the less expensive natural history programmes.

An inglorious demotion, he knew. But he also knew that it made more sense.

They would glide around exploring their environment, these creatures: they were deft, they never punctured the surface of the water, they observed and regarded and absorbed. Their antennae were never idle. Human explorers saw more of their world, but a pond-skater saw everything.

It experienced perfection.

Easy to imagine himself as just such a creature.

In the interests of balance, of course, he had been obliged – 'I'm obliged,' he told them – to give Mr Porter and his adolescent pals the other side of the story, there in the stuffy classroom under the eaves.

'Obligated, sir,' said one of these cronies, from the front row of seats.

'Obligated?'

'It's what the Americans say, sir. It's what my brother says they say,' the student said, drawing himself up a little. 'He's an attorney, sir, in Philadelphia.'

'Oh, an *attorney*, who is *obligated* from afar to correct my English,' Patrick told him drily, and the class laughed. 'Well, there you are now. Well, boys, I'm obligated to give you the other side of the story. Listen up, Mr Porter, you'll like this.'

And he told them. About the privileges accorded explorers down the years. To shed experiences as rapidly as they are acquired. To move on, to have others enter the space that has been created, in order to set this new world to rights. To allow horror and degradation to ensue: think, he told them, of the history of America in the aftermath of the *Mayflower*'s arrival on the scene. Think of the Vikings landing on Irish shores, the Spaniards coming upon the Incas, the British arrival in Tasmania and the Maori arrival in a pristine, pre-human New Zealand.

'Think of my own Cook,' he told them scrupulously, 'and think about the diseases they unleashed.'

'Diseases, sir?' They liked this bit.

'Smallpox, boys, running from island to island, and killing everyone in its tracks. No immunity, you see: they died like flies.' He didn't mention syphilis: he didn't want any parents to hear that he had been lecturing their Catholic boys about stuff like that. He hoped they'd cotton on by themselves. 'Think of the deluge,' he said – and he thought suddenly about the deluge, about Robert and Margaret; about the flood that runs across the fields when a sea wall breaks.

He swayed on his feet: paused for a moment, the boys eyeing him. But no: he was well trained; he kept his talk, cool, cold. He kept his composure.

Better, he understood already, to be a pond-skater. It did less damage. In his fantasy life, he could continue to skate and watch and observe. To experience perfection; to do no more harm to anyone.

'So, what happened to Captain Cook, sir?'

Porter was looking – sly. Knowing, literally. Though, how would he know? Why ever would a Derry schoolboy know about the fate of Captain Cook?

'I mean, did he –'

'Live to a ripe old age?'

'Yes, sir.'

'No, Mr Porter, that he definitely didn't.'

This advantage Patrick was able to wield over some of the great explorers: he kept his distance. Unlike his favourite: James Cook, clubbed to death and then filleted on a beach in Hawaii. His mistake? – getting too involved. He ought to have kept his distance and kept his head, sailed away and stayed away – and then he might have kept himself whole and lived to enjoy a hearty Yorkshire retirement.

'So I suppose the moral of the story, boys, is – what?'

The boys looked at him. They were thinking, presumably, about being filleted, and what that would feel like.

'Mind your own business, boys, of course.'

*

That same summer – mere weeks later – he went to New Zealand. Partly, in fact, to check out Cook's stamping grounds, his base at Ship Cove: this was the official reason he gave, in fact, to his family. To Sarah, who looked sour and disapproving, who complained about the extravagance, the expense.

'Wouldn't Spain do you? Half of Derry goes to Spain in July – but oh no, *you* have to go to the other side of the world.'

'Not every summer I don't, Ma. You make it sound like it's an annual event.'

She pursed her lips and seemed to withdraw her head into the folds of her latest scarf like a tortoise into its shell.

Not *any* summer, he ought to have said – but his mother had a humiliating knack of silencing him, even now in his thirties.

'Good for you,' Margaret told him over the phone. Her voice held its now habitual bleak tones. 'Good for you. Why not. Any other news?'

Yes, he wanted to say. *I want to put half a planet between me and Derry, Ireland, the whole damn place. I have had enough, at least for the time being: enough of my family, of grey streets and obstreperous students, of the present – and of history, of the past, and of my conscience, most of all.*

'No, not really. You?'

A pause. 'No.'

'How's Robert?'

Another pause.

'He's not doing so well, actually. But so what?'

Yes: so what?

July was winter, of course, in the southern hemisphere: not that he minded that; and the New Zealand weather stayed reasonable. Patrick travelled the length of the two islands, staying in youth hostels as he went – aware that he was the object of compassion on the part of young, unwashed fellow travellers, some of whom liked to ask kindly questions of this solitary guy rattling around the communal kitchen, and to regale him with their take on Sri Lanka, on Malaysia, and (to shock) on the drug scene in Thailand, in other places.

'Man!' they would say, scratching their on-the-road beards and hippy braids.

Patrick only wanted to read and be left alone: but he felt obliged – 'obligated!' said a voice from the recent past – to listen to them. Of course he knew he could press the off button and cause them to beat a retreat at any moment, simply by informing them that he was a schoolteacher. In their juvenile minds, teachers and the FBI were clearly synonymous.

Towards the end of his visit – thoughts already tilting back towards lesson plans and staff training days – he fetched up at Picton, and took a launch out to Ship Cove. What to expect? – he hardly knew, though he was pleased with what he found: a curving bay of deep, green water, a beach of white sand; and on either side of the beach the dark New Zealand bush growing down to the edge of the sea. He took the path that led from the cove to the heights above and looked back and down and drank in the landscape and seascape: all green points of land and serpentine fiords – and this little silent cove of deep water in the middle of it all. And he the only visitor that day and apart from the little jetty and a plaque, there was no sign at all of human intervention in the landscape. Entirely alone: and that pleased him most of all.

He remembered this now: now, lying in his blue hospital bed. The afternoon was darkening and there had been no visitors and the pain for a moment was not so very bad: and he was able, he had the liberty, to think a little. To take stock of memories of air and light, to think of colours and textures, gleaming gemstones stitched to the fabric of his life.

What had he felt, there on that silent beach, on the dense, bush-clad hill above? He felt the sheer fact of the distance from home: this was mind-boggling and wonderful in itself. He felt a sense of space in his head for the first time in years, because the life that crowded him in at home was now, suddenly, sloughed off – sloughed off, shrugged off into deep, cold New Zealand waters. He felt he might be in with a chance of washing himself clean there, far from home. To step away from involvement in the lives and deaths of other people.

Patrick had imagined it was too late for him to learn this lesson – the one he ought to have learned long ago. Sitting by Ship Cove that day, though, he knew he would never forget it again. He thought about what had happened to Captain Cook: killed, filleted for the crime of getting too involved. He thought: look what happened to Cook – and look what happened to me. He thought: from now on, I'll keep my distance.

And then the launch returned, and he clambered on board and was brought back to Picton.

All of which meant that a little corner of this tapestry would be stitched and coloured and emblazoned in green and blue: in the dark green of the New Zealand bush, and the cold green and profound blue of its sea, and the wake of a little white boat puttering across the Sounds. Nobody else will understand it, he thought: nobody else was there; this will be my story alone. Private history. Nobody there to report on the meteorological conditions, on the views of the sea, on the sounds of the bush. Nobody in the whole world, for those few hours, but me.

The relief of it. And the understanding that a new chapter might, tentatively, have begun.

He returned home now – and a year or so later came the diagnosis. This had been cruel, it felt cruel still, to be left with a series of might-have-beens.

Patrick moved a little in his blue bed. Time had run out, instead.

*

The bush was silent. Midday, and warm for the time of year, and Patrick shed his coat, his hat, his scarf. The sound of the departing launch faded and he was left in deep silence.

Earlier, lying in his bunk in the hostel, he had listened to the cacophonous birdsong of New Zealand, sounding through the bush which hemmed in the little town. Not a bird he could recognise. It came to him, then, that Cassie might have known. Some of them, anyway: not the native ones, but the others, brought here long ago from Europe. She knew about such things, though he had never bothered to learn from her.

Now, standing on the sand at Ship Cove, the birds had fallen silent; and the sun, winter-low in the northern sky, glared on the water.

He was here to see for himself. To feel for himself: this blessed isolation, this aloneness that was the opposite of loneliness; this self-containment, he thought, that for these few hours was his alone, to be grasped and cherished. He stood by the water's edge, on this beach that was once the centre of the world for a ship's company – each member of which was busily hacking, hammering, stewing and provisioning – and which was now deeply silent and private. The sand ran down rapidly into deep, green water: memories of other waters, other beaches came to him and were thrust away. This is *mine*, he thought: this moment belongs to *me*. Not hedged in or elbowed or crowded by anyone else. Not compromised by one's own grievous mistakes and sins, or those of others – but instead, a semblance of independence and peace, to keep hold of for as long as may be.

He turned from the water and up the beach and onto the trail that tracked up the hill, deep into the bush. He walked slowly uphill, feeling the muscles working in the backs of his legs, feeling fit; *I'm young still*, he thought, though he puffed a little, his face reddening as he climbed. Soon enough, he reached a saddle: the path levelled off and then began to fall away; through the thick growth, he watched it fall and in the distance begin again to climb, following the beautiful contours of the land. No further. He looked back: the ground dropped away steeply back down into deep water; and there was the cove behind and below him, the jetty, the white sand with no tracks on it today but those he himself made. He laughed: Crusoe, he thought, how are you?

Of course he had grabbed at a sense of perspective before now: grasped at a long view back over the landscape of his life. From time to time he had attained this perspective. Naturally: time and experience ensure this. But now he was aware of a ringing clarity: and aware too that he had been obliged to put some physical distance between himself and this still-unfolding life in order to attain this clarity.

The lesson? Well, he thought, I know the lesson: never again to take on the affairs of others – their violence, their guilt and aggression. Their swaying, flailing emotions.

Never, never again, he thought. He looked straight down, to this hillside plunging into deep water. He thought: I might wash myself clean, here. I might be reborn.

*

One of the points Patrick liked to make in class – though there were so many, and he was aware that some of them didn't quite hit the mark – was to do with the trickery of history. These people stalking through history, who knows what they thought? What they imagined and dreamed? 'How can we tell, boys? Our arrogance in making assumptions about these things: we can extrapolate, that's all, but we can never really know, can we?'

The boys sighed.

He thought about the Spanish sailors on that Armada ship, long ago: what did they *think* as they came ashore, or as they felt themselves drowning in cold Irish seas? What did they *say*? Nobody could say – though it was easy enough to guess. 'They cried for their mothers,' he told the students, 'didn't they?' The boys shifted uneasily: this was too emotional. Though probably true. 'And what else? They cursed their leaders, the

Protestant English Queen, the weather; and they prayed to their Catholic God.'

This was more like it – the cursing, the Protestants; the boys perked up. 'And what about all those others – those men in those armies, those women nursing, those camp followers, following a leader around the world? What did they think, how did they feel?' Sometimes they leave letters and journals behind, he told them, if it so happens that they could read and write; usually, though, we never know. 'We have to be watchful around history,' he said. Narrow our eyes, and read between the lines.

He gave one of the nurses a little lecture on historical context, when she came in to plump up the pillows the other day. Or last week. Poor nurse.

*

'And this one?' asked the nurse. Good to have this young fella – God love him – nice and chatty; and she gestured at the latest card pinned to the corkboard on the wall, she peered. 'The white cliffs of Dover, is what it looks like.'

There was a pause. He seemed to fade, right there in front of her.

'Something like that.' He closed his eyes briefly, opened them again.

'Were you there?' the nurse asked. She glanced surreptitiously at her watch.

'Something like that,' he said. 'Yes,' he said, and closed his eyes again.

A painting: a nineteenth-century painting by William Dyce that he saw once. *Pegwell Bay*; he saw it in the Tate once on a trip across the water, and it cast a spell on him, being at once serene, and yet full of unease and doubt and fear. *Pegwell Bay*: it portrayed the white chalk cliffs near Dover, and though he was not English – not at all English – he knew about these cliffs. They were a comfort to the English; they enfolded the English in a warm embrace of happy, supreme insularity. In front of these cliffs the painting showed a family group – actually the Dyce family itself: a father, a mother, a child Dyce; even an aunt or two. But the family, he saw, was spread out thinly across the landscape, and nobody was looking at each other: instead, one figure looked one way and another figure looked another way, the beach was otherwise empty and vast, terribly so, and all the while a comet streaked silently across the sky.

Margaret stood beside him, chafing, silent. They were in the middle of a quarrel.

Patrick stood there in that splendid room in the Tate and looked at the painting for a long time. He knew a little about Victorian art. Dyce, he knew, was a bit of a Christian – lots of Madonnas and Children stuffed into his portfolios – but he was also a bit of an amateur scientist, a geologist, an astronomer. He settled on Pegwell Bay because this stretch of the Kent coast was falling into the sea, eroding year by year, exposing fresh gleaming-white chalk all the while; the beach in this painting was strewn with fallen rocks and debris. He settled on the comet because comets always prophecy Doom. And he settled on his anxious figures because he was living through an anxious time, with Darwin and evolution nibbling away at all those high Victorian certainties: God was suddenly more dead than alive, and his compatriots were spending their weekends at the seaside, slung about with hammers and magnifying glasses, poking around looking for the very fossils which proved – yes, that Darwin was right and the Church wrong.

Patrick stood in the echoing gallery, and thought about all this. So much context. He stood longer than he would normally have stood – deliberately, to annoy his sister.

Poor Dyce, he thought. What could he do? – well, the only thing he could do was to go off and execute in oils a painting about context. It made him feel better: it got it all out of his system, and then he could go back to his Madonnas, feeling Godly and secure once more. Fair enough, Patrick thought – and then they went off to the gift shop, and he bought a postcard of the painting.

'Can we go now?'

'If you like.'

They left the gallery and headed up Millbank, walking briskly east towards Westminster.

'History's a man's game, don't you agree?'

Margaret flashed him a glance. 'Shut up,' she said – or rather shouted, over the din of a diesel-scented London bus rasping by.

His father had told him about the Spanish Armada as they drove out and across the border into Donegal that day. Told *him* – not Margaret, history being a man's world – as they drove up the hill and down again to Kinnagoe. He sketched in a little context, and his son's imagination did the rest. The galleons and supposed treasure chests, the winter storm and the foundering ship, the waiting locals and the drowning men, Philip of Spain in his castle and Elizabeth of England in hers: what a context.

Clang, clang. The bell began to toll in its belfry across the garden. Home time for the boys, though not for Patrick. He was clinging on for dear life.

*

Characters being outlined, he thought. Using one of those soft, black pencils that roughens, thickens their edges; and crumbling, waxy crayons.

In black and white: yes, he thought; some of them. Like the medieval morality plays we studied in university: not to my taste, then, but I can appreciate now the starkness of them, their love of allegory and metaphor. He shifted in the bed: they needed to come to him soon, to do their rounds, to turn him; he was almost past turning himself. In his mind's eye, he roughed in his Robert: his medieval Robert, surrounded by shadows and ivies. His mother, in deceptive pastels; and his father in darks and greys, sensible colours; and Cassie in – pale blues and greys, perhaps. Margaret, caught in a snare of ivy, creeping and binding her feet.

And what about me? He thought: how do I appear? I'm

tumbling down the pecking order: that much is clear. They are making it clear – here in this place. The other day he remembered the impatient someone, a brisk and unsmiling nurse on the bustle in the room, her patience a little stretched. It was, after all, one of his good days.

So she put him in his place. They slapped each other roundly for a few minutes; but she put him in his place.

'Dear me,' he said. 'On duty again, Samantha?' He said, 'Don't they ever give you a day off, to go back to that farm of yours?'

She smiled, a little tightly. 'Sam isn't on duty today, Patrick. You'll have to put up with me today.'

'You sound harried. Busy today, is it?'

'No rest for the wicked, Patrick,' she said.

'Are you wicked, Samantha? I wouldn't have imagined you'd have many opportunities to be wicked.' He said this with a lilting sweetness. He had closed his eyes now – but she was on the attack already. A word or two would do it.

'More opportunities than you, Patrick,' she said – and his eyelids flickered. He said nothing for a moment – and when he spoke again, the sugary tones had vanished.

'Where's my tea?' he snapped. 'It's getting later and later. What time do you call this?'

'I call it four o'clock,' she said.

'Then you'd better go and see what the hell's going on.'

And she went, the not-Samantha, the soles of her shoes squeaking on the floor. He could see a small and satisfied smile curling her lips.

90

And that was that. He didn't come first for Sam or her abrasive colleague or anyone else, not any longer: this was the sad lesson of infirmity. What about inside his own head? – did he still come first in his own head? Hm, maybe not: another lesson, to be absorbed.

Only of the past – or aspects of it.

Which was something: something to grasp on to, as nurses turned him and massaged his buttocks and God knows what else.

'Stop that!' he'd said recently, for someone's fingers felt icy cold on his buttocks. Whose fingers? – but that was the worst thing, the most humiliating thing, for he couldn't recall. What? – someone's hands on your buttocks, on your *own* buttocks? And you didn't even know whose hands, whose cold fingers they were?

It was no wonder he was finding a refuge in the past. And that day: the day of the painting, the Tate, the diesel-belching red London bus – that was the day he met Robert for the first time, his life – even if he didn't know it – turning smoothly and silently on a pivot.

They had gone to the Tate to try to cool down, was the truth of the matter: literally to cool down, mainly, for this was the boiling summer of 1976 and they were red in the face and sweating as they wandered through London. Margaret was living there at the time: she had been unhitched, boyfriend-less, chafing with frustration – but all this had now changed. She had taken up with a new fella.

Robert, from Belfast. Patrick didn't like the sound of him –

not one little bit. And they would be meeting up later that day.

They walked slowly along Millbank, and found a bus to take them to Piccadilly Circus: then plunged along Regent Street to do some shopping. London was looking a little tatty, Patrick thought, in the heat: the parks baked and yellow, the leaves dull and dry on the plane trees. A gallery, they thought, to cool off, and then we'll be ready for some shopping. That ought to do it. Pegwell Bay, first.

'It could be us,' said Margaret. She stood considering the painting: the mercifully cool air hummed with quiet footfalls, with the unshakeable, carrying confidence of middle-class English voices. Supported voices, thought Patrick, who had been reading about supported voices, and who now imagined a room filled with muscular, toned diaphragms. Supported English voices. Irish voices, he thought, hardly ever sound like this: our diaphragms, he thought, must sag in the middle.

Now he frowned. 'Us?' he said. 'What do you mean?'

'I don't really mean like us,' Margaret said, still examining the painting.

'No, because there's only one child.'

She turned, triumphant. 'There! You were looking at the child too!'

He paused. It's true, he was. 'I suppose I was.'

'You were. And so was I.'

She'd been getting deep into psychology lately, he knew: into mother figures and father figures and family dynamics. It all sounded a bit heavy. He watched her turn to the painting, as though to recharge her vision, and then back to him.

'Here we are, two adults, still identifying with the child in the painting. Now,' she said, 'what do you suppose that signifies?'

'Oh, *signifies*,' he mocked, fearing the ocean floor soon to fall away from under his feet, fearing he will soon be out of his depth, fearing he will be at sea amid this mass of psychology that is – surely – coming his way.

'Here we are,' Margaret went on, staking out her position inexorably, 'on our own. Grown up. Have been grown up for a couple of years now. Away from home: we can do what we want. We look at a painting. We see a child – and it's the child we identify with.'

Patrick looked at the painting again: at the crumbling chalk cliffs and the pools in the sand, at the comet streaking silently through the sky. At the child. 'OK,' he said, 'I see what you mean.'

Margaret nodded. 'Arrested development,' she said with a sort of horrible satisfaction. 'Both of us.'

He flinched. 'Come off it.' And regretted the phrase at once, as his sister took offence.

*

'Come off it,' he said, and Margaret felt her temper rise, her face redden with something more than the heat of the day.

'Listen to me!' she said. She felt her temper in her throat, in her chest, a sort of pulsing, beating. She had a quick temper.

Her mother, too. Snapping at her. 'What man would have you, if you go on like that? A fishwife. Who'd have a fishwife around them?'

Well. She had a man now. They'd be meeting him later, in Hampstead, and she was not looking forward to the experience. And now she embraced her anger. The heat, the pollution of the city, her environment: all conspiring against her all day – and now here was Patrick too, contradicting her flatly, unpleasantly. 'Listen to me!'

She began to talk about Sarah. Their mother who never nurtured, who seemed to have no idea *how* to nurture, who undermined them, who didn't seem much to like her husband, her children; who kept them in bondage.

'Bondage!' Patrick blinked. 'Bondage! This isn't the Bible. Bondage,' he scoffed. 'The Jews were kept in bondage,' he said, 'in Babylon.' (Wasn't it Babylon?) 'Not us.'

'She hasn't allowed us to grow up,' Margaret said. 'That's the truth.'

They quarrelled, there in the handsome, spacious room. Other visitors sidled past, or lurked in the corners, under the arches, to listen to their distinctive accents, their Irish voices. They quarrelled – but they often quarrelled. It meant less than the rapt bystanders seemed to think it meant. Later, they walked down Millbank to the bus stop. Still discussing their mother, but this time with less passion. The city was hot – but these two, suddenly, were not.

They did quarrel a good deal. They were bound together – which did not mean they were a pair of ghastly ideal children, lifted from a sickly-sweet Victorian Christmas card. Not at all. They went on scrapping their way through their youth – physically, sometimes, taking lumps out of one another if the opportunity arose. Margaret, being older and bolder, tended to emerge triumphant from these early confrontations. Later, as they were forced to graduate into verbal weaponry – though still sharp ones, cudgels and axes – Patrick managed to finesse his verbal dexterity a little, to rile Margaret that way, to drive her up the walls with anger and frustration.

Temper, said Sarah. So undesirable in a lady.

Leave her alone, said Martin, for Christ's sake.

But Margaret found herself a man in the end – after the longest of searches. The countryside trawled with exceptional thoroughness; and the end result hardly the most prepossessing specimen in the world. Robert: lurking in a dark corner, with tendrils of ivy winding around his ankles.

Margaret blamed her mother for it. For this lack of romantic interest. For the shape of her life. For everything. For all her woes. With justification, as Patrick came to realise. 'I wish we could get to the bottom of it,' he said one day. Meaning: why did their mother withhold her love?

But he never did get to the bottom of it.

SIX

Sarah would take the pan of uneaten porridge every morning, and step out of the back door, and scrape the cold, congealing contents of the pan onto the lawn. Onto the same spot, and for the birds – but the birds would not eat it; and over time a bald patch formed in the grass.

'The birds don't like porridge,' Patrick said one day, knotting his school tie, donning his blazer; Margaret, in her dreary bottle-green school gabardine, was already out the door and away. 'Why don't you put it in the bin instead?'

Cassie was busy with tea and toast; she glanced at him. Martin was absorbed in the football results. His mother, saucepan in hand, paused.

'You'll be late for school. Go on, now.'

He went. The porridge was never explained.

Later, as a teacher, Patrick had a natural inclination for spotting a student – a child – in trouble at home: a child spinning untethered by an absence of love, by violence, by the domestic disorder which comes in a multitude of forms. He had an eye for it: he helped to bolster such children, sensitively, invisibly.

This was the repayment of a debt, yes – but he would have done it anyway. He understood those domestic landscapes that are so crucial, that are everything in the eyes of a child. Mental maps, as he thought of them – thinking of his atlases and charts and books of flags stuffed into a cabinet at home – in which each aspect and factor crucial and comforting ought to have its fixed place, with luck.

In his case, in Margaret's case, no such luck.

Of course there were landscapes and terrains available to them, as to any child. In this case, though, these places seemed lined with trenches, pocked with potholes. It was easy to turn an ankle on such terrain: to go flying, to be bruised and marked. His mother dug the trenches, carved out the potholes; or so it seemed to him. Cassie was there too, but Cassie could not compensate, not completely.

What did he remember?

The suburban house, into which the family moved when the children were both very small: the first house he could remember. A big bungalow, long and low, sporting a breakfast nook complete with comfortable banquettes and a skylight overhead onto which the Derry rain pattered and occasional hailstones clattered, and – best of all – snow occasionally fell, softly and envelopingly in winter, covering the sky overhead with a thick, white blanket. A thrilling early memory.

A high shelf in the hall on which his mother placed her prized copper bowl: it would catch the evening sun and flame out in red and orange.

'Where did it come from?' he asked one day. She had taken a chair and lifted it down with tender care; and dusted and polished it; and now was returning it to its high shelf. A little dent, a notch, shadowed its broad lip.

Sarah glanced briefly down. 'Never you mind.'

What else? His bedroom, with a window out of which he could hop, directly into the long back garden: a pampas grass tossed out there in the wind, with a belt of trees to the rear, screens of shrubs to either side in which a small boy could scout, lose himself, embark on a journey of exploration. There was the gap in the fence where the neighbouring garden could be accessed, where apples could be stolen from an apple tree in autumn; there was a tangle of blackberry brambles that had been allowed to do their own thing, peaceably, wildly, with a tribute of berries annually. And there, the hide colonised by a local tabby who, docile and easy, would allow her belly to be tickled, her ears to be scratched. Here a little boy could lie in dry grass and look up at a screen of branches and beech leaves, into white and blue sky.

Mental maps, as he thought of them, later: incontrovertible maps that stood the test of time and memory, that could not be contradicted; that made their paper equivalents flimsy, anorexic things.

In those earliest days, he put together a map of solidity, of security, compensating for their absence elsewhere. The house was *here* and the garden *here*; the beech trees *there* and the blackberries *there*. He and Margaret hunted in long grass; or he was alone, daydreaming on warm, bare earth. Rain falling in the world outside – as he staked out the dry hide, with the amiable tabby for company. Cassie in the kitchen, the rattling sound of an oven being opened, being closed. Discoveries to be made that were already conceived and understood. Warmth and routine, endlessly fixed and unchanging.

And, eventually, the field notes, the observations that threw up other information, that introduced discord, that could no longer be ignored. The world at length beginning to vibrate and to tremble and then to shake. A body, the body of a young man right there on the footpath, as fifteen-year-old Patrick walked home slowly from school. Not to be stepped over, exactly – for there were soldiers and policemen, and white security tape snapping in a brisk wind – but as good as. A little blood from the neck wound, dark on the tarmac. 'Did you walk straight past?' said Sarah, pressed up against the worktop in the kitchen. 'You always just keep walking. Remember that for next time.' And Cassie, gesturing to a plate of buns on the table.

The outside world, and the domestic world too – the world as a whole, which one day placed its boot, its heel against the windows of the house and kicked, and sent shards of glass flying through the air. And in the process sealed a relationship – in blood, in dreadful gravity; and with manifold consequences.

*

It had rained the previous evening, and after the rain frost – and now, on the following afternoon, the pools of water by the side of the road were still iced over. Patrick set his heel on one of these pools; the disc of ice moved slightly. He brought his heel down on the ice: though it did not shatter, fine, white cracks radiated out from the point of impact.

'You could go skating on that,' he told Margaret, 'if it was big enough.'

She nodded. She was distracted – and with good reason: there were crowds clustered all around them, they were being jostled a little as they walked – and they were walking slowly, with thousands of people behind them and thousands in front. The march was bigger, apparently, than anyone had anticipated.

Which was good.

And something else. It was good craic too. 'This is good craic,' Patrick murmured and again Margaret smiled, nodded. People were having a laugh as they walked: the air filled with buzz, with chatter. This wasn't what he'd expected.

His first march.

Not Margaret's first march, of course. She'd been to some, up in Belfast. Not good craic at all, those ones, she said – and Patrick could well believe it, Belfast being Belfast. They walked slowly downhill, in the midst of the crowd. They passed the cathedral, they passed the swimming pool, they passed terraced houses burned out now, they passed the snapped trunks of saplings, planted in a fit of unrealistic optimism, they passed the derelict bakery. And now the atmosphere began to alter: he could feel the change sweep rapidly through the crowd. The clatter of the helicopter –

invasive, unpleasant, but of course expected, anticipated. It wasn't the sound of the helicopter that caused electricity suddenly to charge the air, the chatter of voices to die to a murmur. He sees faces glancing up and over: a sea of heads snapping up to the left and staring and then snapping back again, snapping straight ahead. He looked to the left himself, and saw snipers, armed, lying rigid on the roof of the Sorting Office building. He looked away, he saw Margaret look away – in disdain, and in fear.

Amazing, how rapidly loud chat could fall away, how rapidly tension and fear could sweep through a crowd. He could feel it. He didn't say much and neither did Margaret: instead, they continued to walk slowly. The sun had long since reached its zenith and was now, on this late January day, beginning to sink in the sky: already, long, thin shadows were stretching from the edges of the crowd. They walked slowly and he took in this new electric charge.

'Don't go,' their mother had said. Especially to Margaret: let Patrick go if he must, but Margaret should stay at home. But no: the days when Margaret would stay at home were long past. She was a university student, she was old enough to make her own decisions. She was nineteen years old.

'I'm going,' was all she said. Their mother pursed her lips at that, but said nothing more. Cassie watched silently from the kitchen door as they donned scarves and hats and winter coats; low winter sunlight glinted red on the copper bowl on the shelf in the hall. They walked slowly into town – a long walk from their suburban home, though not unpleasant on this fine day – in time to blend with the middle of the crowd as it snaked down Creggan Street. The place was packed.

Speeches were to come a little later. They arrived at the corner of William Street and Patrick looked south and saw the road blocked, the usual makeshift arrangements in place: a stage set up on the back of a parked lorry, festooned with placards and banners; and more crowds on the far side, a sea of dark clothing and white faces. He looked east and saw the narrow mouth of William Street blocked by a barrier where it met the city centre, sealed by more soldiers with helmets, more guns. He looked north and saw Little James Street blocked by another barrier, by more men, helmets, guns, by the high wall of the Sorting Office. He looked away and then behind, to the mass of dark clothing and white faces that filled the street behind.

Not trapped, no question of a trap. Yet his instincts began to tighten, to whine, a shrill noise on the edge of his hearing; and he took Margaret's hand. Just in front, the flats rose on one side of the road: three high-rise buildings, incongruous in this flat landscape of small houses and small terraces. The flats were sheer, jerry-built, grouped around a dismal car park. Beyond them, in the distance, the hill crowned by grey buildings jumbled in behind the line of the city walls. There were figures moving on the walls itself: soldiers, of course, with binoculars and cameras and more guns, manning their observation post up there, taking in the scene. He glanced up, and then away. Let them look, he thought brazenly: much good may it do them.

The multitude was still moving behind them, packing the streets still more tightly. Patrick felt crowded, suddenly: his shoulders jostled, Margaret jostled. He loosened his grip on her hand, and took her elbow instead, and they shoved their way out a little from the crowd, stepped towards the nearest entrance to the flats complex: a narrow, shadowed slot between two of the buildings. For a breather. There was another barricade set here – in fact a mass of rubble, three or four feet high, set up this time by the people themselves – and here they stopped, lodged in shadow between the rubble and the sheer wall and a phone box. For their breather.

Patrick turned to his sister.

'Maybe we should go home.' His instincts were singing still higher now: a thin, shrilling whine filling the inside of his skull.

Margaret paused.

'Well,' she said, 'let's just wait, why don't we, and listen to the speeches from here.' She gestured to the coal lorry in the distance. There would be loudspeakers: they'd hear every word from here. And they had the wall as a sort of shelter. Not too many people would congregate here, not many would want to, most of the marchers would want to be in the thick of it, wouldn't they? 'This is grand,' she said. They agreed to wait here, in this narrow slot. 'Happy birthday to me,' she said.

*

They were huddled, twelve or fourteen or sixteen of them now, behind the phone box, beside the wall: neither phone box nor wall nor rubble barricade nor the great frowning side of the block of flats could provide anything like adequate shelter, of course – but nor could anywhere else. There was steep Chamberlain Street, just ahead, a route up and away to safety – but no, because an immensity of ground lay between it and them. Not that there was shelter anywhere from the snipers, not from the bullets slicing through the air, coming from this direction or that direction, nobody could tell from where. From every direction, maybe: for the air was crackling with rifle shots, crackling with tension, crackling with a dreadful, infectious fear. No: no shelter anywhere, but they must stay here, beside this phone box, beside the wall. They dared not make a run for it.

This is all my fault, Margaret thought as she cowered there, on her knees behind the phone box. If Patrick is killed today, it will be my fault.

The air was poisoned too. She could smell the gas – they could all smell it, for there was coughing all around, retching combined with screaming, and gunshots and the deafening clatter of a helicopter overhead. From time to time, people ran past, making a bolt for it – but where? She stayed there, then, on her knees on the stone-strewn footpath, with Patrick on his knees in front of her, and an inferno of smoke and poison and the reports of gunshots filling the air.

The destined bullet found its target in front of her. A man, a man she did not recognise, had straightened up beside her: he had been sheltering there with her, part of this terrified group in the lee of the phone box – but now he straightened up beside her and took a step, two steps away from what seemed to be safety. She saw why: there was another man lying there, perhaps ten feet away – no more – on open, rubble-strewn ground. He'd been shot, but was clearly still alive, for he had moved a little now and again in these last few frightful minutes. And now: 'I can't stand it anymore,' her companion said: and he straightened up and took a step, two steps, and died, the bullet entering through one side of his head and exiting at the other, just at his right eye. The eye exploded outwards – Margaret saw this happening only a few feet from where she crouched by the phone box – and blood and matter flew in the air and struck the wall; and the man fell to the ground. Now there were two bodies on the ground in her direct line of vision; and the sound of human screaming was louder than ever; this and the sound of the helicopter overhead filled her brain. And she reached out and grasped Patrick's shoulder and pulled him back, hard, as he in turn made as if to lunge forward to help the dead man. 'He's dead, he's dead,' she hissed. 'He's already dead.' She pulled Patrick back, hard – and now he was flat on his back, and the women in the crowd gathered around his prone body as though to shield him, or to sit on him, to stop him making a second attempt. They formed a phalanx, though there was no need: Patrick stayed on the ground and made no further attempt to move. The whole world was constricted now into these few feet of grey pavement, strewn with rubble and marked with blood and shadowed by the bleak wall of the nearest block of flats. It was only a temporary respite: they were coming for her and for Patrick; to pump bullets into her head too and into her brother's head. This grey pavement is where we will die, this afternoon; and it will be my fault.

*

The tea trolley rattled in the corridor. A sister rapped an instruction, a nurse turned with a squeak of a heel and clipped away. The door opened.

'Tea, love?'

But there was no movement from the blue bed, no acknowledgement.

'Or is it coffee?' A pause.

What did their mother imagine, how did she feel, that day in Derry as the news began to spread out across the city, from street to street, from house to house? Easy enough to guess: the point is, though, that they had to guess, Margaret and Patrick, because their mother never said. They were obliged to guess. She never described or articulated. Not a word, in all the years that followed.

And Cassie, following her lead, said nothing either: she merely looked and watched and listened.

An aggrieved sigh, and the door closed again. No tea this afternoon.

The front door opened, and closed. There was a short silence – and then the rustle of coats and scarves being shed. Cassie moved first, from the kitchen where she was stationed, looking out into the empty back garden, twisting and twisting a tea towel in her hands. The news had spread. A telephone call, and the flurried arrival at the front door of a neighbour, another neighbour. The distant wail of sirens and the clatter of a helicopter: all noises par for the course – but the neighbour had got wind of something more, today, something greater. Sarah looking and looking again at the front door: though what did she think she would see? Nothing to see, Cassie thought. But useless to say anything: better to stay quiet and wait for the news to come in.

And then the front door opened and the children appeared, and took their coats off. Cassie dropped the tea towel, she felt herself move forward, as though on wheels: through the kitchen and into the hall and she herself said nothing, thought nothing, only felt a wash of relief course through her. Her head was light, her heart was beating painfully.

'We're alright, Cassie,' said Margaret and she took Cassie's hand and tried to lead her back into the kitchen, to sit her down. Everything was alright now, wasn't it? But Cassie could see the expression in her eyes and the whiteness of her skin, and now she glanced back at Patrick, and his expression and pallor were the same: set, fixed with shock and horror. 'We're alright, Cassie,' said Margaret again. But Cassie felt now a pulse of – something, of terrible recognition. A gust of her own memories:

and now she sat, and Patrick, responding, rattled the kettle and familiar sounds took over; and now Sarah bustled down the hall and into the kitchen and asked if everyone is – and you need a cup of tea – and what happened? And the story began to be told, and Cassie closed her eyes. I know what happened, she thought. She thought: it is always the same story.

She kept her gaze on the floor, for fear of what she might see if she looked up, and at Sarah.

And when on the following day, on the Monday morning when the man arrived to deliver and hang the new living-room curtains – yellow-gold, and heavy, handsome curtains – Sarah threw him out of the house. She gave him his marching orders: and only Cassie there as witness.

If the children had only been in the house, if they had only been there to see and hear this for themselves, they might have changed their minds about poor Sarah. A little, anyway: they might have given her more credit.

'Served them right,' said the man. 'What were they doing there, anyway? Looking for trouble, that's what. They had it coming to them, so they did.' Brazenly. Cassie's head swam.

Sarah had ordered the curtains at vast expense. 'They'll last us a lifetime, Cassie,' she'd told her, a little defensively, 'they'll have to.' But she looked now at the man standing on his stepladder – the department store made the curtains to measure, and lined them, and delivered them, and hung them too, bringing their own stepladder, filling the room with a golden glow; it was a full service – and now suddenly she took the man's metal measuring tape that lay nearby and flung it into his face; and he teetered, there on the ladder.

Well, what did he expect?

The man uttered an oath, but he had no time to say anything more, for Sarah's tones stopped the words in his mouth. 'Take your curtains, and get out of my house,' she said, 'and don't come back.' The man descended the steps, and she took them and pulled them through the hall, and opened the door and flung the ladder out of it; and the folded curtains after them; and the man said not another word and was gone inside two minutes.

They managed without any curtains for a few weeks and Sarah made an excuse to the family, and the story was never told. I wish she would tell it, Cassie thought. It might change some minds.

*

Cassie.

Well, of course Patrick was thinking about Cassie.

He thought about her each time they came through the wards with the tea, the coffee, with the Digestive biscuit balanced on the saucer: tea and coffee and Cassie went together with an absolute inevitability. She provided layers of – something in his childhood. Of what? Strangeness and comfort combined. Strangeness, for she seemed to put something of a spoke in the wheel of a nuclear family: mother and father and two bright children. Although that was an exceptional fact in itself: that was a strange sort of family, at that time and in that place. What? – only two children? Catholic families tended to aim for the stratosphere when it came to children, with six, seven, ten the usual numbers; Cassie's presence, then, provided just one more layer of strangeness to an already strange situation.

But comfort too: always there, always rattling around. Making up for what their mother could or would not provide.

She was an orphan: he and Margaret knew this. She had been slotted into their mother's family – 'placed', they would say now – back in the summer of 1937. She was sixteen at this time, their mother some years younger. This much of the story had they pieced together over the years: slowly, looking through paperwork and gleaning the occasional slender fact from their mother herself. Her own mother had died in the spring of the year: her father would normally – this was the Irish way – have been expected to find himself another wife, and fast, with the resources of the community placed at his disposal to locate one and seal the deal as soon as could be arranged.

But it turned out that their unknown grandfather wasn't in the mood. He didn't want to find himself another wife: he had been more than satisfied with his first one, and didn't much care for the idea of a substitute. His house needed a woman's touch though, that was certain, and his own daughter was still too young to do what was needed.

These were the facts, put together slowly.

'The nuns sent her,' their mother said: and Patrick and Margaret, whispering and imagining, came to see a huddle of

111

nuns, all habits and wimples, crape and veils, black and white, cooking up a conspiracy between them. This solution? – to pluck a likely-looking girl from the county orphanage and establish her in their grandfather's house as cook, housekeeper, washerwoman and general help. Someone not uppity, someone who could be relied upon not to get ideas above her station. They imagined that to the nuns who ran the orphanage, their grandmother's early death must have been quite a blessing, no two ways about it.

Cassie would do! Cassie was immediately lined up to step in. What an answer to prayer! Sure, what else would she be fit for?

Cassie: a little slow, a little dreamy, and a dab hand with pastry. The children loved her: she was their fixed, calm centre. They exploited her every opportunity that came along: exploited her goodness to the hilt, running rings around her, demanding she make cakes and soup and sandwiches. She existed to service their needs.

Although sometimes they bit off a little too much.

*

Patrick placed his hands on the counter-top – and sprang, lifted himself. Then knelt and reached for the biscuit cupboard. His mother had slipped something in here earlier – something: a packet of biscuits, of chocolate, he'd watched her from the doorway. Now she was gone, away for an hour or two. 'Back in an hour, Cassie,' he heard her say. Gone to the butcher?

Gone, anyway: now the coast was clear. Now he and Margaret had the place to themselves. Cassie wouldn't mind, Cassie didn't count.

The package was there. Blue, with white stripes. Sweeties. Maybe mints? They were new: he'd never seen them before. The Rich Tea tin was there too, but he knew already that there was nothing to be found there. Only old, soft biscuits. Nobody would want *them*.

He felt Margaret behind him and turned, precarious on the counter-top; his knees hurting already from the press of the hard surface on his kneecaps.

'You're not allowed,' Margaret told him piously – but he had his answer, flourishing the contraband package; and she moved forward, rapidly. 'What are they?' She examined the package. *Goodies*. 'What are Goodies?'

'Let's open them and see.'

In a moment, the package was ripped open. Little discs of chocolate, with an odd powdery bloom – but chocolate just the same. And now they heard Cassie in the hall. Her soft slippers flapping on the wooden floor, as always. She shuffled through the hall, she came into the kitchen.

Very short, very small. Patrick was almost taller than she was, already; Margaret was taller, definitely. They measured their height, last week, then measured Cassie – and how they had crowed with triumph.

Now, they didn't bother to hide the package of Goodies. Cassie wasn't their mother: she wouldn't snatch, she wouldn't raise her voice, she wouldn't skite them across the legs.

Most likely she wouldn't do anything at all.

'We found them, Cassie,' said Patrick.

'*Goodies*,' read Cassie.

'Do you want one?' he asked generously. But she shook her head and smiled a little.

'I'll have a cup of tea instead,' she said, and she flapped softly across to the sink, filled the kettle, looked out of the window. The garden was alive.

*

The garden is alive. There's the sun shining on the water in the bird bath that she filled early that morning, when she had the house to herself, the garden to herself, the birds shrilling and singing. Now the afternoon garden is silent, but still alive. The sunlight is white, thought Cassie, on the water; and green through the leaves. I'll make some tea, she thought, and go outside for a few minutes; and leave them to it. And suddenly she laughed: she laughed and laughed, there at the sink, until a tear rolled down her cheek.

The children stared. 'What are you laughing about, Cassie?'

She shook her head. She made her tea, still laughing, and went outside.

*

The chocolate buttons – the Goodies – tasted… strange. But definitely chocolate.

Later, they were sick: both of them, just a little. 'It's your own fault,' said their mother, 'for sneaking around the kitchen the minute my back's turned. And it'll teach you to ask before you eat.' She had given the Goodies to Roger, the black Labrador who lived over the garden wall. She had a soft spot for Roger, who was plump and friendly and glossy and who didn't answer back; and she often bought him dog treats. The Goodies were new, but Roger liked them already. 'You should have asked Cassie,' added their mother, snapping on a pair of rubber gloves to clean up the little bit of vomit on the floor. 'Ask next time.'

*

Sarah, who came to visit once or twice a week. Who ate grapes and crunched on the seeds. Who was very much alive: who had become the sort of person who was determined never to grow old, never die, who was determined to outlive the whole world.

Patrick was trying to make sense of this, too. He was trying to make connections.

His mother would outlive him. That's pretty definite, he thought. That's looking like a good bet. The rest of the world, he thought, I can't speak for.

She moved about these days in disguise. On a permanent basis. She had gone in for fleecy pastel wools in her widowhood: not quite shawls – that would be too weird – but cardies and scarves. Yes: to act as a disguise. And it seemed to work too.

People treated her like a sweet lady. In the past, she'd had an eye for expensive, hard-wearing tweed suits: the sort the rain would run off, as though it were metal-plated. It stood out, in a place like Derry: people would look at you, and that was presumably the point.

Now, though, the nurse took one look at her pale blue or pale pink wool and rushed to fetch a cup of tea, to make a fuss of her. Patrick kept his eyes closed and refused to say a word. And prayed – in vain, needless to say – for the end to come: death, he thought, would be preferable to this.

The day before, she had been on top form.

*

'Tea,' said Sarah. 'Tea would be lovely. If it isn't too much trouble.'

'No trouble at all,' he heard the nurse say. He heard her leave the room: he heard the door swing open, he heard it close, he heard shoes squeak into the distance. He kept his eyes shut. Other senses took over: he heard his mother sigh and settle herself in the high-backed chair; he smelled her disguise, her perfume of jasmine and rose.

The disguise, he thought, is absolute. The room was silent.

Presently, the nurse returned. A clink of a cup, a saucer, the tinkle of a teaspoon. The nurse was – she must be – busy: but his mother ensured, now, that she stopped what she was doing, that she follow up the cup of tea with conversation, with her time and energy channelled in a new direction. Any

116

news on my son? – the first, polite question. No: the only one, for his mother held information at arm's length: even now, in this extreme environment, where questions and the needs of others must be paramount. She sipped her tea and focused on her own concerns; and he heard the floor squeak and squeak again, as time ticked on dreadfully, as the jobs mounted up, as the nurse – he could sense it – grew more and more desperate to get away.

His mother had a trick: he had seen it deployed a thousand times. She would reach out and grasp a wrist: she took it and held it, so that the person simply could not get away without being unpardonably rude. Patrick's eyes were closed – but he knew she was doing it right now, doing it to the nurse. There was a strange breathlessness in the nurse's voice, and he'd heard this before too. The girl was all at sea.

'Never?' said his mother, sounding surprised. 'Well now, there you are. That seems strange, I must say, in this day and age.'

She was talking about southern Spain: about some Costa or other, the one she visited last year.

'I –' said the nurse.

'I know,' his mother said. 'Each to their own, dear: you're quite right. Or her own, in this case. But the *sunshine*. And the Alhambra –'

His mother spoke of the Alhambra. The nurse did not know about the Alhambra. Patrick lay and listened, with a strange, bitter satisfaction. At least, he thought, at least it isn't only me. At least she from time to time selects other victims too.

Well, serve her right, probably. Nurses and medical staff need metal plating themselves, he thought, and they all too frequently display it to me. Since when was a little lady so impossible to handle?

So he told himself. But of course he could never handle his mother. He never could – so he could hardly bitch about other people not being able to handle her either.

I could never handle her, he thought. Margaret could never handle her. He, in fact, had been a bit better at it: Margaret was reduced to jelly by their mother, or to gasping, wordless fury, or to supplication – to a range of states, in fact, and none of them in any way constructive or flattering. Bawling at her mother as she stumped from a room, a door slamming in her wake; or incoherent in the face of a patronising expression; or, or, or. 'Why would you do something like that?' That being: German at school, or art, geography, history. Brown bread baked from scratch. 'Sure, I wouldn't bother, if I was you: you'll never be any good at it. You'll have people laughing at you.'

And later: 'Those hips: couldn't you do something about them?' A fishwife. Who'd have a fishwife around them? And what about that hair?

Poor Margaret, he thought: that was how it was, for her. No wonder she settled for Robert: done to get away and stay away.

Armour plating. How odd it sounded: to describe one's own mother as armoured. And yet it was the image that came always to mind. The tweed suits repelling water, the tough skin repelling love, the words, the language crafted to keep one at a distance.

The eyes – that had something different to say, though impossible to tell what. Interpreting what the eyes had to say would be a life's work. Nobody would have the time.

Margaret might have made the time, had she been given a little encouragement. But none was forthcoming, and that was an end to that.

She was always clear-headed, his mother, with an iron constitution and an iron turn of phrase. Honed, no doubt, from many years in a girls' school, where iron turns of phrase came in very useful. And she also could boast of a generally iron will: she spoke her wishes, and they tended to come to pass.

And perhaps, he thought, perhaps I ought not to slap her down too hard. Not too hard. My mother kept the family together. This is a fact, he thought, of history.

'And I loved the local food. The seafood,' his mother told the silent nurse. 'We export most of our fish to Spain. I say we should try keeping some of it.'

Patrick lay silently, and listed facts as once he had listed capitals of the world. The objective was the same: to create and maintain order, to feel on top of things.

Margaret, he thought, tried to drown me in the sea off Kinnagoe beach on a summer's day long ago, when I was six years old and she seven or thereabouts. This is a fact of history: she denies it, but I claim it as an unalterable truth. Then she saved me. That was our relationship. This is a fact.

My father had a stroke four years after that day on the beach. Another fact. My mother took over the management of the family, of its finances, of everything. Another fact.

Martin was still young, when it happened: only in his late-thirties. It happened on the night of the 1964 General Election.

'They've booted them out, they have, they have!' Martin said excitedly. 'They've put Labour in again. At last! – well, just about.'

He was watching the results on what he liked to call 'our new suburban telly'. 'Our suburban telly for our suburban house, our suburban dream,' he would say, waving a hand at the long windows overlooking the patio, the still bare garden. 'Who'd have thought it, ladies and gentlemen? We've made it at last.'

He liked to talk like this in front of Sarah, who was the mover and shaker behind the shift from a Victorian terraced number close to the city centre to this new suburban house, this bare, unformed garden. 'More room for the children to play,' she said, and Martin replied, 'ah yes, in a mud bath, a nice mud bath that I'll be working for the next thirty years to pay off.' Sarah tended to leave the room at that point: the children, smiling uncertainly, joined in with his jolliness. Now he was crowing happily as the election results rolled in: 'That'll teach them,' he was saying: and then he had a stroke, just like that. Patrick and Margaret had been allowed to stay up late to watch the telly, and that proved to be a mistake – for they were right there when Martin keeled over on the hearth rug in front of them.

Nowadays, Patrick thought, we'd be hauled off for trauma counselling. Back then, we were told to – to get on with it, something like that. Which they duly did. They scratched their heads and got on with it.

And it didn't kill him. It was a relatively minor stroke, and the doctors were hesitant in the matter of connections with the General Election results. No, probably no connection between the two. And no, it didn't kill their father – though it didn't make him stronger, either.

And the family tended to be a little anxious around politics, after that.

A minor stroke, so it was classified: but Martin could no longer work; and so Sarah was obliged to pick up the white man's burden. That was the phrase she herself used. 'The white man's burden for me, then,' she said, standing in the living room of the new house, which would have to be paid for somehow. That, as Patrick reflected frequently, was another of her phrases.

'We could have paid for the old house in about five minutes flat,' Martin said.

'Ah well,' Sarah murmured. 'No use crying over spilt milk now, is there?'

And she picked up, in fact, the white man's burden with gusto: Patrick understood this later. She drew on the mathematics degree she had taken in her late twenties. She drew on a facility with numbers in general and a general sense of organisation – and was appointed bursar at the girls' school down the road. And yes: it soon became clear enough that she quite liked having a good job to go to in the mornings and that these new arrangements were right up her street. And she quite liked having an infirm man to leave in Cassie's care at home. It appealed to her, in all sorts of ways. Patrick saw this early on.

He was himself sensitive to memories of his father's early illness. He was too young to have a father figure transform into someone who seemed not always there. Too young to have a mother transform into a breadwinner. Too young to – wondering at the vagaries of the world – assume something of the burden of being the Man of the House: having to cut the grass and clip the hedges, grumblingly, since his father was no longer up to it.

'Why don't you do it sometimes?' he said sourly to Margaret. But these were jobs for a *man*, she reminded him with relish.

'You can't have your cake and eat it,' she said.

Cassie was still there, of course, to provide the cakes. At that point she was still around: physically strong and able and profoundly domestic, and still had a way with pastry that nobody could better.

So Cassie did the cooking and the cleaning; and Patrick did the garden; their mother went out to work and their father sat around, nursing his health. Patrick knotted his tie and went to school, and Margaret clambered into her tunic and gabardine and went to hers; and they both did very well. Robert was not yet on the horizon, and so the world continued to go round and round.

Martin had taken on Sarah when not many men would have done so. She was an odd one, it was universally agreed in the district; too odd for most, even if that Cassie one was left out of the equation. Certainly Martin's mother thought so, and told him bluntly what she thought.

'What would you go and do a thing like that for?'

'What's wrong with her?' Martin had been a blithe young man, with a socially useful career as a GP mapped out from an early age. He was one of a rare breed in this part of the world: a Catholic family with means enough to put their son through grammar school, and then through medical training, and all without financial distress to themselves. Without noticing, even, was the word around Derry. They lived in one of the fine old Georgian houses close to the city centre, with plaster moulding and ceiling roses and a brass knocker on the glossy front door. They thought well of themselves.

Martin was already qualified, in fact, when they met, after the war. Sarah wasn't qualified: she was qualified to do nothing: she was becalmed. 'What will she do?' said Martin's mother, who was a great believer in female emancipation. 'She'll marry me,' said Martin; and his mother pursed her lips and turned away. 'The breed and the seed of her,' she said. Martin left the room. He slammed the door. Sarah's life took its decisive turn that night: she was persuaded out of her digs one night by an old school friend. 'We'll go to Borderland,' said Isobel. 'Come on: we'll paint the town red.'

'So this is what you meant about painting the town red,' Sarah said when they arrived. She looked around: the walls of Borderland were red: a strange, dark red that soaked up the light. The band was playing and the atmosphere lively; the place was packed. People were having a good time, but Sarah herself was not likely to join them in this. She'd made her mind up about that. She was a sore thumb.

'Come on,' said Isobel. 'Aren't we here to have a good time?' She did not herself seem to be having a good time: Sarah's mood was infectious; no man was coming near them. Isobel's foot tapped the floor – not in time to the music, but nervously, a nervous bounce on the sticky timbers. It had been kind of her: she hadn't seen Sarah for months. Isobel thought she ought to show willing, to be kind.

Maybe now she was regretting her kindness.

'You need to dump me.'

Isobel turned, frowned. 'That's right,' she said. 'That's what I need to do. I need to just dump you.'

'I'm giving you smallpox,' said Sarah.

'Shut up, will you.'

'Typhoid,' said Sarah. 'Bubonic plague. Infantile paralysis.'

Isobel turned away. 'Stop feeling sorry for yourself,' she said over her shoulder, bluntly. 'It's very unattractive.' Sarah stared, said nothing, blinked. 'Clear?'

'Clear,' Sarah said at last. 'Clear.' They laughed, the two of them, for the first time in the course of the evening and at that moment, the two young men who had been observing them from the far side of the room, made their approach. They were well spoken, well dressed; around the room, other girls stared with displeasure; they knew a catch when they saw one.

*

Martin could not account for it. He leaned with his friend Danny against the red walls of Borderland and observed her

124

through the haze of cigarette smoke. Martin could imagine – or rather, he could not imagine – what his mother would say if presented with such a girl. Such a girl! A country girl, out to grab any man. Was Martin mad?

He was. Danny, leaning beside him, cigarette in hand, seemed to understand – later, he reflected that if Danny hadn't been there, if Danny hadn't supported him, then he would never have plucked up the courage to step across the floor, with so many beady eyes tracking his step, and ask this girl to dance. His life would have turned into another channel. Though, Danny had his eye on her friend and had a stake himself in this adventure.

'We'll ask them to dance, come on,' said Danny. He drew on his cigarette. 'Come on,' he said again, 'before someone else does.' Which was a foolish thing to say. Nobody was going near these girls – but Martin too felt an urgency just the same, a prompt to get in there just as fast as possible. Danny stubbed out his cigarette, clicked his tongue in irritation. 'Come *on*, Marty,' – and now the deed was underway: his feet were on the move and the eyes of the room swivelling and focusing; the girl looked truly, genuinely, frankly dumbfounded as he presented himself in front of her and asked her to dance. She flushed, nodded; beside her, her pal was already being whisked away.

*

Behind his closed eyelids, Patrick saw the daylight begin to fade, heard the texture of the background hospital sounds.

move up a gear; dinner was on the way. He heard his mother wrapping up, heard the nurse gather herself to go, to get the hell out of there.

'Patrick?' Sarah said. 'I'm going to go now.'

She gathered herself up; she left without fuss. In the blessed, relative silence which followed, he continued to dredge up his now worn mental maps. Even in this place, on this ward, in this bed – dusted off with ease. Recalling various events of childhood, events like that trip to Kinnagoe, visits to other beaches, assorted picnics with Thermos flasks and battered Tupperware containers filled with ham baps – picnics to be consumed in the car, more often than not, with the rain bouncing off the roof, and condensation fogging the windscreen. A family unit intact, after a fashion.

Intact, Patrick thought: *intact* in this case meaning a righteous mother, a humiliated father, a marriage far from simple or mutually satisfying. People tell themselves that children notice little or nothing, he thought: when the truth is that they notice everything, every last thing. They are sponges, soaking up the ether. Certainly he and Margaret soaked it up: but they were also aware that their affairs were being managed well enough, that their needs were being met. That they had three adults in their family and not simply two: that one of them was in the kitchen from sunrise to sunset, and that they were as a result better off than most of their friends.

That the lid was on, though it rattled from time to time ominously, and that all was well.

That the map of their lives was laid out on the table, or spread on the floor: clean and clear and unarguable in its portrayal of past and present and future.

But as they grew, it began to dawn on them that this map of their lives, past and present and future, was perhaps deceptive. That its clarity was false: that the myths which helped to structure all of their lives – myths of sanctity, of togetherness and security – had in their case little bearing on reality.

A devastating idea – even if, in their case, it dawned slowly, in fits and starts. Because they needed the myths – more than this, they needed the myths to connect in some way with reality. Patrick began to imagine another map – a palimpsest, he thought later – laid over that map: a palimpsest, with marks in dark indelible ink. These marks soak through the pure fabric of the map: they stain and mark; and all the while the edges of the map grow grubby and soiled with handling, with use, with life.

And of course he was well able to listen and watch and absorb all the while – well able to observe as hand grenades were aimed and flung from one room, to explode in the next. A man's body lies splayed across a footpath, to be sidestepped, to be stepped over. Who knows what a child remembers and absorbs? And who cares?

Sometimes, nobody cares.

*

'Don't say another word,' Sarah said. She stood in the kitchen doorway, watching Martin. His newspaper flung away, its leaves scattered; his reading glasses on the table, as if flung too; his cane on the floor; the air crackling with anger. Cassie had vanished, as if into thin air; along the hall, her bedroom door closed quietly.

Cassie gone, Patrick gone, Margaret gone. They had the place to themselves. Plenty of words thrown back and forth already, exploding like so many mines in the landscape of this house. And now more words hovered, momentous, almost spoken, ready to detonate.

She regretted her language already. Sickness and incapacity; overwork and a house to run: slick phrases, spoken easily, spoken to goad and injure – and Martin had flung the newspaper across the tiled floor; had taken off his glasses and thrown them onto the table. And now he took aim in his turn.

'Who would have taken you on?' he said. 'Nobody, that's who. You were too much of a handful. But I took you on,' and he lowered his voice and gestured along the corridor, '*and* her,' and now he raised his voice again, recklessly, 'and is it any wonder, is it, that I got a stroke out of all that?'

She stared at him.

'You'll always have making up to do,' and now, though he had lowered his voice again, the force of his words were, if anything, greater still. 'You'll always have,' he said, throwing her trust, her confiding words long ago, back in her face, 'and you know it.' He reached for his glasses, bent for his scattered newspaper. 'So get on with it,' he said, winding up now. 'This is your lot.'

Sarah looked for another second, and then turned and left the room.

The pampas grass rustled and swayed. The sun was warm and the ground dry, hard; and the bristles on the pampas snagged his sleeve, snagged Margaret's sleeve. They were crouched, the two of them, behind the pampas; its leaves covered them like a scratchy blanket.

'We shouldn't listen,' she said piously, with the tact, the law-abiding attitude of age. The kitchen windows were wide open: they could hear every word. They stayed where they were, they listened until the conversation ended, until the silence that fell was worse than the shouting had been. The kitchen was silent: no rattling of dishes, no clatter of pans. Cassie was simply not there; and when they peeped through the rasping pampas fronds, they saw their father's black, glossy cane lying across the floor, their father's stockinged feet at the table.

'Come on,' Patrick said, and they scurried from the shelter of the pampas, rapidly across the grass and into the jungle of longer grass and trees and shadows that lay across the back of the garden. There would be shelter here, dappled sunlight and dry ground and the friendly, purring tabby, perhaps, to stroke and tickle. But even as Patrick scurried into the long grass, the warm air filled, his head filled with angry voices, with the hard clatter of his father's cane flung to the floor. The blackberries will be gone, he thought, and the tabby and her nest will be gone and the apple tree next-door will be – it will be cut down, someone will have cut it down and left it there, lying on the grass, and the leaves shrivelling away to nothing.

He stopped for a second, his head swam; it will all be gone.

'Go on, go on, what are you stopping for?' said Margaret and she dug hard fingers into his back. 'Go on, go on.' And he stumbled on – and there were the long curtains of blackberry brambles, and there were the blackberries, green and small, all over there. You can't pick them yet, but there they are. The apple tree would still be there too, he knew now without having to look – and there was the tabby stretched out and sleeping in her shady den; and she woke and saw them and stretched, her claws going out and going in; and she yawned and Margaret, on her knees, stroked the tabby's soft fur; and the tabby began to purr.

Patrick saw all this. He stood in the shade, and saw green sunlight shining through the beech trees. Margaret turned from the tabby.

'What are you looking at?' she said. 'You look funny.'

He shook his head. 'Nothing,' he said. But there was a trembling that he never had felt before, a shaking in the ground. Perhaps there will be an earthquake, perhaps someone will come with sharp shears and cut, cut, cut the blackberries away before the berries turn from green to black, perhaps there will be an explosion. 'Nothing,' he said, and now he too knelt and buried his face in the tabby's warm, soft fur; and felt her purring. Nothing.

SEVEN

'Let's go back the longer way. I'll direct you.'

Kinnagoe and the Spanish Armada was behind them now: as the car climbed the steep slope from the beach, the road turned sharply back on itself once, then twice, and Sarah looked from the passenger seat straight down the green hillside onto black rocks, white sand, turquoise shallows. The deeper sea was a dark, dark blue: somewhere out there the Armada ship lay on the seabed, undiscovered, its timbers gone, its metal remains barnacle-encrusted.

Martin had been going on about this lately, to the children – but of course people had always said: this been the story; she could remember such tales from childhood. The surviving men came ashore onto the beach and the locals were waiting for them – and what happened then? Eaten, said some – said malicious young men, intent on terrifying their younger listeners; but her father frowned.

Long ago, now.

'Eaten?' he said. 'Were the Irish cannibals? Were our ancestors cannibals? Is that what you're saying, girl? Eaten, is it?'

'I didn't say it!'

'Eaten, indeed. Marched off, is what happened to them, and handed over to the English. Which was bad enough,' he added, as though debating with himself, 'but what choice did they have?'

Now Sarah gazed down onto the beach. She remembered these old stories, remembered her father's actual stories. Then she pulled in a deep breath and blinked, and glanced over her shoulder into the back seat, at Cassie, at Margaret and Patrick, red with sun and slack with tiredness after a long day in the open air. 'We'll go back past the farm,' she decided suddenly. 'Left at the crossroads,' she said and settled back into her seat. Cassie stirred. Martin glanced.

And at the crossroads, they turned left.

After a few minutes, another ridge and now another view opening up: Lough Foyle in the distance, a sheet of water, blue and silver in the westering light; and bluer hills beyond. There was the church spire and the beginning of the town, and there! Sarah thought: there was home ground. She gestured then, suddenly, to the right: the land here fell into a shallow valley, in shadow already on this summer evening, into a landscape of small fields flecked with rushes. 'There,' she said to the quiet back seat, 'that's where I lived and Cassie lived when we were growing up.'

There was a short pause and then questions began to bubble. *What age were you?* and *where did you live?* and *where's the house?*

Again, Martin glanced at her.

'Do you want me to turn in somewhere?'

'What? No. Why would you turn in?' She looked across at the fields, her voice resuming its habitual sharp tones. 'There isn't anything to see.' The house was still there, as it happened: but in someone else's hands now. It had been tarted up, so she had heard. Running water, now, and the works. Well, it would, wouldn't it? The Stone Age was over.

She spoke quellingly, and the children were duly quelled; Cassie looked; the temperature inside the car, having crested, dropped. Martin drove on, Sarah looked out at the fields skimming by.

It had just been a notion and she regretted it already.

Patrick piped up.

'You're a closed book,' he said, 'so you are.'

She turned, stared at him: this little boy, all bare, sunburned legs and a red face.

'Says who?'

'Says –' But Margaret elbowed him in the ribs and he said, 'nobody. Says nobody.'

Sarah twisted forward again, and said nothing more.

A closed book? The injustice of it all.

Her children knew that a family had existed, didn't they? Nobody could say that she didn't pass on information. About a father, Brendan, whom she had just about tolerated; and Cassie, devoted Cassie, who was still here, still with them. A farm: they knew about this too. This was all known: had been discussed, even, around the kitchen table. Even her mother, her long-dead mother, was mentioned. A closed book?

'Six, seven,' Sarah had told them recently: the meal over, her hands on the green-and-white checked oilcloth spread across the table.

'Six, seven?' cried Patrick. 'Six is my age!' He paused to think about this.

Margaret asked, 'Can you remember her?'

'I remember her well enough,' Sarah said. And then, 'and that's when Cassie came to live with us.'

It was so easy, she thought – as the children's eyes swung around to Cassie – it was so easy to deflect.

Though it was true: Sarah could remember her mother fairly well. Time blurred the edges, certainly: certain elements sanded away over years. She thought, once: what colour were her eyes? God knows. Was she tall or not so tall? – though nearly everyone is tall to a child, she thought, so no point even thinking about that one. But her mother had – she had dark hair, very dark, and very pale skin; a dusting of freckles in summer. Freckles, Sarah thought, and long, capable fingers.

So yes: she remembered her well enough.

Certain memories emerged from this jumble of snatches and threads. A mild evening in late spring: the fields greening, everything growing as it should, a dry spell of weather, though not too dry; all well. Sheets floating on the line strung out across the farmyard, her mother sitting on the doorstep, a girl cuddled close – just the one girl. The hawthorn hedges lining the long driveway in bloom, white and creamy-pink, and their sharp and almost acrid scent filling the air. 'Look, but don't touch,' her mother said, as she had said so many times before.

'Never touch – see the thorns?' The little girl saw the thorns, she nodded. 'And never, ever break a branch and bring it in the house. Never, ever.' The little girl said, 'why?' – but she knew the answer. 'Because of the fairies,' said her mother. 'The hawthorn belongs to the fairies and it belongs outdoors, where they belong. You don't want to make them angry.' The little girl nodded. 'Will you remember that, Sarah?' The child nodded. She knew the fairy ring in the field, that her father would not plough, that he skirted, walked around. A *wide berth*, he called it. 'Give it a wide berth, Sarah,' he said, 'and I will too, and that's the best way.'

And now her father appeared, around the corner from the barn: he picked the child up and threw her in the air and caught her and set her down again, gently on her sturdy legs; and they were laughing together, young mother and young father and little girl, all laughing together, as the sheets floated in the soft evening air. 'My great girl,' said her father, and he ran a brown thumb along the child's temple. 'What a great girl.'

This was what Sarah remembered – as if she herself had not been there, as if the cosy child was some other little girl, some other unrelated little girl, as if Sarah was hovering elsewhere, maybe near the floating laundry, watching. Perhaps this was why she remembered so well – because of this sensation of feeling like a viewer, a peeper, a watcher. There were other memories too and they were the same: as though she was touring a picture gallery, taking in this or that framed scene from history, in the days when her father still stood tall and upright, when he laughed and took her hand and her mother's hand. It was all too long ago.

She thought, after some years had passed by, that perhaps it had begun with the farm. This stealth, this caution. Knowledge of the farm coloured the opinions of others, long ago. She was the child of a farmer; there was always plenty to eat; there was land; there was a natural advantage there, over other children, other families. A dead mother was a disadvantage – but being of farming stock provided a balance. She understood how people thought: and it made her wary.

What else: red-checked cloth on the table; and the gleaming copper bowl with a wide lip that was her mother's pride and joy: set on the broad window sill in order to catch the scant light. Her dowry, she called it once. 'All I had with me,' she said ruefully, and her father laughed and gently touched her hair with a finger. 'I wish this house wasn't so dark,' she remembered her mother saying: only once; and her father sighed and nodded. 'I know.'

The farm: it was not a pure blessing, in spite of what people thought. Much of their land was damp and low-lying: rushes sprouted instead of good grass; endless labour was required to keep the fields drained. And the house was low too, as well as dark; the chimney smoked. Her father took these facts to heart, more and more as time went on: he took them to heart as he took to heart her mother's death: in silence, for the most part, though with occasional bouts of incoherent anger, with the heel of his hand punched and punched against the wall.

Sarah took them to heart too, in the shape of a recurring dream: of water seeping into a drainage ditch in her father's fields. It is choked with rushes, this ditch, and very deep; and she is standing in it. The water rises, passing her ankles and her knees, her waist and eventually her neck. As it reaches her chin, she begins to scream: the rushes close in and stops her mouth. She woke always in a sweat, tears in her eyes. And around the table, after her mother died, conversation had come to dwell on drainage ditches: in their sparse conversation, in their thoughts, in their sleep. After all, their collective destiny depended on such facts.

All this she remembered.

Of course there were other events, other occasions to remember – years after her mother passed away, after Cassie had come to live with them; and not all of them sour and sad. A morning or a summer evening, say, on the beach. For they had their pick: beaches and coves below the fields; rocky foreshore, the lighthouse up the coast. Warm sand and calm, icy water, an apple pie spiced with a few cloves, knocked up that morning by Cassie; and out at sea, a ship slipping past on its way up to the docks at Derry. Or another spring evening, and the smell of green grass in the air and the noise of corncrakes calling, a *creeeeak*, a rasping in the long grass. Brendan sitting on the step, cleaning – something, his boots maybe; or sharpening a blade; Cassie on the step too, quiet, her face turned up to a bright sky.

And later, once the war began, the sound of explosions would bring them together. 'Don't worry, Cassie,' fourteen-year-old Sarah would say, 'it's a torpedo, it's a ship, out at sea, it won't come to us.' There was an echo of an echo in the walls, the faint breath of a vibration in the granite on which the house stood: the ship, the explosion was near, very near, and Cassie shivered in the bed. 'A torpedo,' she whispered in the darkness, turning the word over and over, 'a torpedo.' A ship was sinking, out there: in a day or a few days, bodies would wash up on their beach; anything could become normal, given time. 'Go to sleep now, Cassie,' Sarah said; but the two girls lay awake in the darkness, and thought about the ship sinking, a few miles away; the fire and the panic and the rising water. In the next room, surely Brendan lay awake too; for the following morning, there might be something approaching tenderness, gratitude, palpable in the air.

Harmony springing from sources expected and unexpected, in other words – even if these episodes were few and far between.

What else? As the car, with Martin at the wheel, had crested the hill, as one view – sea and hills and Scottish islands on the horizon – had sunk away and another opened up, Sarah looked across the rushy fields. An old photograph: a family photograph, which – she often thought – surely must have been an unusual household item back in the day? A photograph of her father and her grandparents there on the kitchen wall, with his brothers – long since emigrated and forgotten – taken long, long ago, at the turn of the century. Black and white and severe, the lot of them – even her father, then aged ten or thereabouts: uptilted chins, stern expressions and uncomfortable Sunday clothes, all collars and wires. Sarah pulled a face herself. Think of the expense of it.

'What?' Martin said.

She shook her head. 'I was just thinking.'

Her grandparents – her father's parents – had farmed those same boggy fields: Sarah had put this part of the story together herself, slowly over the years making sense of her father, slowly learning to forgive and understand him. As she looked out now on these fields and views, it was easy enough to see them through his eyes: to see that these prospects had been open to him too, as he made his way as a boy down to school. For a few scant years, until all that ended and his parents set him instead to work on their farm's wet fields.

These gleaming views of ocean and land and sky: how he must have drunk them in as he made his way, a little boy, along to school. And when school ended for good, when farm chores began, how his world must have shrunk and shrivelled, as he stopped taking in these views.

'What was her name?' Margaret asked, leaning across the table, her hands on the oilcloth. 'Granny's name: what was it?'

'Mary.'

'Mary what?'

'McCallion. Mary McCallion. A local girl: a townland or two away. He married her in, what, I think it was 1922 – and I was born three years later. But no more children, after that.'

Patrick and Margaret studied her across the expanse of table; Cassie leaned against the sink, watching them, watching her.

How her father must have seen in her mother a second, magical chance: Sarah had no doubts about that; her memories were too clean and clear. And how betrayed he must have felt when she died, from causes mysterious, neglected. How the family were observed now, and pitied: a certain amount could be done for poor Brendan and his motherless daughter; help given, up to a point, on the farm. These were specific troubles, and they could be remedied; it was the unspecified that caused trouble. 'Don't be telling her too much,' Brendan told Sarah, when Isobel came visiting. 'Don't be letting on.' Letting on about what? 'Just don't be letting on.' Sarah took to keeping her cards close to her chest, holding Isobel, holding everyone, at arm's length.

God knows what people thought. Sarah had traced and imagined it all.

'And that's when Cassie came to live with us.'

The children's eyes swivelled to Cassie, who had turned again to the sink.

For this was the solution found – rapidly – for Brendan's pressing domestic problems. A girl picked, plucked from the county home at Lifford: a parentless girl of fourteen or so. A bit simple, they said – but a good girl, no trouble at all. Clean and quiet; not much talk out of her. She could run the kitchen, at least; she had a good touch, a dab hand; she made the lightest, the flakiest pastry. Cassie came to the farm: for Sarah, a strange presence at first, but one who she became fond of, grew to depend on, grew to love, in time.

'Is she a bit simple?' said Isobel.

'Not as simple as you.'

But, all water off a duck's back, for Isobel.

And for Brendan: an answer to a prayer on the domestic front.

All this Sarah knew.

Later, another photograph was arranged, to hang beside that stern earlier photograph on the wall. Brendan arranged a family photograph of the three of them, taken in a studio in Derry and hung on the kitchen wall. A little less stiff, perhaps, than that earlier one – though not by much: in this photograph he was seated stiffly on a heavy mahogany chair, against a pale backdrop, and staring – a look of belligerence, almost – into the camera; Sarah herself smiled self-consciously; Cassie, in her Sunday best, broad-shouldered and broad-faced, sweet-faced, looked into the distance.

*

'Smile now,' the photographer commanded. 'Like this,' he said, and he smiled, exposing yellowing teeth. His smile faded as he glanced and then looked for a beat, two beats, at the hot scene before him: at Brendan, scratchy and reddening on this summer day in thick wool, his Sunday suit; at Sarah and Cassie in hats and Sunday best too; at the heavy, black mahogany chair that formed the empty centre of this family group. 'I need,' he paused and rubbed his jaw, assessing what he needed, blinking a little at the challenge ahead of him. 'I need –'

They had taken the bus into Derry on this August afternoon for the express purpose of having a family photograph taken; braved the covert looks and (more usually) stares of their fellow passengers; elbowed their way through the Saturday shoppers to the photographic studio on Waterloo Street. 'Like this,' the photographer said again, pleadingly this time, and now Sarah tried to oblige. Not very successfully: the photographer's tired face fell a little in disappointment. The small room was sweltering. She pulled a wider smile and he straightened up and brushed his hands down the front of his shirt. 'That's more like it.'

But it was an embarrassing episode. At any rate, embarrassing for her. For her father too, probably. The photographer, fifty-ish and stout, had no idea how to handle Cassie. I ought to be used to it by now, she thought, the way that some people can't manage Cassie. In their usual place, among their usual people – the shopkeepers, the neighbours and farmers – folk usually could muddle through: she was one of their own, after a manner of speaking, and they were used to her odd ways: the way she avoided catching anyone's eye, avoided conversation, avoided company. The photographer, though: he was unused to all of this – and his way of managing her was the especially embarrassing way: by treating her, behaving around her, speaking to her as though she was a toddling infant; and how to organise a family photograph when one of its subjects wouldn't or couldn't look at the camera? I don't know, Sarah thought: I don't bloody well know.

'Will you not smile?' the photographer coaxed; and now

he appealed to Sarah herself. 'Will she not smile? Can you get her to smile?' Sarah smiled even wider, she smiled for two – but she could see that Cassie looked trapped, cornered; smiling was the last thing she would ever do. And then the photographer decided to take matters into his own hands, to organise them, to make a success of this stiff, stilted tableau. 'This way!' he said, 'I need you turned around,' for Cassie was angled now into the corner, into the wall. 'This way!' he said again with a sort of dreadful jollity, and then he took – grasped, really – Cassie by both elbows and began to manoeuvre her into position as though she was a piece of heavy furniture, to be slotted or managed.

Sarah watched this as though from across a suddenly opening gulf in the floor of this hot studio; Brendan too watched, seemed frozen. Cassie might scream, she might bawl: she could not bear to be touched; there was no way of knowing how she would react to being hauled around. Instead, mercifully, she froze – as though, it seemed to Sarah, she suddenly *was* a piece of furniture – and seemed to bow to this handling. He moved her around, then, to the left, out from the wall, towards the mahogany chair. 'There!' he said again. 'That's lovely now. And your da there, and you,' he pointed at Sarah and then at the floor, 'you just there.'

They came to, and moved, taking their places: Brendan seated on the heavy mahogany chair, the girls on either side. The mahogany chair was, they knew, the photographer's pride and joy: most of the people in the area who could afford to have a family portrait taken – not many – came to this man, and the mahogany chair therefore featured on many a local wall. 'And now smile,' the photographer instructed again, looking up and nodding and smiling himself with relief. 'Nice big smiles,' he said.

The photograph was taken, and they thanked him and left, bursting from the airless studio and onto the street. They walked across Waterloo Place, each taking long breaths of air. Sarah tried to lower her shoulders, to wash away the tension. Brendan – for this was the next stage in this exhausting afternoon – was taking them for tea and buns in the Golden Teapot: and so they took their places in the windows of the cafe, and had their tea, their buns and watched the crowds milling outside. 'That wasn't too bad, was it?' Brendan said, and he looked at them with sudden, unfamiliar appeal. Cassie, seemingly utterly concentrated on the jammy bun before her, said nothing; Sarah nodded and smiled again, the muscles in her face tired and aching from the efforts of the previous half-hour. 'It was nice,' she said, and she smiled and smiled, and Brendan looked down and in silence addressed his own jammy bun. There was a lump in Sarah's throat as she looked at them: at the table, the tea cups and buns, at the street scene outside. There seemed an embargo on every word, on everything she might have said.

Then Cassie looked up and popped the tension. 'It was nice,' she said and now she smiled at last, the unfamiliarity, the tension of the photographic studio suddenly sloughed off. 'And these are nice buns,' she said. 'Thank you.' And now Brendan seemed to smile a proper smile, a normal smile, and he sat back with relief into the red plush material of the seat. The tears were very near, but Sarah had her own bun on which to focus, her own tea to stir; and the tears to manage, and the pressure in her throat: they passed.

The photograph arrived a fortnight later, neatly parcelled, silver framed and tied with brown twine.

'It's nice,' said Isobel.

There they were in their Sunday best: Brendan smiling in the chair and Sarah smiling a little madly; and Cassie, her chin tucked well in, looking off to one side.

'You've a nice smile,' said Isobel.

The photograph was hung on the kitchen wall; and never referred to again. For a long time, Sarah wondered about it: about its very existence, about Brendan's motivations for summoning it into being. It could not have been commissioned for the usual reason that people commission such items: to place on a wall in order to demonstrate familial togetherness and normality – because people seldom came to visit, no, they never came to visit, except for Father Lynch, and even he had his visits rationed. And besides, the family had already had a branch lopped off: why, she thought, why frame the reminder, the remainder, the stump of it, and hang it on the kitchen wall?

Eventually – at last she thought she might understand why her father had arranged the taking of the photograph. It was his gesture to Cassie: a sort of groping towards a declaration of love, of tenderness, of gratitude, of familial unity. Wordless – naturally – but at least well framed. It was not such an amazing, unexpected message to try to deliver: and maybe, she thought with pain, maybe it says more about me that it's taken so long for the idea to occur. She wondered, then, if Cassie had ever come to the same conclusion.

*

Help me, Cassie thought: help me, help me. The man was pulling and grabbing and tugging; smile, smile smile. I need Sarah to help me, I need someone to help me. But Sarah can't help; and Brendan is about to burst; I can feel it in the air. All the way on the bus he has been about to burst. He wants this to happen and he doesn't want it to happen; he wants someone to be here who can't be, who'll never be here again. Tears stung her eyes, but, but – he wants this to happen, he wants this to happen for me, and I can't cry. She took a breath and held her breath and allowed the man to pull her round, to drag her across the carpet to the chair sitting in the middle of the floor. There, stand there and smile, smile, smile. I can't smile, this is all I can do. It's all I can do. Brendan said we could go for tea after this: I'll have tea and something sweet, with a crunchy sugar topping, or smooth white icing, and split and filled with blackcurrant jam. The Golden Teapot, Brendan had said: we'll go to the Golden Teapot; they say it's nice, and we'll have a nice tea to ourselves. Smile, smile, smile, but I can't smile. Brendan is too sad, Sarah is too sad, for me to smile. To smile would be a sin. I can't smile.

*

Her father had wanted so much for her. Sarah knew this. Brendan's hunger for success, for education: these had been undiminished by time – and his clever daughter should have all that he had been denied, should win scholarships and attend the University, should have every opportunity to absorb the marvellous world.

She should be a credit to her mother's memory.

But he came to his senses in the end.

Brendan did not at first reckon with the scarcity of money, or scholarships, of opportunity – but yes, he came to his senses in the end. And more embittered, and more extreme, blaming now the British for his woes and the woes of his country: the British, who still clung to their little harbour in this far corner of Ireland. She remembered how he clung to this idea, as the only certainty in an uncertain world. When they left, life would be better: he knew this.

But they would never leave, not really. And he knew this too.

Well, they gave up on their little harbour, at least. Brendan made sure of witnessing their final departure, in the autumn of the year before the war began: he made sure the two girls did, too.

*

The spring of 1938. Sarah stood with Cassie on the crest of the hill and looked out over Lough Swilly. The fort at Dunree loomed. *Powerful*, she heard a woman murmur, meaning dramatic – and powerful it was: the engineers who built the fort and harbour here (to keep Napoleon at bay, she knew this from her history lessons) surely had an eye for drama, for power: the weathered grey buildings perching at the end of a high promontory, water stretching on either side. The lough narrow and silvery – sleek, she thought now, like a fish, like a seal – and flat calm on this windless day, with the peak of Inch Island amid its flatlands far away to the south, the open Atlantic to the north. As she watched, a cormorant glided, landed on the surface of the water with a brief flap of wings and an explosion of ripples, dived, vanished, reappeared far away. On the opposite shore, the hills were blue-grey and indistinct in the misty air. Cassie took her hand – and Sarah turned, smiled at her. 'Isn't it good, Cassie?' Cassie nodded.

Sarah's stomach rumbled: ages since their early breakfast, and then the roads were full and slow, the whole county seemed to have turned out to see this sight. But they were here at last; she could wait a little longer for her sandwiches; and she looked around at the crowd gathered all around her, gathered wherever they could get a good view. They were massed on the hill around them; massed on the curving shingle beach at its foot; massed, precariously, on the ledges and rocks below the battlements of the fort itself.

And what a crowd. There were people here from all the neighbouring districts; even a scattering of families come by bus from Derry. 'To bear witness,' the same woman said, sounding important. But it was odd: it seemed now that there would be little by way of public ceremony – yet the local schools were closed, all of them; and there were announcements from the altar the previous Sunday, and the one before that and the one before that too. The day of the handover was given, and the time; clear enough what Father Lynch expected people to do. 'This is a moment of *history*,' he'd said from the altar. 'The British are giving up. They're going home.' They were surrendering their last toehold in Ireland – and there certainly was excitement in the air, a giddiness that she could feel just by standing here, taking it all in.

Sarah was conscious of a little confusion too: the British *weren't* surrendering their last foothold in Ireland, were they? They were just there, just down the road. But she knew to hold her tongue, to keep her expression neutral.

'What time?' she asked again; and her father murmured, a few other people in the crowd murmured, noon. They were ranged across the crest of the hill: below, soldiers – '*our* soldiers' – had closed the approach roads to the fort. 'This is as close as we can get,' her father told her, 'so we might as well make ourselves comfortable,' and he took off his green-flecked tweed jacket – his good jacket, he was too warm, his face reddening a little bit – and spread it on the heathery ground. He sat and Sarah and Cassie sat and others along the ridge followed their example, and sat too. Her mind strayed from history: she worried about the stew Cassie had made and left for tea; gone too long and it would dry up. She sighed; Cassie glanced at her.

They were all there, the great and the good amid the crowd: a teacher or two, and a priest or two; one or two posh shopkeepers from the town. Sarah knew all these; her father knew other priests, farmers, other shopkeepers from other towns and from elsewhere in the county. He nodded, said hello; she and Cassie bobbed their heads, bobbed them again. Father Lynch appeared: clever, full of facts – handy at such a time. He looked now down onto the fort. 'The French,' he said. 'They built this to keep out the French. Poor Wolfe Tone: they caught him out there on the water.' He smiled, too brightly, at Cassie; he turned to Sarah. 'Do you remember, Sarah?'

She remembered, how they caught him and dragged him to Derry and then Dublin, where he opened his – what, his windpipe? – with something – with a pen knife? – and he died a horrible death, a ghastly death; they did this at school. 'Well, no more British ships on Lough Swilly,' the priest went on in satisfied tones, 'not after today.' A pair of grey warships was floating just off the fort, resting, lining up on the grey water. 'Getting ready to move off,' said the priest, 'in an hour or two. And that'll be an end to that.' He pointed to the strange flag fluttering above the battlements. 'The royal ensign,' he said, bobbing up and down on the heels of his polished black shoes. 'That'll be coming down.' She nodded. He knew everything.

And in fact, it took less than an hour or two. After half an hour, her father opened the waxy packet of sandwiches and they ate; and a few minutes after that, a volley of shots; Cassie was shushed; and the flag slid down, and a tricolour was raised in its place. The grey ships moved off, smoothly on the water; in a matter of minutes they rounded the point and disappeared into the open ocean. A single Irish ship took their place, resting just offshore; and that, it seemed, was that. 'Time to go home,' her father said. He sounded flat, somehow; she felt flat too; the crowd was quiet, sober as it looked out across the water, as it broke up. Cassie said, 'Are we going home now?'

Father Lynch reappeared.

'We got rid of them, girls,' he said. 'At last,' he repeated: Sarah watched him there on the ridge of the hill, the shadowy water, the view of blue hills fading now into afternoon mist. He paused, rubbed his jaw. 'At last,' he said again and seemed now to gather himself. 'And no last-minute problems either,' he added with more energy. 'It was the last-minute problems that I was afraid of, but everything went well in the end.' He finished gathering himself now, and looked at Sarah indulgently.

'And what did you think, Sarah?' He paid no attention now to Cassie, who paid no attention to him.

'It was a little quiet, Father. I expected something more exciting.'

Her father looked at her too, but Father Lynch merely sucked his teeth thoughtfully.

'Well, Sarah,' he told her, 'the event is exciting enough in its own way. That's the thing to remember.'

'No, I know, Father – but maybe the government should have made it more public. I mean, more of a ceremony; something like that.'

Now everyone seemed to be looking at her. Cassie took her hand. Father Lynch nodded, spoke in bracing fashion:

'Indeed, Sarah, but that's not really the point. The spectacle isn't really the point, is it? Not the main thing.'

'I know, Father, but surely –'

Her father cut in. 'How will you be getting back, Father?'

'Dr Harvey has kindly offered me a run home,' the priest told him. He nodded across at the doctor and then nodded at them, dismissed them, began to move away. 'So I'll bid you good day.' The two men strode off.

Her father said: 'You can never just hold your tongue, can you? Always this cleverness. He didn't want to hear you, didn't you see that?'

Sarah blushed, painfully. 'He asked me and I told him. There's nothing wrong with that.'

'It isn't your place to go talking back and giving cheek to anyone – and to priests least of all.' He spoke quietly, always a bad sign. All the same, Sarah opened her mouth once more.

'Be quiet, Sarah.'

Cassie turned, stared.

'I only said –'

'We'll be getting back.' He took her arm firmly; she wriggled, for his grip was painful, but he merely grasped her more tightly and pulled her along. 'Come, Cassie,' for Cassie was hanging back, agitated, threatening tears. 'Cassie,' he said again, 'come.'

The evening at home was quiet, quieter even than usual. They'd been away too long; the stew was ruined. 'You're spoiling it for yourself,' Brendan said once, between breaths. Scholarships were slipping away: the priest didn't like girls

152

to be too clever. She took the beating silently. That was the first time.

*

Brendan watched the priest approach, picking his way through the thinning crowd, over the rocks and springy, blooming heather.

'Well, Sarah? What did you think of all that?'

He felt a small welling of pride. Father liked to distinguish the girl, liked to pick her out of the crowd. She was clever, she read and studied hard; she'd be up for the County Scholarship, maybe, in a couple of years. But Brendan's fear was pressing this pride away. Too few avenues available to his daughter: what her ambitions might be, he could not say – but whatever they were, she would most likely have to put them away. His finances could no longer cope with the expense of her schooling; if the Scholarship didn't come along, they'd have to make other arrangements for her. That was clear.

'It was a little quiet, Father. I expected something more exciting.'

He watched as the priest and his daughter wrestled politely. Again, a tentative flutter of pride, shot through with pain; others were watching, others observing her brains, her will; again, he set these sensations firmly aside; he must maintain his neutral, impassive expression. 'The spectacle isn't really the point,' the priest said – though not with heat, Brendan saw, but rather mildly, with amusement. With appreciation?

153

– though no, there was a look in the priest's eye that Brendan saw, and understood. An intervention was necessary: too many people were listening, and Sarah already getting a name around town for being too clever by half. It was a deadly game, this: for the future might keep her here; she must be roped in for her own sake.

He took her arm and rounded up Cassie and they moved along smartly towards the distant station; and he felt – not for the first time – a sensation of heaviness in his throat. God knows, he was familiar with this sensation by now: he might have wept once, though never in public – but he lost this ability, long ago.

*

Cassie thought: the sea was grey, only a little while ago. It's silver now, the silver of a fresh fish on the slab in the fish shop, bright and then dark. I know what the dark is: cloud – one cloud and another cloud and another – on the water. And the ripple lines on the water, from splashing fish. She looked at the silver sea, thought of rippling fish: live fish, she thought, that nibble my toes in the sea, if I stand still – and I know how to stand still, I can stand still longer than anybody I know, Sarah says so; and the fish nibble and nibble, and then suddenly I wriggle my toes and the fish rush away. I like live fish, but I like dead fish too: and she remembered now the trout, they had trout the other week, its skin crisp from the pan, fresh and lovely with potatoes and greens. Father

Lynch is here, but I don't have to listen to him going on and on and on, because he doesn't like me, he doesn't speak to me, not really, so I don't have to speak to him either; and that's better because he is so boring and boring and boring. And now Cassie looked at Brendan and saw his face and his eyes and she reached for Sarah's hand. 'You mustn't cry, Cassie,' Sarah told her last week or the week before, 'you mustn't cry, there's no need to cry, nothing bad will happen,' and she'd tried not to cry, and she tried not to cry now. No need to cry. Brendan held out his hand. 'Come, Cassie,' and she felt the ripples and she didn't cry.

*

'You didn't need to stop,' Sarah said – for Martin had pulled the car into the side of the narrow country road. 'I only wanted to look.'

'Thought you might like to look properly, though: look around you,' he said. 'You haven't been up here in a long time.'

Sensitive Martin.

But the car was parked right up against the fuchsia hedge, which was typical of him. Sensitive, but bad at parking. Martin didn't in fact drive much at all, in spite of his pride in this handsome new car: usually it was Sarah who took charge of the driving, and Martin had no great skills at the wheel. Perhaps there was an opportunity, though, in this latest example of poor parking: it would be too difficult to get out, to get free, to negotiate; better to keep on going. So she shook her head.

'No need.'

Too late: for Cassie had already pushed the back door open and was clambering out, her face red and burned from the sun; and now her children were following, drifting along the hot surface of the road, looking down over the hedges to the sea. They would get bored in a couple of seconds, Sarah thought, and eager to head for home. But in another second, she had the door wrestled open – 'sorry about the parking,' Martin said – and the hedge dealt with; and now she too was out on the road's warm surface, looking out over the fields.

There was nothing to see – and everything, of course. The heat, even on this cooling evening, was rising from the tarmac: the view was quivering, hazing before her eyes. Cassie was looking over the hedges: and the children, seeming now to sense an opportunity for information, for knowledge, were pressing in, foisting questions on her. Where? And when? And who? – all flung through the hot air. Where did she play? And what fields had belonged to her? And where, exactly, was the house, and could they go to see it? They sensed weakness, today, and vulnerability after a long day of heat and sunshine: they wanted, they demanded answers about history, family, the past. She stood in the quivering air: her body seemed to be heating, its edges melting into its surrounding – and now she shook her head slightly, and gestured to Cassie.

'It's too hot, Cassie, to stand here. We need to go home.'

Time to round up these red-faced children, and deflect any questions. Time to go home.

'Can we get ice cream?' Patrick asked. 'On the way home.'

Sarah nodded. Yes: they could get ice cream, they could get anything, if only these questions ceased, these views – of the past, of the world – were taken away.

Her poor father, she thought now. Time had blunted the sharp edges, the bruises and the pain.

Christine was quite old enough to cycle home like this, alone.
There was no problem: this was a quiet town by Lough Foyle,
a blue-winking, flat-calm glimpse of which could be seen at
the bottom of the hill. Hardly anything ever happened here.
Only the seasons happened, and the weather. The weather
had happened earlier, with bucketing rain while they were in
school – and there on the far side of the lough were the same rain
clouds, now fading and retreating more with every moment,
clearing from the distant basalt cliffs at Benevenagh – black
cliffs but glistening gold now in the westering sun. A beautiful
evening. A tang of frost in the air, already. The weather was
over now, for the day.

The house smelled of apples. Her mother was delighted
with the McDonnells across the way: for they'd had a bumper
apple harvest this year; and had delivered a box of Bramleys
on Sunday afternoon. The box was stowed with pleasure in
the garage; and now the garage, the whole house, smelled
of apples.

What will we do with them all? So she'd asked. Don't worry, love, and never fear: we'll find a use. So said her mother: you don't need to worry yourself about that.

She'd heard them talk, later. She's a little worrier, that one.

But Christine wasn't worried now. She was glad she had on her warm anorak, zipped up to the very top. There was stew for dinner, and maybe an apple pie. Stick to your ribs, her dad told her: he made his stews the night before, always; he made the best stews.

She looked across the fields as she cycled – at the lough and the cliffs, and the town below, from which she had just cycled: white houses and dark slate roofs and the Green on the water's edge, with its bandstand and its stone seats and its white shingle beaches and its little spring that gushed from a rock carved into the shape of a horse's head, and poured across the path in its channel and emptied into the sea. But now, as Christine turned her bicycle off the country road and into the lane that led to her house – a couple of hundred yards away, no more – these views vanished and the hedges closed in, meeting almost overhead. They hadn't been cut, not really cut, for some years: everyone had become a little lackadaisical, she had heard her mother murmur, in the matter of hedging and ditching.

Not that Christine minded: in fact, there was something exciting about spinning down this tunnel-like lane, this lane she knew so well, with the hedgerows cool and dripping, and the hawthorn bright with red berries now at summer's end. It was quite exciting – though she was too old to say so. She knew better.

She was practically grown up.

She knew about the hawthorn. Maria Coyle had brought a bough of hawthorn into school, in May, to decorate the May altar. And Miss McNamara had grabbed it, they said afterwards in the playground, really grabbed it, like a cat grabbing a rat, and snatched it from Maria Coyle's hand and taken it out into the playground and thrown it over the fence: just like that! All in a minute. Then she had come back in: and now she had a big red face, though not as red as Maria Coyle's face was – no way, José, they said afterwards in the playground; Maria's face was a whole lot redder – and she took Maria Coyle and she said, 'sorry, Maria'; and someone said that the hair that grew out of the big mole on Miss McNamara's face stuck out like a bit of wire, as if it had had an electric shock. 'Sorry, Maria,' Miss McNamara said, and then she rested the palm of her hand on Maria's head; and Maria, who had been about to cry, didn't cry, because Miss McNamara told them a good story – about the hawthorn and the fairies and the fairy rings that had hawthorn planted on them. 'Why hawthorn?' said Miss McNamara – and Christine had put her hand up, and 'yes, Christine,' said Miss McNamara; and Christine had told them why.

She had told them why, because she knew why: there was a fairy ring in the field along from their house; and her mother had told her why she must never go near it; and especially must never touch the hawthorn that grew there. 'Because of the fairies, Miss,' Christine had said. 'Because the hawthorn is the fairy tree, Miss, and they don't like us to touch them, or take a branch.'

'Or take a branch; that's right,' said Miss McNamara. 'Or anything like that. Now,' Miss McNamara said, looking around the class, 'who believes in all that? Who believes in the fairies?' Nobody put up their hands; nobody at all, and Miss McNamara laughed. 'Well, I don't either – but I'm still not going to annoy them!' Then she turned around to Maria Coyle and said, 'Well, Maria, and isn't that right?' – and Maria, who'd looked like she was about to cry, to burst out crying, suddenly didn't look like she was about to cry; she laughed instead, and Miss McNamara laughed and all the girls laughed. And Christine laughed.

I laughed too, she thought as she cycled along, and it was far better that Maria didn't cry. She didn't know, that was all; that was the only reason. Christine laughed again as she sailed down the lane: she laughed aloud, ducking her head from time to time to avoid snagging her hair into hawthorn branches that dipped and dripped into her face again, and again and again. It was far better that Maria didn't cry; I was glad that she laughed instead, that Miss McNamara made us all laugh. That was ages ago, she thought: ages ago, now. Months and months ago.

In the school lobby this afternoon, the statue of Our Lady had been surrounded by red autumn leaves and red dahlias from the convent garden. In the spring it was May flowers: bluebells picked from the hedgerows and crowded together in those big glass coffee jars given in by Sister Perpetua's brother who owned the cafe in town. 'He's a bit of a wheeler-dealer,' her parents said. 'A bit of a wheeler-dealer,' they said, 'that one.' These big glass coffee jars were all over the school; they were always being used, all year long. In the autumn, the *big girls rehearsed a musical, and the younger girls had to find branches and stems for the stage. And in the Christmas concert, for the local St Vincent de Paul, they had branches sprayed red and glittery white. And bluebells stuffed into the jars for the May altar.*

The bluebells wilted fast. The jars were kept topped up with water, of course, but the bluebells wilted just the same.

And now, autumn leaves. Christine had hardly looked at them today: not that she was in a hurry, because she had time to kill. She just didn't look at them, that was all. Instead she'd grabbed her bike, they'd all grabbed their bikes if they had bikes, they'd all turned this way and that way, heading for home. She'd free-wheeled down the main street, through the town square, over the bridge with the sea at her left hand, then up – what a puff – up, up, up the steep road that climbed from the lough, up to where her house stood on the crest of the hill, with its big garden. Plenty of room, everyone said, for a growing family. How many times had she walked and cycled up here? Oh, it was dozens, hundreds of times in her life; and now that she was a big girl, she was allowed to do it on her own.

There were houses, people, traffic coming and going. She was nearly home.

And now suddenly there was a van there on the lane, behind her, on the hedge-shadowed lane, where there had been no van a minute ago. Where did that van come from?

No time to wonder. Christine fell backwards and for an instant she felt pain as the back of her head hit the ground – and then, nothing at all for some time. Or almost nothing:

a blur of pain, swimming in and out of pain; and water, and darkness. And movement: for a little while, it felt as though she was moving.

For a little while. But her head, her mind, were shattered: and before too long, she reached oblivion.

EIGHT

Robert on the railway, picking up stones.
Along came the engine and broke Robert's bones.
Oh! said Robert, that's not fair.
Oh! said the engine driver, I don't care.
How many bones did Robert break?
One, two, three, four...

Two children squabbling in the hospital corridor: shrill voices raised – outraged, furious, complaining. A boy, a girl, two girls; the boy being blamed. And a mother's ineffectual shush-ing.

'Shush, shush! There are sick people here!'

'But he –'

'I never did!' – the boy's voice, raised and wailing in distress.

'He did, he did!'

'I didn't!'

And now the mother's voice. 'James, that's enough! Be quiet!'

And now a nurse's squeaking shoes running: the family bundled away; and Robert opened his eyes. There was the room, the bed, the thin outline of his brother-in-law's body under the blue coverlet, the beaky profile, the loose skin, the plastic tubes.

*

Run, boy, run.

The clearances were beginning. Belfast voices crowing. They were coming.

Stones rained. The families on either side of them had left Bombay Street in daylight, taking the advice of the priest, the police, their own bawling instincts. 'Let's go too,' Robert said. He smelled fear in the air – but his mother was bloody-minded: and she'd dug her heels in. She'd not be thrown out of her own house by anybody. They'd take her out in a box, first.

That was her decision. She had a little time to think about its consequences.

First, for a moment when the kitchen window came in; then again, as they stood in the narrow hall, as the walls of the small front room glowed in the light of the flames. They were coming: the mob – though the firemen weren't coming, they wouldn't come, so they had heard. Bombay Street could burn, first. And it was burning as they left: there was a screen of young men and boys holding the line to the left as they scurried like rats to the right, to shelter, with bags, with bundles, with whatever they had been able to lay their hands on; screams and whistles and bellows.

Run, boy, run: stones raining over the screen: and Robert turns to look, sees flames, sees crowds, sees a red light in the sky and a Red Hand and a union flag amid the smoke and the flaming light. And turns again, and sees the blood running from her scalp down and onto his mother's face. A stone has met its mark; and there is a hotness of vomit in his throat. She stumbles, picks herself up, catches his hand and they run.

Run, boy, run.

*

They never went away: these memories, these sensations of humiliation. That little boy out in the corridor, pecked and blamed and scolded: that was it, in a nutshell. That was me, Robert thought, and he ran a hand over his forehead, over his skull. That was me.

Robert on the railway...

The skipping game – but he had run into the crowd, fists flailing. He had learned not to waste time in words. Yes, he had learned early to use his fists. His dreadful temper: he had never tamed it. Instead, the world flamed red before his eyes, and then black; and before he knew it, his fists met their mark.

How many bones did Robert break? – many bones, in fact: many bones over the years, the bones of other people. He never broke his own. The little, petty humiliations year by year: well, the thought of broken bones had corrected the balance a little.

And now the figure in the bed moved, woke. Eyelids flickered, eyes focused, looked, and looked away.

'Oh, what did I tell you?' – a reedy voice, a petulant voice. 'I told you not to come again.'

Robert leaned forward in his chair.

'I came to say sorry. To tell you I'm sorry.'

A pause, a beat.

'Don't be telling me. Why are you telling me?'

Which was a point: why was Robert sitting in this over-heated hospital room? Why was he saying such things?

'And I thought I told you not to come back,' Patrick added. High, yes: reedy – an old man's voice in a young man's body; but still capable of loftiness, of a little of the astringency of old.

'I mean I want –' said Robert, but Patrick had already closed his eyes again, and now he moistened his dry lips and spoke again.

'I know what you want. You want me to shower you with admiring kisses. But it isn't me you should be apologising to. Go away, Robert,' he said, mildly now. 'This is pointless. Apologise to someone else – as if *apologising* will do it. And call the nurse: I want some tea.'

True: this was pointless. Robert grasped his coat and left the room.

*

Too much. Too much.

So Patrick thought. He opened an eye to check that the

unwelcome visitor had departed – and yes, the coast was clear. Another bolt of material, duly stashed away. Too much material: this fabric going on and on, unfurling dementedly. Like, he thought, one of those rolled-up parchment maps flung across tables in adventure films, pirate films, revealing itself in a cloud of dust.

At least those rolls of parchment tended to show the way home, the way to the treasure, to Shangri-La. But there was no treasure trove, no Shangri-La at the end of *this* adventure, Patrick thought. My ma and Robert have taken care of that, between them. This adventure cost too much, too much in materials and labour and tears. Too much in consequences – too much for anyone sane to want to embark upon it.

It was too much. And he laughed, then, stretched in his blue bed: and it wasn't as if he had all the time in the world, either. Which was the problem with memory, with history: too damned much of them both. They expand, they go on expanding, exponentially, especially once they are paid the smallest amount of attention. They're like – and here he paused – yes: they're like certain children and domestic pets I've come across, squalling, pawing and poking, running around hissing and flapping, like ganders in a farmyard. They can never be satisfied.

But the children analogy was hardly in the best of taste. He knew that too.

'You know those balloons,' he said to Margaret – this was lately, he thought; the days continued to blur now – 'that people have trouble blowing up?'

'She moved her chair a little closer to the bed. 'I think so,' she said. 'You can't start them off, sometimes, is that what you mean?'

'That's it,' he murmured.

'You need a bicycle pump.'

'Mm.'

'So, what about them?'

He said after a pause, 'Well, once you get started, the things sometimes seem to go on and on, don't they? It's like you can never get them filled. That's what it's like.'

She looked at him. 'What is?' she said. 'What what's like?'

'So I scratch myself,' Patrick murmured, 'and wonder what I have begun.'

'What?'

'You know, in Sisyphean fashion.'

'What?'

'Oh, nothing.'

She rolled her eyes, then, and edged the chair back again.

But Patrick was also aware of time ticking ever onwards, of the impossibility of resolution. So that he need not worry, necessarily, about the final product, about its shape, about consequences. And God knows, he thought, surely the consequences are clear already? I'll just keep on rolling along.

Before he got sick – just before; in his mind's eye, it was barrelling along the motorway in his direction – he had come across the theory about the butterfly's wing. Everyone was getting excited about it and he could see why. He talked to one of his senior classes about this theory.

'For the sake of argument, let's say down there on the grass.'

Those closest to the classroom windows glanced out and down onto the lawn and then back at him again. The rest of the class just kept looking at him.

'So, the idea is that the movement of a butterfly's wing down there on that bit of grass here in Derry will, given time and the correct set of circumstances' – and he paused for breath now, aware of the disinterest in the room, ploughing on through air that had the consistency of thick soup, 'create consequences undreamt-of in the here and now.' He paused again. 'What do you think of that?'

They didn't think much about it, apparently.

'So,' he said, 'an iceberg calved in Antarctica, a flood in Australia, a dust storm in the Gobi –'

'That's in China,' said one of the boys, unexpectedly.

'That's right. And if there's a dust storm in China, a dust storm that maybe – what, say it stops production in one of their electronics factories. Say the sand gets into the air conditioning system. What does that mean?'

They were all paying a little more attention now.

'It might mean – say it means that you won't get the new Walkman you wanted. There might be a delay.'

A delay? Now he had their attention.

'And all because a butterfly took it into its head to have a little spin on our front lawn. What do you think of that, boys?'

There was a movement through the class, a ripple.

'Yeah. That's pretty cool, sir.'

It *was* cool, he thought. I really *get* this theory: I really do. I really get it: I can apply it to my own life without even having to think about it.

It is the most appealing theory I have ever come across.

This was the point of history: that in the movement of a butterfly's wing lay the potential for the world – or portions of it, at any rate – to turn on a pivot.

His father had understood this. The name of the theory had changed in the, what, quarter-century since that day on the beach in the summer of 1960, but the substance remained the same. His father said that that poor ship of the Spanish Armada wouldn't even have *been* beating its way back home to Spain via Scotland and Ireland if it hadn't been for a series of curious, frustrating delays back in Spain in the spring and summer of that year. The fleet was late taking sail: already, the commanders were doubtful about the whole enterprise. Then, as the Armada reached the Channel, the season turned with a snarl: summer ended abruptly, too early, and an autumn storm howled down from the North Sea: the great, top-heavy ships could not manage such narrow, stormy waters; the vengeful English navy went hungrily to work – and the rest was history.

So I might say, he thought, that the movement of a butterfly's wing late in the sixteenth century caused a shipwreck off the beach at Kinnagoe; thus inclining my father to visit that same beach on a warm summer day four hundred years later; and causing me to be nearly drowned by my sister.

Or not, she would claim.

So yes, he thought now: the theory appeals. Of course it

appeals: he could apply it always to his own story. This flutter of a butterfly's wing created movements: a wave, and another wave, rippling from one house to another, from this place to that one, from person to person, era to era. They ripple, he thought, and they submerge me. And his family, his mother, his sister, her husband: each of them also entangled.

He thought: I had my own personal history. So too did my father, and Margaret and Cassie, and my mother; all of them.

Even Robert. Yes: Robert too.

But Patrick's mind shrank from this topic.

Margaret had filled him in – or tried to. Robert had a history too, it seemed. Quite the back story.

'They burned him out,' she said. Out of his house.'

Margaret had told him the stories that Robert had told her. The mobs, the howling, the stones. The flames at one end of Bombay Street. Being kicked out of their own house. 'Can you imagine? You went marching for the likes of him, we both did.'

But that was a long time ago. And it was different, when these people appeared in the flesh. In this, at least, he was his mother's son. My father, he thought instead: take my father. He was happy enough to yarn on: he was an open book, especially in his final years; he had come to terms with fortune and misfortune and ill-health and destiny, shoving them all aside as equally irrelevant. Or take my sister: I knew as much about Margaret's life as anyone could know: when she married, she necessarily moved out of my orbit – a little, and not decisively and later she moved back in again; and besides, I had the insight of years to fall back on. As for my mother: well, he knew least about her: just bits and gleaned scraps. Nothing so very substantial. Ditto Cassie, though that's because I never took the trouble to ask a few questions.

But sometimes, all this – *stuff*, these episodes and disparate, all this *stuff* came together in a way that made another shape. And of course later, usually: at the time, they were too much in the thick of things to make out any shapes with clarity. Sometimes. Looking back, he could see clear shapes emerging from the darkness: an episode here and an episode there which made perfect sense, where the ripples, the connections were clear to be seen. When characters came together, when stories merged and melded.

Such as: one September night, just a couple of years ago, when Margaret and Robert came to the house for dinner: a birthday dinner, for Margaret's birthday, in their parents' suburban house. He could recall it with much clarity because his father died shortly afterwards. It was the last time they would all be together – and it was as if his mother had divined the future, because she cooked a fancy meal.

He could even recall the menu. Fillet of pork stuffed with apricots, with a home-made lemon meringue number to follow. And a birthday cake, festooned with mandarin orange segments from a tin. In his mother's eyes, tinned fruit still counted as fancy.

And not all together, either. Cassie had passed away by this point. A mere postscript, Patrick thought: after all that care, there she was dangling on the edge of the family; dropping off without anyone much noticing. All there together, then, except Cassie.

It had been raining all morning, but it stopped as he drove home. When he parked the car in the driveway, he paused for a moment to take the place in, to smell the air. The leaves were starting to fall. Cool enough in the evenings, already, for fires to be lit: he could smell coal, a little turf, hanging in the still air. And the air also full of the freshness that follows rain; though with an undertow of falling, decaying leaves; a beautiful, heady smell of autumn. Mushrooms sprang up on the lawn overnight: he remembered that, too; a glimmer of white under the trees when he opened his window the following morning.

Coal smoke and turf; decaying leaves and fresh rain lying slicked on the grass; roasting meat.

And dreadful hindsight.

No wonder, of course, that I remember it all so well. The date, the day of the week, the occasion, the weather. Even – yes, even the phase of the moon.

*

The rain was over, at least for now. The sky was clearing, and a pale gibbous moon was rising. He pulled neatly into the drive, parked behind his father's car, beside his mother's car, saw a house that gleamed like a Christmas decoration in the autumn twilight. Was every lamp in the place switched on? It seemed so: the darkness was being pushed back by the glint of the copper bowl on its high shelf; by the light shining from the windows of the hall, the dining room – all places normally in darkness. The house welled with light. He locked the car, and stood on the gravel for a second: the rain had stopped for now, but from the garden came a sound of oozing, like a heavy sponge; the soil murmuring to itself, the whole place trying to find a way of dealing with, of shedding this superabundance of water. The eaves of the house dripped; the trees dripped, his mother's azalea bushes dripped in the darkness.

Patrick stood on the gravel and looked at the illuminated house: then, on an impulse, slipped through the car port, past the high slatted gate which lay, tonight, wide open, and into the long back garden. Here too, when he stood the garden seemed to ooze – but instead of listening, he was now looking: standing just outside the pools of lamplight on the white walls of the house, on the wet grass, on the path. He looked through the wide, uncurtained windows, and there was his sister: there was Margaret, a gin and tonic in hand, the picture now of relaxation after a long day, her toes pointing towards the fire. There was Robert, sitting in a chair pushed well back into the corner; and there was his dad, saying something – what? Pointing, gesticulating at the drinks cabinet, at the half-lemon rolling on the board, at the tongs, the gently sweating little bowl of ice and his cane on the polished floor. A punchline delivered.

His sister, her husband, his father – and there now, his mother coming into view, slim, upright and purposeful in her movements. His dad – what, he made another comment, laughed, Margaret laughed; and now suddenly his mother glanced into the darkness, her expression familiar.

Set, tense. Immeasurably sad.

He had not created it, this expression, none of them had created it – but he wondered if in some way he added to it, day by day. A familiar thought: this sense he had had since childhood. He watched as his mother's expression flicked back into a tense smile, as she turned and said – something, and sat down with a plump in her chair. And now he moved, slipped through the car port again; now he jangled the keys in the front door, now he eased off his boots, and closed the front door behind him and went in to greet his family.

*

The gin and tonic hit the spot. 'That really hits the spot,' Margaret said, and she clinked the ice in her glass, 'it really, really does,' and Martin smiled and offered a top-up. Margaret put a hand on the rim of the glass. 'Not a bit,' she said, 'or I'll fall off the chair. Before we even eat.'

'Which reminds me,' said her mother. 'I must put on the potatoes.' She slipped away.

In full martyr mode, Margaret thought, tonight: she is revelling in this volume of work. 'What can I do?' she'd said, presenting herself in the kitchen door – but her mother had chivvied her out again: she had everything in hand; have a drink, she said, instead. Now she sat, uncomfortably aware of a genteel rattling of utensils from the kitchen. Her mother could do sound effects better than anyone.

Robert had entered, and sat. Had offered no assistance: and now he too sat with his drink, clinking gently from time to time the ice against the glass.

'Actually, Daddy, you know what: I *could* do with a refill.'

Her mother bustled back from the kitchen. 'Another one? Are you sure?'

Margaret took a breath. 'I'm sure,' she said, and her dad did the necessary. 'You're red in the face, Mum,' she said and her mum replied sharply that opening the oven had heated her face right up.

'I sometimes wonder,' she said, 'how do chefs manage if they wear glasses? All that steam!' And then she glanced quickly out of the window, into the black garden.

'OK, Mum?' Margaret regretted already her bitchiness – but her mother brought it out in her, no question – and after a moment a short reply, 'Fine, fine, nearly there now.'

Robert still sat, quietly in the corner. Not a man of many words, but more than usually silent tonight. He put a hand over his glass: no, his drink was fine for the moment; and her dad retreated, for the moment vanquished.

And now a jingle of keys and Patrick appeared. Margaret thought – not for the first time – that he looked older than his twenty-something years, tall and thin, the beginnings, already, of a stoop; his hair already receding. She hugged him briefly, aware of his sharp shoulder blades, so different from her soft roundness, so unalike they were as siblings. He had already nodded at her husband, distantly; she was aware of Robert's eyes on her back. She was thirty years old today: and there was her cake, all white cream and tinned mandarin orange segments, ready and resplendent on the sideboard.

From the kitchen, a clatter of dishes, of pots and pans.

*

The dining room table was already decked: a red paper table-cloth and red matching paper napkins; paper party plates and glasses – and on the sideboard, Margaret's impressive birthday cake, three layers of chocolate icing and the '10' picked out in white piping. Cassie had gone to town. 'You're going to town on this one, Cassie,' her dad had said, earlier, 'You're looking serious.' Cassie laughed at that – but she had been serious, she had gone to town with the cake. 'What do you say to Cassie?' said her mammy, and Margaret said, 'Thank you, Cassie.' And Cassie had given her a hug – one of her special hugs, that lasted for a long, long time. 'You're ten, love,' said Cassie. 'Ten!'

'This is serious. This is a double-digit affair,' her dad said.

Yes: this was a serious, double-digit affair – and Margaret was serious too. Her party dress was new, her hair brushed and her shoulders set and now she clutched her hands to her sharp elbows. Four o'clock, the invitations read, and four o'clock it was, right now: the girls arriving any minute.

She looked around the room. Her house was the best house, she had the best house in her gang, she knew this: the best and the newest. She knew the other girls thought this:

she'd noticed, already, the way the girls looked around its new rooms and wooden hall and glossy parquet floor and big back garden; her mammy's copper bowl shining with red light on the high shelf in the hall; the long, long back garden. Most of the other girls lived in the town, still: there were some new houses outside the town, but not many. Margaret knew they were jealous: she'd seen the look in their eyes and in the mammies' eyes when they came to visit. They wanted to live here, in this house in this street, they wanted to live here too.

Veronica most of all. Veronica, the queen, the bully, the one to keep as a friend if she could, if she could. Nobody wanted Veronica as an enemy. Margaret was afraid of Veronica; she knew too that Veronica was – she was inching close to getting rid of Margaret from the group. So, this house was Margaret's secret weapon: the house and also Margaret's strange mammy, of whom so many people seemed afraid, or unsure of themselves around. Veronica herself was afraid of Margaret's mammy, she was specially nice to her, specially polite to her, though, even though, Margaret's mammy was not really specially polite and nice back, and this too kept Margaret safe.

Though, she hoped Veronica would not laugh at Cassie. Later, at school on Monday. She hoped not.

Her mammy came into the dining room. 'All set?' she said. Margaret could've done with another hug – but a hug was unlikely, on the whole; her mammy was not a hugging kind of lady. Instead she smiled. 'All set,' she told her mammy – and then several things happened at once: the front doorbell pealed; and the back door slammed shut, sending a draught into the house and setting a few paper cups flying and a lampshade swaying; and Patrick jumped into the room. He was filthy: he was covered in dirt; and the girls were waiting at the front door.

'Make him clean himself!' she hissed at her mammy. 'Make him, make him!' She did not want the girls to hear her shouting at her dirty little brother; and now there was the bell again; and she whisked into the hall. There were faces behind the rippling glass, many blurred faces. She took a breath and opened the door, and there was Veronica, standing and waiting at the head of the posse. A few mammies lurked behind: the plan was that they would stay in the kitchen and drink tea, while the girls had a birthday feast – a *Feast*, said the invitation, *for Margaret's 10th birthday* – in the dining room.

'Come in,' said Margaret, for she could hear her mammy manhandling Patrick along the hall and down the step and into the bathroom. The coast was clear. 'Come in,' she said, and she opened the door and Veronica came into the hall. 'I brought you this,' Veronica said, raking a stare around, and she handed over a little parcel, wrapped and ribboned excitingly; and now the other girls filed in too, one by one, and soon Margaret's arms overflowed with presents. 'Thank you,' she said to one and all, 'thank you.'

Later, when the girls and their mammies left, with the front and back doors and all the windows wide open to let the smoke out (but it lingered and clung just the same: her mammy said that the curtains would need to be taken down after all this, and sent away to be cleaned), and the neighbours dispersed from the street outside – later, after all this, Margaret sat on the dining room floor and cried. The floorboards were strewn with wrapping paper and ribbons, for they had just reached this point in the ceremony when the smoke began to billow from the sitting room. But the food remained piled on plates, the cake, with its chocolate icing, remained uncut – and now Patrick appeared, sidling into the room, his face once more smudged and dirty. But so too was Margaret's face – smudged and dirty from smoke and tears; and so had been Veronica's face when she left the house – smudged with smoke and tears. For good reason.

'Why did you want to ruin my party?' Margaret wailed now: she had drawn her knees in close to her body, and now as Patrick sidled closer, she aimed a kick. He skipped out of reach – but half-heartedly, not triumphantly, for he too had been crying, at first in the sitting room amid the smoke, and then in the hall, the girls eddying around all the while in scandalised formation, and then in his own bedroom.

'I didn't mean to,' Patrick said.

'You did so mean to.'

What had happened was this: Patrick had taken Veronica's coat and another girl's coat and stuffed them into the fireplace. No: not merely into the fireplace, but into the actual fire burning on the sitting room hearth. Nobody knew a thing about it until a dense black cloud of smoke and an acrid smell issued from the room and into the hall – for the coats were not burning with a quick, hot flame, but rather smouldering, and releasing horrifying amounts of black smoke, the blackest.

Suddenly the house was filling with smoke, and Veronica was screaming, screeching and the other girls and even some of the mammies were screaming and screeching too. The rooms, the whole house were filled with screaming.

Her own mammy soon put a stop to that. She appeared with the bucket from the back yard, and she elbowed her way through the crowd and without saying a single, solitary word doused the fire in the fireplace with water, and that was an end to that. The coats hissed; they still looked horrifying, there in the hearth. Like black, twisted bodies. And yes, her mammy didn't say a word the whole time: not a word; she stayed silent until the fire was out and the windows and doors opened; and then the kettle went on again; and only then did she say anything at all.

'I'm sorry,' she said. 'I'm so sorry,' she said, looking around. 'I'm afraid Patrick has been showing off.' She took in the scene. 'I think we all need more tea.'

Meanwhile the girls were crowding into the sitting room and then Veronica began screaming louder than ever. She had seen her coat: ruined, soaking, blackened and reeking in the fireplace; and she turned and pointed a finger at Margaret.

'You did that on purpose, Margaret Jackson! You did! – you did it on purpose!'

There was no way back from this. She was out of the group now.

'I didn't mean to,' Patrick now repeated. This was so obviously a lie that Margaret didn't know what to say: the fight had gone out of her, suddenly, gone out of her legs; and sensing this, her brother crept closer, within range. She pulled her legs in tightly – her dress was covered with sooty smudges, it was ruined – and wrapped her arms around her knees; and now Patrick sat down on the floor too and burrowed his small, dirty face into her shoulder.

'I didn't mean to. I didn't mean to.'

'You did so mean to,' Margaret whispered and then she did what she always did: she pulled him closer still to her, and they just sat there. This was what she always did, always, always, when things happened. After a moment, she sensed her mammy's eyes on her, standing there in the doorway, but she kept her own eyes tightly closed; and when after a few more moments she opened them, the doorway was empty and her mammy gone.

And it didn't really matter. Not really. Patrick was sniffing into her shoulder and snorting back his snotters and his tears, but all of this, it didn't really matter. She closed her eyes again. Cassie was coming along the hall: she was shy of strangers, she'd stayed in her room, so Veronica hadn't seen her. And now she was coming again, shuffling, padding. Surely she would get a hug from Cassie. Surely everything was fine.

*

But in the kitchen, tucked out of sight from her family – for the fridge protruded a little, and unsatisfactorily, not sleek and streamlined like the rest of the kitchen, she would have to see if something could be done about that – Sarah had

184

set down carefully the stack of plates, was gripping the edge of the counter, was looking down at her knuckles. A young woman again – a girl, really, though she didn't think so at the time – and Cassie was hovering at her shoulder. What to do, what to do? There was nothing to be done. Nothing, no: not a thing. And then the moment passed. Everything was fine: the pork, the potatoes were fine. And the family was fine – and only Cassie absent – and again Sarah felt a gust of something, dizziness, wretchedness – pass through her. Five years dead, and still Sarah felt unanchored, untethered.

'Begin again,' Cassie told her long ago. 'You can begin again. Can't you?'

The sound of the explosion was caught, still, in her ears, a high, shrill ringing; the fire puffed out a little turf smoke; in the black outdoors, the frost was settling on the farmyard. 'And what will you do?'

Cassie's clear, light laugh. 'Follow you, maybe. But I'll look after Brendan, first.'

Brendan?

'He gave me a home. I'll stay with him, until it's all over.'

And she was as good as her word, Sarah thought. She had a promise to keep and she kept it, and then she came to live with me; and died too soon. Too young.

*

Patrick accepted a drink. And what happened then? In a few more minutes, their mother called them and an evening of

185

gluttony commenced: roast stuffed fillet of pork, accompanied with home-grown steamed potatoes; and followed with lemon meringue pie and ice cream, with cheese and crackers, and coffee. And then the over-stuffed birthday cake, cream and mandarin oranges and more cream.

Strange, the memories that cling. He remembered that the dining room curtains stayed pulled back, so that light flooded from the house, shining in long, white squares across the back garden, the sodden lawn. Shining, he remembered, onto the pampas grass that my mother had planted years and years ago in the middle of the lawn, that was indestructible. What a scene, as though we were on stage, stuffing ourselves: how must we have appeared to a watcher, as potatoes were passed and cream spooned, wine poured and more wine, silently, on the far side of the glass. Margaret blowing out the candles on her cake, with a flourish.

The memories that cling – bolstered with hindsight. He remembered too that on that same night, a bomb – not a huge bomb, though big enough – exploded in a car parked in front of a shop in the city centre: the damage of course substantial. He remembered the Indian family who owned the shop: well, they would have wondered if it'd be worth, this time, clearing up and applying for the compensation package, worth beginning all over again. They did apply, they did clean up, they did begin all over again: they did, he thought, because he bought a jacket from them a couple of months later.

Why remember that bomb? Of all the bombs, why that one? I remember it, he thought, because a few minutes after

Margaret blew out the candles on her birthday cake, the windows buckled the way they always did when a bomb exploded. The sound wave travelled along the river from the city and collided against the walls of the house, and the windows bulged in on us: bulged, but did not quite explode. We were too far away from the explosion for our windows to come in on us. How complacent. Still, the sight of them, moving inside the uncurtained frames: this was not very nice; the sort of sight, he thought, that stays. We watched them buckle, and then there was the usual short silence, and then we got back to our cake.

Something else Patrick remembered – though no, not remembered, because he was not aware of it at the time. Yet there it is in my memory, he thought, as though I was actually there. He shifted uncomfortably in his blue bed. Along the coast, further up Lough Foyle, another family was also sitting together. Sitting in trouble. Yes, he thought, poetic license is needed for this one – though not much, because later I drove past the house and took it in, got some sense of its layout. Its glassed-in porch, filled with wicker furniture, a caned-legged table. I got a sense of the place. And the trouble with the family, it was this: their youngest girl was gone. Was missing. Out there in the darkness, all hell was breaking loose: her father was combing the lanes, the police were involved already; the foreshore of the lough had been searched already, in the fading evening light. The house was filling up: neighbours making tea, the inevitable priest, a policewoman. The lane outside the house was jammed, as for a wake – which in effect it was.

The child's mother was sitting in a wicker chair in the chilly porch of her house and weeping and weeping for her daughter; her husband was outside in the darkness, trying to keep it together. In the warm living room, her remaining daughters sat, dry-eyed and silent and rigid, and wrapped their hands around their elbows, their knees.

In his memory. He thought: chances are.

His was a lucky family that night, in comparison: lucky them, that night, gathered together under a tight roof, clinking the ice in their drinks, and living off the fat of the land. What a lucky, complacent family. Were they not? To be sure, they blinked, they jumped as the wall of sound from the bomb blast, rolling down the river from the city, collided with the windows of their house. They watched the windows swell visibly, ripple inwards: they felt startled, as always, wondering if one day these windows would shatter and blast inwards. But sure, they recovered rapidly enough. This was merely an aspect of everyday life. It was nothing to cause undue alarm: and there was a birthday cake to deal with, besides.

Patrick, searching through his memory, remembered now how watchful his brother-in-law was that night, how little he took part in the conversation. Even less than usual, that night. But now – no: this was with hindsight. His memories in this regard were not to be trusted.

NINE

Patrick looked out of the window into a silver moonlit night.

The garden was – changed, somehow. Not as it might if snow had fallen, or a light mist come down, altering the life, the dimensions of the place. It had changed completely. The lawn no longer broad, substantial: instead, it had become hemmed in with plants. Plants crept out across the grass: some unfamiliar, white-flowering, their blossoms catching the moonlight; others he recognised – dead nettle that grew rapidly and choked invisibly, ivies set on strangling in silence the plants around them. Tendrils moving along the ground and winding into the surrounding trees, round and round their trunks; and the trees unfamiliar too, with silvery leaves and smooth bark that shone white in the silver light. The moonlight, the garden, the world, now: all was silver and shadow-dappled.

What is this place? Does it belong to him? – no, not to him, that much was certain; and his eyes filled with tears at the thought, for he knew that here at least, in this garden at least, he had sometimes felt safe, comfortable. In hides, in dens, behind curtains of blackberry brambles. No longer.

His mother was responsible, somehow. And Robert. They had arranged all of this. As a treat, he knew, somehow: arranged as a treat – for him, in secret and silently, without saying a word. We won't say a word, he heard them say – though indeed, neither his mother nor Robert was anywhere in sight. We won't say a word, they repeated; and now here they were – here they were in sight now, standing behind him, framed, paired in the doorway. Patrick opened his mouth – but no, they were having none of it; would not meet his look, for one set of eyes flickered away and then another; and now they were gone; and the door closed silently.

He returned to the window. He looked out for some time: then, he caught the clasp on the window frame and opened it wide and slid out into the garden. The moonlight was more distinct here. Harder: the silver light filling the air was gone now, replaced by a clearer white and black – the white of the moon, the black of the hedging, enveloping shadows, the white gleam of leaves, the black of shadowed trunks and stems. The tendrils of the unfamiliar plants crept across his bare feet – but no, they did not wind around his bare legs, he would not be throttled by them, he knew that he was – not safe, no, but not in danger of death either.

Not yet.

He looked again around this white and black garden, and now he saw something else: that each of the trees, each of the shrubs was dead. There had been only a semblance of life: for the trunk of each tree, the stem of each shrub had been severed – a clean cut, surgical, close to the ground. The moonlight had deceived him: he must bend, now, to see the minute signs of incipient decay in the form of shrivelling leaves, as though the plants were frozen by a frost. In no time, he thought, each of these leaves will wither; there will be no more pretence. In the morning, the decay will be complete: when I look out of this window in the morning, I'll see death. This was not a shock: he seemed to know it, as though he'd anticipated it, seen it countless times before. There was no sorrow now: this was simply the way of it.

Yes: they – his mother, Robert – had caused the whole thing: the occlusion, the creeping shadows and the disturbed, fitful light; and the clean slice in the trunks of these living things. They never stood there in the moonlight, they never actually figured at all, they'd vanished behind that closing door – but as is the way of dreams, he felt the message, as one might feel a blow to the back of the neck.

Carrying this knowledge, he slipped back across the grass to his window, let himself in, fastened the clasp once more.

*

'Well!' said the nurse. 'What happened to you, then?'

She fingered – not unkindly – the brushed cotton on the collar of his pyjamas. The paisley pattern, bottle green and sky blue – an odd choice, this nurse thought, not very attractive, poor fellow, who bought those for him? – was darkened a little: by perspiration. The temperature of the room was held at an even, pleasant level; the window was closed; she moved a little closer to feel his forehead, her mind swung to her thermometer, held at the ready.

'It isn't anything – clinical,' he murmured.

'Oh?' said the nurse. She'd be the judge of that.

'Of course, you'll be the judge of that,' he murmured. His eyes were closed; there was little spark in him today. 'But it was only a dream. A dream, night sweats; happens all the time.'

'Oh?' said the nurse again, this time with a glimmering of professional curiosity. She had a little interest in dreams.

'So, nothing to worry about, I suggest,' he said. He sighed, a hand moving up slowly to touch in his turn the soft paisley cotton. 'You might change these, though,' he said, and his body moved a little, straightened slowly and with effort. Preparing itself for this latest, miserable, small indignity.

There was more he might have said. The room is too light, the curtains unlined, skimpy, insufficient; the silence insufficient too, making sleep an endurance pursuit. No wonder I bitch at you all. Last night, though, I managed something approaching a deep sleep – and this was the result. He might have said – but all of it unwise. He held his tongue.

It hovered, this dream, on the edge of his sleep. Always had – for years and years. It had changed its complexion with the years, naturally enough, morphing with circumstance: at first, his mother ran it as a solo operation, dominating proceedings like a Colossus; and when he was younger, before he knew the names of certain plants, the masses of creeping foliage

192

had presented itself as an undifferentiated mass of leaves and stems and tendrils. Knowledge, then, sharpened the dream – which just proved, he thought, that a little knowledge was certainly not always a good thing.

When Robert met Margaret and she opted to marry him, the dream took on a changed form. Following their meeting in London, following the disturbed realisation that this unprepossessing character wasn't about to shuffle away once more into the shadows – following this, Robert seemed to make common cause with Sarah: in his head, the pair of them moving smoothly to colonise his subconscious mind. And so the dream began, and lurked stubbornly – for years now, morphing and altering in complexion, but remaining essentially, tediously the same.

This, Patrick had very often thought, was like having a tapeworm. You didn't *choose* such a guest: you simply inhaled or ingested an egg – and there it grew, arranging itself happily, settling down for a good feed. This is what it felt like, to him: as if he had his own personal tapeworm. He had read in the paper one morning about a woman who managed to get a tapeworm lodged in her brain. It stayed there – oh, for ages, getting up to all sorts of terrible mischief. He spread some more marmalade on his toast and realised that he could identify easily enough with the poor dear.

And yes: in the mornings, after yet another repetitive episode, he would wake to feel himself wet: his pyjamas – and then when at length he decided was too modern for pyjamas, his tee-shirt – damp, unpleasantly moist. If the dream woke him in the middle of the night, as it occasionally had the power to do, he would find the cloth saturated, and sometimes the sheet saturated, sweat trickling in runnels on his chest.

Deeply unpleasant – not that there was ever anyone to share the sensation of a night sweat, to offer comfort in the darkness. No chance.

Patrick always – always, always – for a moment imagined that this dream was real. Always, always did: always it took his brain a moment, two moments, to recover something of a grasp on the actual world. Then he would cross the room, his pyjamas hanging damply, and pull the curtain – or rather, yank it across – and open the window and pull air into his lungs, as though they were filled with some pestilence or miasma of disease. And then: then, he would shove his dream aside: until the next time it presented itself.

And always there was a next time. Over and over this episode recurred; and over and over he shoved it aside.

Patrick told himself from time to time that at least the whole phenomenon was a sign of his mind's independence. It did its own thing, it made its own mind up, it sifted and sorted and judged. Well, perhaps: but this was a profoundly unconvincing argument, most of the time – though occasionally it retained a little power. He could see why: he had never been good at having things his own way. *If Patrick has his way*: not a sentence, he thought, to make a blushing appearance all that often in his life. *Patrick will do as he's told*: this (of course) from his mother. *Come on then, Patrick*: reluctantly, at school, when chosen last at PE. *We're not going*

194

anywhere, not really: this from the boys at school, slipping off at home time for a bit of craic. *Let Patrick have his way*: seldom. No, never. He learned how to manage; later, as a teacher, he observed that all such children learn fast, and with such skill. Fleet of foot, speed like quicksilver: they learn how not to be hurt. Some of them in the process learn how to hurt others. Then they became adults. He watched all this, and said nothing.

At least, he thought, at least my dream had the – something, the grace to change itself, to adapt itself a little to the changing circumstances of my life. At the beginning – when he began to dream it as a child in their little terraced house, the first house that had no garden worth speaking of – the garden in the dream was small, walled, circumscribed. He was still able, though, magically to step from his bedroom window on the first floor straight into that walled place, crammed with silvery plants and darkness.

Later, when they moved – exchanging that barely remembered house on the red Victorian terrace on the hill for the long, sprawling, modern bungalow with its skylight and big back garden – the old dream and his new life, his real life, seemed to come to some hellish accord: in the new house, his bedroom was of course right there on the ground floor; how easy to creep through the bedroom window, creep outside into a moonlit garden! Although aspects of the dream of course adapted themselves too: the shape of the window, the form of its clasp, altered as the dream retold itself; the one became a ghostly facsimile of the other.

And later still, Robert joined his mother, there behind the closing door.

Robert. Medieval Robert, shadowed Robert, placed there in half-darkness on the tapestry, placed in the embrace of sullen-leaved ivy. Their mutual dislike was absolute.

He had had such little practice at liking Margaret's boyfriends: little practice at putting together a bland, dissembling face, false smile, falsely firm handshake. There had been none. Robert was the first and the last, really.

Margaret had finished university and at once left Ireland for London. Magnetic London, a place with jobs, with air to breathe. Air with a different flavour, as Margaret put it. She would go to London, she would do her own thing, she would like it in a place with choice, with anonymity. She went – as it turned out, for a couple of years.

The famous summer of 1976: the summer of the heatwave. The summer that Patrick, now at the unripe age of twenty-one, was visiting from Ireland, staying with Margaret, dragging her through the comparatively cool, echoing halls of the Tate to look at Victorian painting. The summer that she in turn ushered him onto a hot London bus on Millbank for the short – but stifling – journey up to Piccadilly Circus, and then on to Regent Street to do a little shopping.

Margaret was living alongside half of Ireland: as she wrote in one of her infrequent letters home, she could have gone to a hoolie every night of the week, had she been minded to do so. Or pub crawls through Kilburn. But hoolies and Irish bars were not quite her style – or his, come to that: marches and killer demonstrations were one thing; but their mother had schooled them too rigorously in ways of thinking and behaving for hoolies and smoky Irish dives in Kilburn ever to attract.

She lived, for her two or so London years, in a little flat in a little street at the bottom of the Caledonian Road. Caledonian Crescent: a dinky little half-moon of Georgian houses around the corner from King's Cross: fallen on hard times, to be sure, but pleasant enough, and handy, too. Not at all bad, if you could avoid the King's Cross prostitutes plying their trade; and the druggies shooting up on the basement steps. She didn't have to step over these druggies though, because her little flat was the first floor of one of these Georgian houses: the druggies, then, could be circumvented easily enough; and with time she even found herself on nodding terms with some of the prostitutes.

Patrick, watching the nurse slide a needle into his arm, watching a drip being administered, was reminded of the glint of a syringe on those basement steps, long ago.

He was distinctly green about the gills on the evening he arrived. Fresh out of university: in Belfast, which meant home to Derry each weekend on the bus; set aside the political ferment and shaves with death, and you could almost say he hadn't seen much of the world. And he had never been to London before. On that first evening, they went for a walk to see the local colour – the anarchist bookshop and the Greek grocer at the end of the road, both places soaked, to him, in extreme exotica; and then up the road, through the thick, hot air to see the gloomy walls of Pentonville prison

197

– and then back; and Margaret made something to eat while Patrick hung around the windows and looked down into the London twilight as the first of the prostitutes took up her station nearby.

'I could watch them all night,' he said, absorbing like a sponge the girl's get-up and hair and carriage.

Margaret said, a faint pulse of pride in her voice, 'A couple of them are my friends now.'

'Friends!' Patrick said in pious horror.

She backtracked a little. 'Well, not friends, maybe. But during the snow back in January, a few of them set fire to a litter bin – you know, for warmth – and I was coming back from the tube, and one of them called me over –'

'Called you over?'

'For a gin.' She laughed. 'It was like the Girl Guides, you know, around a brazier.'

She stopped. He was staring.

'Maybe not really like the Girl Guides,' she ended, limply. 'Not with the gin.' She added, 'And there was no tonic.'

An explorer's heart? His exploring heart ought to have pulsed a little at the thought of hanging out with a clutch of prostitutes on a London street. But no: he preferred even then to skate around, to leave behind any sights disagreeable, challenging, unpleasant.

'So what did you do?' he said.

Margaret glanced over from the cramped little kitchenette, a pan in her hand. She shrugged a little defensively. 'Joined them.'

'Joined them!'

She spun from the little hob: put the pan down smartly on a cold gas ring; the overhead grill tinkled faintly. 'For God's sake, Patrick! You're not in the suburbs now! And you're my brother, not my mother!'

Which stung. He felt a gap at that point: not one of emotion, simply of experience. She drank neat gin with prostitutes – well, she had once. And she had a boyfriend now, and he would have to meet this boyfriend the following evening. At the age of twenty-three, Margaret was an adult at last. More than he felt himself to be.

How intimidating.

The theme of the summer visit to London, in hindsight, was one of intimidation. He was intimidated by the anarchists and Greeks, the prison officers and gin-swilling prostitutes of the Caledonian Road – and so in turn he set out to intimidate Margaret. It was easily done: their mother had softened her up, over the years. She was duly intimidated, a little, by the Victorian art that Patrick insisted she look at the next day – before she rallied, applying her psychological insights to *Pegwell Bay.*

And then another form of intimidation. It was Patrick's idea to meet this Robert person and go for a walk on Hampstead Heath: he had a plan that involved showing off his knowledge of culture and history, to put this new man in his place. He and Margaret quarrelled their way through the hot day, then, through London's grimy landmarks: in the Tate and then in Liberty; then again on the top deck of the red London bus as it jerked its way through Camden Town in the gathering rush-hour traffic. And then, at last, the rendezvous with Robert outside Hampstead Heath station.

Patrick's wickedness had not been leeched from him as a result of that long, hot day in central London. If anything, it had been concentrated still further: super-concentrated. He decided they should go the long way round to the Heath: climbing up the hill from the station to Hampstead High Street in the muggy evening air, passing under its barely heeded quaint gas lamps, before turning onto Flask Walk and down into the trees. Toiling, sweating, climbing: all in order to explore the area's cultural heritage. To show off Patrick's education, and to expose this new man's relative absence of same.

He was irked by his presence, yes. Of course he was. By his existence. By the look of him, his simian look, he thought then, and by the sound of him: that harsh Belfast accent capable of slicing through steel. By his presence in Margaret's life. In – though here Patrick's uptight Catholic sensibilities paused, retreated from the scene – in her bed in those nasty Caledonian Road digs. And so he would get to him. He would wind him up.

*

Robert eyed the boy walking along in front of him. The brother: young, younger than he had imagined, and young for his age. Tall, skinny, not much to him at all. Walking like this: a few steps ahead. Who was kidding who?

As he watched, the brother gestured at a house.

'That's it,' he said. 'That one.'

Margaret slowed, looked, took in the house, the scrubby garden. Robert stopped too, not that he had much choice. They stopped, they caught their breath in the hot, polluted air. They looked.

'Doesn't look like much to me,' Robert said.

The boy slid a glance. 'Doesn't it?'

'No.'

But something had altered here, in this moment. Robert heard his accent, his tones, his entire Belfast voice and manner carrying unpleasantly. Suddenly. *Doesn't it?*

How did the brother manage that?

They looked at each other.

Though the tone was set just a few minutes before. The bus pulling in (late) and the introductions (awkward) in the middle of a cloud of diesel fumes, of anxious, clucking mothers and grannies and grim fathers getting their bearings, looking for the entrance to the Royal Free Hospital. Margaret tense – and then this proposal to go looking for this damned house.

'We might as well,' the brother had said, 'we're practically there already.'

'Might as well.' Margaret flashed an anxious glance: and Robert shrugged. But he knew the brother's game. As long as he didn't begin to recite some damned poem outside the house.

And now here they stood. No, no recitation. But if anything, the brother looked far from crestfallen. He looked – pleased.

'Not up to much, this place,' Robert said, 'is it?'

Margaret looked at him again. Pleading, a little.

But now the brother spoke. 'I suppose it depends on your perspective.'

Oh, *perspective.*

'Let's walk on, will we?' Margaret said – and they walked on, labouring now up the High Street. It should be fresher up here, there should be a breeze – Robert looked back into darkness, a tunnel of limp-leaved plane trees on the slopes below; there should be a breeze – but no: the air stifled. And he was too warmly dressed, besides: a leather jacket he could not now take off for fear of showing the circles of sweat leaking from his underarms and onto his blue denim shirt. The wrong fabric, the wrong shade. They trudged up the ever-steepening High Street – and turned at Flask Walk and now he was aware with relief that the ground was beginning to fall away again, and that in the distance, ahead of them now, the trees on the Heath were swaying in something like a breeze. A pair of teenage girls clicked down a flight of stone steps from some other street, some other lane: they cut in front of them and walked ahead, talking busily, and he took in their tight jeans, packed arses, bare arms.

Surely, he thought, Margaret will focus on him soon. Surely she will gather her attention together and take him in soon. The brother is – nothing, he is nothing, there is nothing much there. But – and Robert saw the way the brother had of carrying himself, a way that set Robert's teeth on edge. An upward rush of temper. Young, yes – but there was more to him than that.

The girls walked ahead along Flask Walk, they extended their lead. Robert quickened his pace now, forcing the others to do likewise: his footsteps clattered on the Hampstead cobbles, echoing a little in the narrow lane. The echoes ran up and ran down, they bounced on the dark brick houses to either side. The girls disappeared into the shade of an avenue of lime trees. He'd catch himself, he'd get himself together once they were on the Heath.

*

This was a mistake.

Too soon for him to meet any member of her family: too soon in particular to meet Patrick, to take on the freight of this relationship.

It entered Margaret's mind, as a sort of pale consolation, that at least Robert wasn't meeting her mother: that at least she wasn't about to set off across the Heath with Robert on one side of her and her mother on the other: arm in arm, stride matching stride, like a troupe of chorus girls. She almost laughed, before the reality grabbed her, roughly, that this present situation was bad enough. That these two did not, could not possibly get along. That Robert's best side was not being brought out: that it took an almost magical combination of forces to bring out this side, and that this combination was not at this moment present.

That this manifestly was no laughing matter.

That her brother was discomfited by this stranger with his rough Belfast accent – and that as a response he was at his worst, his most superior, his most acid.

That she was hot and tired, and grimy and sweaty, after her day in the West End, and exhausted by this unwise climb through Hampstead. Keats and his house had not been worth it. Patrick should not have insisted on it. They should just have gone straight to the Heath and stayed there.

That she could do better than Robert. That she shouldn't be with a man like this, a man nobody else would take.

She caught her breath, pushed this thought away.

At least Robert hadn't swung for Patrick.

A pair of young girls appeared ahead of them: fourteen, fifteen, they talked confidently, they laughed. They certainly hadn't been trailing around central London all day long. The world was their oyster. She eyed them as they clipped ahead, laughing: she felt old, just looking at them, like someone's aunt. But the Walk was opening up a little now, Flask Walk turning into Well Walk and she took her eye off the girls: she looked to her left, at rampant, flower-laden gardens sloping in front of marching Georgian houses, and to her right, where the houses were narrower, and set directly onto the street. Margaret caught glimpses into these worlds as they passed: in the depths of one house, a woman setting flowers on a table in front of a window, through which a view of London opened up magically; in the depths of another, a family at a table before the same view. English families, in this English city – and now she thought of the big, rambling bungalow at home, of their table set beneath the skylight. She thought painfully of her mother. She peered, looked away, walked on.

The girls vanished into the shade of the lime trees that lined Well Walk. Patrick was pointing out this feature and that feature; another Keats reference, the eponymous well, the health-giving qualities of Hampstead well water, dark with iron. He was talking away, lecturing away: she murmured a question or two and then tried to fade him out – but this was impossible, so aware was she of Robert's nerves being screwed up and up, a spring ready to explode outwards, releasing who knew how much energy. And now the dark, brick-built eighteenth-century houses gave way to bigger houses, showier and more exuberant Victorian mansion houses in red brick, and now at last they reached the end of Well Walk and crossed the road and passed through the narrow gate and entered the Heath, where the trees were immediately dense, cooling, shadowing. And she felt an immediate relief: at least, she thought, I can keep my face a little hidden now.

How could this have ever been a good idea? Margaret had had an ideal of tranquillity, and had imagined that it might be found up here on the Heath, on the windy summit of Parliament Hill, amid the kite flyers and dog walkers, with London indistinct and silent below. She had imagined tranquillity – not that this was a quality familiar in her life. And now she was here, under the shadows of the trees on the Heath, with twilight not far off. Tranquillity though: this remained unattainable. It would always be unattainable. She felt caught, suddenly, in a web of relationships: these two men who flanked her; her mother and father, in distant Ireland.

She would be better off on her own – but no: her soul flinched at the idea.

Never alone.

She cleared her throat. 'Will we make for Parliament Hill?'

*

'*High thinking, plain living and small economies*. So they said.'

Margaret murmured, 'Who said?'

'Some commentator. About Hampstead at the turn of the century. Gas lamps and poets and intellectuals. The Hampstead women bought their necklaces one bead at a time, from a bead shop on the High Street. Not much money, you see, but they needed to keep up appearances.'

Patrick was filled with malice. A spirit of wickedness, his mother would have said: ready to sweep away any happiness, any smoothness or comfort or tranquillity. He pointed to the old well still in place there on Well Walk.

'Dark as sherry, they said, with the iron content. You could draw the water right here. Set you up for the day.' He thought of cholera, himself, and typhoid: these were his associations with London pumps and wells – but iron and in particular sherry served his purposes better at this moment than typhoid and cholera.

Robert might be at his ease around typhoid and cholera. Sherry, though – never.

Not much going on with Robert at the moment. Patrick watched him lope along in his heavy jacket, silent. He seems to have run out of juice, he thought, our simian friend. And she was silent too.

Never mind, thought Patrick. There was a whole lot left to say. He moved on to Well Walk itself.

'And Keats again: he lived at Number Forty-Six, and DH Lawrence in Number Thirty-Two,' he rattled on, winding up the tension, 'and Constable lived – somewhere too. Somewhere along here. Maybe it's been demolished.'

Nobody said anything. A hot, dirty breeze rattled the dry, heat-struck leaves of the lime trees: and it occurred to Patrick that in fact, he was not, now, enjoying this very much. He had checked his references, he knew all these irritating facts in advance, Margaret had filled him in on Robert's background with quite enough detail for him to set about pressing all the correct buttons. And he had been pressing them and watching the result.

And yet now the results were in, and there wasn't much satisfaction to be had.

They left Well Walk behind and entered the Heath: the heat at first seeming greater under the splay-leaved chestnuts and sycamores; but as they walked further, first downhill under the trees and through clearings where great logs lay along the edges of the bare clays, and then uphill through beeches, through brighter and greener light, so the oppressiveness of the evening seemed a little less and the breeze a little more evident. And now they broke through the trees entirely and walked through the upland and there was the summit of Parliament Hill itself: there were the dog walkers and the kite flyers, yes, they were all there; and the Post Office Tower and the dome of St Paul's, and the thin, indistinct line of the southern hills running on the hazy, pollution-clouded skyline.

They sat.

They sat, the three of them in a row, on one of the benches scattered along the crest of the hill; and Patrick felt – like a fool, like a knave. He felt – vicious. No: there was no *feels* about it: he had been vicious with Margaret, for no other reason than spiteful jealousy. Robert was – not up to much, that was a certainty – but Robert was hardly his priority here.

*

A year or so later, Margaret made the move back to Derry. London was now out of her system, after eighteen months or so. She retrained as a teacher – nobody could say that they were alive and fizzing with imagination, the Jackson kids, in their choice of careers – and that seemed to be that. Everyone would live happily after all.

Everyone including – Robert. Yes, Robert came too. They married: a very traditional wedding, big and splashy and the reception in a hotel in Donegal. There was no convenient brother to act as best man, and Patrick found himself wondering if he would be asked: of course he would have declined, but instead Robert sidestepped the question and dredged up some old North Belfast school pal (as unprepossessing as Robert himself) instead. And that was that. Yes: everyone would live happily.

Patrick had spent the previous months praying to a – he now assumed – non-existent God for this awful man to fade away out of his sister's life. To be knifed one day by a prisoner escaped from Pentonville, to fall under a train or be run over by a London bus or have his throat cut by someone, anyone. Then, when they returned to Ireland, to fall under a local bus. Or simply to walk away from Margaret and go and live a life of his own – though this would be less lurid a fate and certainly less satisfying.

Of course, Patrick thought, of course we sometimes read history backwards. Inevitably we do: I do it myself all the time, he thought – and this in spite of the fact that I am a history teacher and so have even fewer excuses than most. I spice my memories of the next few years with little bits and grains of knowledge that in fact came later: later, when it was evident to all of us what sort of man he was. We all understood how unsavoury he was: that he liked, from time to time, to have other women; that he barely made the effort to hide these inclinations. That he had a temper and that Margaret was, from time to time, made into his punching bag. We came to realise this – though we never dreamed what this temper would eventually bring, what he was ultimately capable of doing to other people.

At the beginning, however, Patrick was aware only of a fixed dislike that had its roots in pure prejudice. He disliked Robert: his coarseness, his accent, his – yes, his class, his origins. He didn't want to like Robert – he would have disliked Robert had he been a hero, a Titan, the toast of the town – so the situation was all very straightforward.

209

And of course he wasn't a hero, a Titan or the toast of the town. He was the opposite of each of these, which made the situation more straightforward still.

What the rest of the family thought: of course little was said aloud, but it was easy enough to read the smoke signals, to listen to the tom-toms beating quietly in the hills.

*

'The breed and the seed of him,' said Sarah. It was the taint of him; she caught the smoke and the reek and the shattered glass of Bombay Street; she caught the people who lived there. She wanted nothing to do with it. Martin stirred in his seat. 'Sarah, not that kind of language.' She kept her language to herself, after that.

*

The door to the sitting room was open: as Robert hesitated, on the threshold of entering, Sarah spoke. 'The breed and the seed of him,' she said. Her voice carried: could it be heard? – she didn't care; she hoped so; that much was clear. She was sitting in upholstered, centrally-heated comfort; outside, the grass had been cut in neat, geometric lines; the pampas grass tossed in the wind. He heard Martin move uncomfortably; the leather creaked and squeaked. 'Sarah, not that kind of language,' and then the soft tap of rubber on wood, as he and his cane made their way across the floor.

Robert slipped back into the kitchen. *The breed and the seed of him*: he'd heard enough. A flame of anger rose and was choked down.

*

'Have you seen my cane, son?'

Patrick shook his head. 'Which one?' His father had over the years amassed a small collection of canes: solid, heavy oak; an elegant blackthorn switch; even one in glossy, fine-grained hornbeam, imported from England.

His father rubbed a jaw. 'Well, at this point, any of them. How can a man lose, what, three, four canes?' A pause. 'What do you think of the handiwork, son?'

At Robert's handiwork – and they stood, the two of them, and looked up at the new wooden shelves: rubbed with fragrant linseed oil, smoothly finished and handsome.

'Impressive, it really is. And there's us,' said his father, 'not knowing one end of a screwdriver from the other.'

'Badge of honour, surely,' said Patrick. And his father turned, frowned, displeased at these grudging words, these ugly tones.

'Give the fella a chance,' he said – and turned. 'You owe it to your sister. Left it in the living room, surely,' he said, and turned, and left the room. The door closed with a firm, a too-firm, snap.

'Married!' said Sarah, as if the news was a surprise. She sat down heavily on a kitchen chair. Cassie moved to put the kettle on. 'Married,' Sarah said again, and she shook her head. A few minutes passed: with tea inside her, she spoke again. 'Well, that's Margaret for you,' she said. 'She'll not be satisfied until she has the whole town laughing at her.'

*

'No more tea for me.'

Cassie's hips ached, now. She moved slowly along the hall. My hips ache, she thought: the days are too long for me, now. Poor Margaret, she thought, settling for that one. She reached her room, closed the door behind her, opened the window wide. The garden was dusky – but there was still birdsong. She closed her eyes, listened. Poor Sarah, and poor Margaret, she thought: it will hardly end well.

*

Just give him a chance.

Margaret moved through her day: walking, teaching, cleaning, cooking.

Just give him a chance, she said to herself. They can do that, can't they? She thought: me, I'm giving him a chance. Can't they give us a chance?

*

I often wonder, he thought, how differently events might have played out, had Robert been given more of a chance. There was danger here: in taking responsibility away from him, in taking it on oneself. He knew this. But he wondered just the same: the thought moved and nosed through his brain, like a living thing, like a worm.

TEN

Sarah tied her scarf – one the colour of buttermilk, today, and heavily, smoothly luxurious – more firmly around her neck. Patrick's room was held at its usual careful temperature, neither hot nor cold. Just the same, though, she was feeling the cold, feeling her age. She was feeling the horror of this situation – though damned if she was going to show anyone, by word or movement or expression.

Her son was fading.

'Fading, fading away,' the ruddy-faced hospital chaplain had told her, with odd lilting gaiety, as though about to break into a child's verse. The medical people said the same, of course with more gravity. The clock was ticking, was the message being delivered in various ways: she should prepare herself; the family, the whole circle of her son's acquaintance, everyone should make the necessary preparations.

'Thank you,' she said. 'How long?'

At this, a thoughtful purse of the lips. 'Still difficult to say: but, a fortnight perhaps?'

'A fortnight,' Sarah repeated. And, 'A fortnight,' she told Margaret and Robert. First with the information: and now they nodded too and Margaret blinked. A fortnight. Maybe less? A week. Imagine.

Now, sitting at the end of the bed, Sarah felt a thin, whispering draught issuing from – somewhere, she could not say from where, in this sealed, controlled world; and she gathered her buttermilk scarf around her neck more snugly still. Here was Patrick's beaky profile, his emaciated skull; here were drips and tubes and bright lights, metal and hard, impervious plastic to be wiped and sterilised, as necessary. She could hardly bear to look – at Patrick, at the inhuman paraphernalia that surrounded him now. She could hardly maintain her composure – and yet she would. She must. I must, she thought. It was an article of pride. No other way would suffice. Pride and a rhino's hide had kept her alive all these years: it must see her out, now.

Her father had beaten her again one frosty autumn evening. Again: and with his leather belt. She had left the door to the barn open: the cows had wandered out into the wintry fields. Brendan discovered them – and came pounding across the frosty grass at her.

His belt was already in his hand as he burst through the kitchen door.

The cows he left out in the field as darkness fell. Beating her took priority, it seemed, over getting them safely back inside.

'I'm sorry, I'm sorry!' she screamed – she was cowering beside the dresser by now, her arms and hands protecting

216

her head – and he was screaming too as he laid into her with leather and metal. Behind the door, Cassie was crying.

'Stop making that noise!' he bawled, 'Stop it, or you'll be sorry.' But she was already sorry.

There would be no scholarship for her. That had been made clear – obliquely; the priest had put out the word.

She flung out her arms again as Brendan's belt hissed through the air and found its mark: and her hand caught a glass on the dresser; and it fell and shattered on the flags.

Her skin was bruised and reddened that night – and she took to her heels, leaving home, her father, Cassie: leaving it all behind her, replacing it all with a Derry in the throes of war. At least, she'd thought as she ran down the dark lane and away from the farmhouse, at least I'll find a job, do something for myself – and she did too, though not without some trouble along the way. Jobs were abundant in the militarised wartime Derry of the day: they were handing them out like sweeties.

And Cassie – Cassie she left behind. But she knew, somehow, that Brendan would never hand out such a punishment to Cassie. Cassie kept the household running, Cassie wasn't a child of his, Cassie was altogether too fragile. It would be like picking up a piece of thin china or porcelain, and throwing it against a wall and expecting it not to break. Cassie would break. It would be unthinkable.

Sarah, on the other hand, seemed to be made of stronger stuff. She could be beaten at will. She went out into the world, and into a war, and found herself a job.

The doors of the mess hut faced south and east: and the sun, rising over a low shoulder of hills on the far side of the river, shone red into Sarah's eyes. The hut was freezing, as cold as the morning outside: soon, the other women would arrive and begin complaining about their nipped fingers, noses, toes. But Sarah preferred the cold. She never had minded the cold rooms of her youth – just as well; she had had no choice in the matter – and she didn't mind it now: took pleasure, in fact, in her chilly surroundings, in the cold air in the nostrils, in her breath rising in clouds into the air. Better this than being wrapped in false heat that dried her skin, fogged her brain and soured her temper. She was alone, and she liked this too: liked to be in first and have a few minutes to herself, before the clattering and banging of the day began. So she stood behind the long counter and enjoyed the cold air and the low, red sun shining into her eyes.

And it was a beautiful morning – clear and frosted and perfectly silent. Earlier she walked over the crisped grass, walked through the very earliest light and watched the thin threads of mist drawing up from the city below. Up here at Creevagh, high on the hill, the whole of Derry was spread out for inspection. The river was stiff with shipping; grey corvettes and destroyers clustered along the wharfs; barrage balloons hanging high in the air. To the north, the river widened into Lough Foyle; and there was Benevenagh in the furthest distance, its black cliffs misty and indistinct at this hour. All around her were more of these curved huts: half-sunk into the churned-and-frozen ground, rank upon rank, mirroring the rows of shipping below; piles of earth to left and right. This hospital base was still new, raw: cheerless in the tail end of the Derry autumn just past, when little streams of muddy earth ran and gurgled along the new paths, and sometimes straight into the huts themselves.

There were Canadians here, and Americans: recuperating from this ailment or that one. Some had barely escaped with their lives from a crash, from an accident; some had survived a torpedoed ship. They complained bitterly about the weather, the Canadians: you'd think they had never felt a cold day, the amount they grumbled about the Irish climate. They described sweltering summers at home; then, in the next breath, they described iced-over lakes and bays, the Rideau Canal at Ottawa, said one with a sigh, iced over and turned into a stage for skimming sledges and skis and all the rest of it; the colour, the racket, the hot chocolate stalls on the ice.

'What are you complaining about then?' Sarah asked them at these times, over the clatter of the mess hut. 'It's never too hot here, is it? That's a good thing, if you ask me.' They laughed, she went on. 'And it's cold there, it's cold here. What's better about the cold at home?'

But it was different there, apparently, it was a different kind of cold. 'The cold is dry,' they told her with heart-breaking earnestness. 'You can't feel it in your feet.'

You're supposed to be fighting a war, she told them, not sitting around comparing different kinds of cold. The Americans went on about home too, on and on: the damp and the cold here is killing us, they told her; it's breaking our lungs and our hearts.

She measured out oats, set them to steep. The hut was warming now, warming nicely. The first men along in – what, twenty minutes? – time to get a move on. She gave the still-cold porridge mix a stir and then walked to the door of the long hut. Many people had been up and about for hours, of course, many never went to bed at all: guards and nightwatchmen and all ravenous by the time the first meals appeared; vehicles on the move, men going to and fro, the sun still low and red, the sky a pale, washed blue, the mist drawing off. Too often the day dawned fresh and blue; and then – she knew the rule – the rain was bouncing off the roof by eleven o'clock. Today, though, was going to be a beautiful day.

It was hardly difficult, this work: she knew this: the usual, the same old pattern of a bit of cleaning and a bit of cooking; not much variation from one day to the next. Plenty of men around: more and more men flooding in each week, more and more ships coming and going from America on the convoys; and these men needed cooks, they needed cleaners. They needed female company. *Not my company,* she sometimes thought: she was perfectly aware of her few words, her lack of small talk and amusing chatter, her sharp edges. Surely they were perfectly aware too – though nobody seemed to mind. She took pains over the morning porridge, which was hot enough, which was free of lumps: and perhaps this helped.

And she revelled in the routine. The cooking and the cleaning, the occasional trips into what was suddenly now a modestly glamorous and colourful Derry, all this became wonderful to her. She sat in the Golden Teapot on afternoons off, drinking tea with other girls, and laughing her head off. It was – it was normal, all of this; she had made it normal.

She had made herself normal, for the first time.

And here was Anthony now. She liked him. He was delighted to be here, he expressed his delight with wide smiles that showed amazingly white teeth. How long might he be stationed here? – well, with the war, Anthony shrugged, you never could tell. That was the thing. He might be sent away, to Europe when the time came, or maybe North Africa – there wasn't exactly a shortage of places, after all, to which he might be sent – or over to England. He was young and able-bodied and, to her eyes, so very tall; he could hardly avoid some move, somewhere.

In the meantime, though, his medical training was coming in very useful: truth to tell, he said, he was delighted to be avoiding the convoys; really, he thought he was stuck with them. When he came in with the *Nerissa*, he thought that this was it, for him; over and back to Newfoundland, over and back with the convoys: 'Those damn convoys,' he said, stretching his arms behind his head luxuriously, 'and anything's a bonus after that.' He didn't even mind the climate too much: he was from Winnipeg, 'too hot and then too cold and always too windy. A change of climate,' he said, 'this is just fine.' The door of the mess hut was closed now, shutting out the sun, and the place warming up very nicely indeed. Though, the porridge needed stirring.

And in the meantime, her companions had arrived – Derry women who needed to make a few extra shillings a week – and the hut was filling; more men and more: some bleary-eyed after yet another raucous night on the tiles, some fresh and upright. They were given porridge and tea (a little stewed, but no help for that) and more arrived and more. Anthony inclined his head to her with mock courtesy as he queued to be served. She felt like a co-conspirator. She was. And now she had promised to go to the regular Friday dance at the Guildhall. That's how a part of this place she had become. She had promised Anthony she would go: as a friend, of course. Only as a friend.

They had met – no, he had saved her – only a month, six weeks before. He had saved her from something. She could not say from what: her imagination flinched. It might have been lice, it might have been bed bugs. But it might have been the something else that the nuns had liked to hint at: he might have saved her from specifically that.

'Where did you meet?' one of the Derry women had asked, casually enough, one afternoon. She'd been eyeing them, wondering what was going on.

'Just on the street,' Sarah had replied. Which was the truthful answer: and the woman, repelled, had moved away.

But what could she have said? That her father had laid into her with his belt, buckle and leather and all? That she had packed a bag and left there and then, running along the lane and past the white gate posts and down the road and past the curtains and eyes of the town, catching the bus to Derry with a few seconds to spare?

No. The truth would hardly do at all.

When the bus had stopped, there in the middle of Derry six weeks or so previously, she had had no plan. She gathered herself together, took the handle of her bag, made her way stiffly to the door: the few other passengers shuffled ahead of her, disembarking, vanishing into thick darkness. This was the last bus of the evening: it was after ten o'clock: it had been delayed at the border by customs officers searching for contraband butter stowed in bags and under hats and sewn, patty by patty, into trouser linings. And there in the centre of Derry, the blackout was adhered to rigidly; she could hardly see her hand in front of her face. She clasped her bags closer, clambered down the steps and into the enveloping dark.

A stiff wind blew, and she jammed her hat more tightly over her ears. She could hear a thin, faint wailing: the sound of the wind as it squealed through the barrage balloons suspended high above. She knew this, she had eavesdropped on a conversation on the bus, had listened as they described the eerie sound – 'it makes me want to squeal back,' one woman had said to her companion – but still, the sound came as a shock to her, there in the blackness. The skin crept on the back of her neck. Maybe, she thought, I shouldn't be here at all – in spite of everything, in spite of how bad home has become, maybe I should have stayed there, maybe I should have lived with his fists. Maybe I should have.

But the long cuts and grazes on the back of her legs would not be ignored: they had caused her continual pain as she sat on the bus, they stung now as she walked – and she remembered the scene in the kitchen that same evening: the whip of her father's belt, and his grunts and oaths. She shook her head: these memories caused her brain to grind to a standstill; no, she was right to leave.

But perhaps – perhaps she should have timed her arrival in Derry for early in the morning. Maybe she should not now be walking the streets of this blacked-out city late in the evening – but no, she was glad she left. Maybes and maybes: she walked faster towards the commercial streets a little distance away, where lights leaked from behind blind windows. She would find something, a dosshouse or something like that – though what was a dosshouse like? – maybe not too pleasant – but she was certain there would be somewhere – there had to be *somewhere* she could stay – and then get a good night's sleep and then she'd see. Then I'll get a job, she thought, and then I'll see.

The blackout made for treacherous walking. She blundered along dark streets, more than once tripping over bicycles and lurking, slinking dogs and sliding on a frozen puddle, and without so much as a single lamp to mark the way. She came across a police patrol: there was no curfew that she knew of, but they stopped her anyway, shining a torch briefly in her eyes, settling down to pass a few minutes with questions.

'And so, where are you off to, Miss?'

'I'm just back from my auntie's house in Donegal,' she gabbled at them. 'I'm going home now.'

'And where's home?'

Where was home? Sarah racked her brains in the darkness.

'Chamberlain Street,' she said at last. She could remember

toiling up Chamberlain Street with her mother once, on a shopping trip years before. There was a pause, the sound of a smile as he replied:

'Well, you'd better get back to *Chamberlain* Street, then, hadn't you, Miss? Shouldn't be out walking on your own, should you? Not at this time of night.'

'No. I'm going home now.'

'Course you are.'

Sarah heard them laugh as she whisked away. She thought: they can hardly think I'm up to no good, can they? Some kind of spy? – and she blushed as she realised what they actually thought – what? a girl out walking the streets on her own, near the docks, at night? She quickened her step, as a wash of fear came over her. She must find somewhere to stay. Would the patrol help, maybe? She turned to call after them – or rather squeak, for her throat was constricted now with panic. But they were banging on a front door a little distance away: light was shining from around its blackout blinds. The door opened and sharp voices read the riot act to some morose householder, silent and invisible in the smoky darkness. Quickly, she turned the corner and out of sight. No: she would be better on her own. Her panic dissipated as quickly as it had gathered. They would hardly have helped her anyway.

Another corner and now she was on the quays. One side of the wide road was studded with pubs of all kinds, most of them noisy with men's voices and dense with smoke which leaked from the doorways, which she could smell as she passed quickly along. She had been here before, of course: the quays, the grey river and great crowds of gulls hanging in the air. She remembered. Too dark to see much, but of course she also knew – she'd seen the photographs in the *Journal* – that the quays had changed a good deal recently: changed beyond recognition. The moorings on the other side of the road were thick with frigates and destroyers – she could see bulky shapes looming out of the night.

And here on this side, the footpaths were crowded: men standing outside the pubs and all of them shouting and singing in a medley of accents: English, she could hear and Scots and Welsh – and was that American? All sorts anyway – and for sure no place for her. So she strode on, skirting or pushing through knots of men – and sometimes women too – and ignoring the ribald comments thrown her way, keeping her head down. Maybe it was all good-natured enough, but some of it didn't sound so – not that she was about to stop and see. But I'll have to go in somewhere, I'll have to ask for help, eventually: so she thought, as snatches of songs and fiddle music, along with the forbidden light, leaked from the doors and windows.

The crowds began to thin as she moved along and she came to a final pub – smaller than the others and, it seemed, a little quieter too. She hesitated outside in the frosty darkness for one more moment – before gathering her courage and plunging through the door, through the heavy curtain that hung across the entrance, blackout fabric and draught excluder in one. Into the room, which was small and dim, with only a lamp or two fixed to brownish walls. It took a moment to accustom her eyes to this dim light – and now she took in the rest of the room, the threadbare red and black carpet, the handful of men hunched over the short bar, the groups of others – servicemen, it seemed; mere boys too, some of them hardly shaving yet, hardly older than she was, surely? they should be in their beds – sitting on small wooden stools around the few tables. A country pub, a *shebeen* like a place or two she could think of back home, filled with farmers on mart day and close to empty the rest of the time. A *shebeen*, lacking only the turf fire; here in the middle of the city.

Well, at least she need not lift her skirts and run. She had the measure of such places, didn't she? What would Father Lynch say, she thought suddenly, if he could see me now? A harlot, a Jezebel – a Bibleful of words; and look what happened to Jezebel in the end – and she girded her loins and ploughed her way through the thick air and her fright and up to the bar. The elderly barman looked her up and down. *Jezebel* too: she could read his mind.

'Well, love?'

'Well,' she said and a moment's silence.

'Cat got your tongue?'

Another man, sitting to her right – and a Scots accent. Young and smiling at her – not a very nice smile. A red, congested face and a belly a little too big for him; Sarah turned again to the confused barman.

'I'm sorry to barge in,' she said, 'but I'm looking for some-where to stay tonight. I don't know anyone in town; and the hotels are too dear for me, I'm sure.' Though no reason to be sorry – this was a public house. She was entitled to be here, she must be careful not to sound grovelling – and it wasn't her fault that her voice sounded shrill, reedy; that her words came out in a gasp, almost a sob.

The barman opened his mouth to speak, but his Scots customer jumped in first. 'I'm sure we can find somewhere for you to stay.'

She didn't look at him. 'I wasn't talking to you.'

He raised his eyebrows. Then, mockingly: 'Well, beggars can't be choosers, can they? Neither can tarts, though maybe Derry girls are getting choosy these days, are they? Lots of men to choose from: too many, maybe. The war's not all bad, is it?'

She said nothing, but turned again to the old barman. But the other was not yet finished and continued in lazy, mocking tones:

'There's always room for nice girls plying their trade. Bed and board for services rendered, is that right?'

'If you've nothing to say,' Sarah told him abruptly, 'then hold your tongue,' and she turned away once more.

'Bitch,' she heard him say: and now, suddenly, she could take no more and blindly she turned and pushed through thick air to the thick curtain over the door. It enveloped her, as the darkness had a little earlier, and for a moment she felt as though she was beating against it, like a moth on a lightshade; and then once again she was on the freezing, black street. But she had caught the raised voice just the same: the altercation springing up from the black-and-red carpet behind her; the new, exotic accent; and the disgust in his tones. And now the curtain parted behind her: and dim light and cigarette smoke leaked out, and this same voice, same accent.

'Excuse me, miss? I know a place.' She half-turned towards this voice in the blackness. 'A job, even, if you want one.'

And that was Anthony, from Winnipeg, as she learned later, Winnipeg which was too hot and too cold and too windy. The next day, having as if by a miracle acquired a job and a bed – there in a Nissen hut full of them – and a routine, she thanked him, and said what she had to say about bed bugs and lice; and something worse than bed bugs and lice.

He shrugged at that. 'Never happened. Don't worry about things that never happened.'

She did worry, though, just the same. She worried later, at the dance.

*

The stained-glass windows of the Guildhall were blacked out on this Friday night. Of course they were – but to Sarah, standing on the city walls and looking down and across the square at the building's looming façade, observation of the blackout seemed now to be distinctly half-hearted. The great oak doors were standing wide open, and light and noise were pouring out like liquid into the night; the building was already clearly packed with people, with more lining up to go inside. Gaggles of folk chattered and laughed on the slippery cobbles of the square, their breath white in the frosty air: certainly nobody seemed disturbed by the music, the noise, the floods of light. Was there a war on?

True: most of the people milling around were in uniform, but this was just about the only sign of war. More noticeable was the jolly atmosphere, the loud screeching laughter, the catcalls that threatened to drown out the music. The sailors in uniform in the icy square below were for the most part arm in arm with Wrens or beaming local girls, and the entire crowd was jostling to get into the building, shouting, pushing. A few solo men, with only bottles of liquor for company, staggering and stumbling around the fringes of this bellowing mass of people. And this was – well, it was ironic, for weren't these Friday night entertainments organised by the local Temperance Society? You wouldn't know it, she thought: little sign of temperance in a place like Derry at any time, and especially not on a Friday night.

She felt a little nervous as she looked out and down at the scene before her: tea and buns in the afternoon was one thing, but she had avoided these dances; in fact, avoided being out at night at all. But Anthony had asked her to come with him: and he had been so kind, so jolly, that she felt obliged – no, she wanted, in spite of other sensations – wanted to go. And now here she was looking out from the city walls on this bitter night, and pushing her hair from her eyes.

They had been walking on the city walls for some minutes: to get some air; she'd been stuck inside all day; and he, he said, filling out forms for most of the afternoon. It was pleasant to be in the icy air, to take in the view before plunging into the dance. But too soon, he nudged her in the ribs. 'We should go,' he said. 'Can't stay here all night. You'll catch a chill.'

'One more minute.' She paused, taking note of her tense body, trying with all her might to make it relax. 'Look – it's like every last one of them down there is drunk.'

Sure enough, a little gaggle of sailors and Wrens was reeling around the edge of the cobbles below. As they watched, one of the men pitched a bottle against the city walls; it exploded and glass flew as a ragged cheer went up into the dark air.

She flinched.

'We should go.' He paused, glanced at her. 'Do you really want to go?'

'Oh yes,' she said and looked at him quickly, 'of course I do.' It would never do to behave like a nun or a schoolmistress, after all, and fret over smashed bottles. They could do what they like, these people, so long as they didn't smash bottles into her face. She imagined her father, sitting with Cassie by the fire in the kitchen at home. She thought of his belt, and heard the blood beating and roaring in her ears. She managed a smile.

*

Anthony watched her smile, he smiled back – with relief, with a good deal of relief: for she had seemed abstracted this evening; all the way down from Creevagh she'd seemed preoccupied, quieter than usual. But now she blinked, smiled, seemed to come back to him, to the present. He led her down the narrow, slippery stone steps from the city walls and into the square.

He led her through the melée, through the oak doors and up the broad carved wooden staircase. He led her into the Great Hall, which was brilliantly lit in spite of the cigarette smoke, packed, noisy; the long sheets of stained glass were hidden behind black blinds, but the great organ and polished wood gleamed under the chandeliers. It was all very grand: Sarah stopped again, she seemed flustered.

She seemed flustered, but he knew better than to shepherd her. Some women just do not like it, his mother had told him, they cannot bear it; you need to watch for the signs. And he had already led and directed her – through the square, through the crowds – more than was perhaps wise. Some girls did not like it – and she was one of these girls; he knew this already. So he stood instead and watched her: she seemed glassy now, she seemed removed; and he stood and watched and waited.

Already he had told her about himself, about his family, about Winnipeg, about the flat plains and the cold and the heat. 'Don't worry,' he said, 'I won't pile it on.' She laughed at that, a relieved laugh: the other boys really piled it on, with their stories of mountains and lakes and blue skies and dry, powdery snow. 'Go ahead and pile it on,' she said. 'It's all a far cry from this,' she said, and gestured around at the Nissen huts half-sunk into the earth, at the sound of autumn rain drumming on the roof, at the rivulets of muddy earth outside, cold feet and cold hands.

He didn't pile it on, though: for every toboggan, he said, you could count a pathway and a shovel, sweat and the snow up to your knees. It isn't, he said, all toboggans and frozen lakes.

'I hardly know what a toboggan is,' she told him. Imagine a boiling summer, he said and clouds of dust that blow in from the prairie ('I hardly know what a prairie is either,' she said) and along Winnipeg's wide, straight streets and the Red River running low and brown; imagine the grass in August turning a brittle yellow. The snow and winter fun, he said – that's all true, but there's more to it all than that.

He asked questions too. Easily, at first: naturally, interestedly. What about you? And what about you? But he sensed a barrier there, he wouldn't push or probe. He waited, instead, for her to come to, for her to come out of herself. She might.

*

After a few minutes of this glassy standing and staring, she came to: the roaring in her ears began to ease, the painful sensation in her throat to sink away a little – although perhaps she was simply becoming more adept at thrusting it down with her heel, thrusting it back inside herself. Certainly she knew how to keep her eyes dry now. Her father was far away. She looked around. Anthony had been standing quietly all this time and waiting for her and now he raised his eyebrows, took her hand, squeezed it gently.

'Not a bad place, is it? All in all?'

She laughed. 'Oh no. Not bad, all in all.'

'Right,' and he tugged at her arm, 'come on then. Chop chop.'

Sarah laughed now, and allowed herself to be pulled gently along. They made their way along the edges of the hall: and soon enough she met people she knew from the base, from the kitchen, from the hospital. She began to relax, she was happy to step out onto the dance floor. And she was a good dancer: she had learned the steps in the kitchen long ago, to tinny music from the old black wireless. The steps came back to her at this moment, as they quickstepped and waltzed around the hall to the honking notes of the show band. She was a good dancer – better, in fact, than Anthony, whom she began to guide confidently.

Later – back on the base, one bed among a row of beds, unable to remember how she got there, how she got home in one piece – later, she lay shaking. She could piece together certain parts of the evening: shards, elements in a jigsaw. But the night as a whole – no. She was dancing inside, then was outside, walking across the frosty, cobbled square. Her hand was taken, then raised voices and a brawl and pieces of glass flying through the air – and the story, everything, fell to pieces. She could not remember how it happened.

The Guildhall was, suddenly, too hot, too noisy and crowded – she had to get out. So they retreated, down the polished wooden staircase and through the echoing hall and back out into the square. Now he took her hand: he meant nothing by it – or rather, he meant everything. But no harm: he meant no harm. They had danced, or she had danced and he had followed, was the truth, until their faces were pink and shiny and their clothes damp and reeking of tobacco fumes.

But the air became grey with smoke and the hall steaming hot and they had retreated down the stairs and out into the chill, damp air – and now he took her hand.

She said nothing. She looked at his hand and her hand and she said nothing. It was almost pleasant, wasn't it? – and after all, they had been dancing, been hand in hand, arm in arm, for the best part of an hour. So this was – fine, she thought: and a moment later, she was pushed violently and she careered into Anthony's chest and they both fell; and there was a ferocious splintering, a crack of glass on the cobbles, and she screamed.

A glass bottle had exploded on the ground close to their faces. Splinters of glass pierced his temple; she saw thin streams of blood on his cheek. He lay there, dazed; she raised herself on her hands and looked around, looked up.

'So it's another fucking soldier, is it? Come to save us all.'

A man was standing a little way away. He was tottering a little from side to side and as Sarah scrambled to get up, this man aimed a kick roughly, drunkenly in the direction of Anthony's head. He missed and now Anthony rolled hastily, out of range of the heavy boot. Sarah pushed herself onto her heels, sliced her hand on a piece of glass, saw the man lose his balance and fall against the Guildhall's red sandstone walls. 'Bastard,' the man said. 'Bastard.' He was drunk, but not roaring drunk: he could still unbuckle his belt in a second and in another second whip it through the air. 'Bastard. Fucking bastard. Coming over here and telling us what to do. Fucking bastard. You and all the rest of you bastards. It's not our fucking war.' Spit flew from his mouth and he wiped his face with his sleeve and aimed another lash of his belt. It hissed as it flew through the air and caught her arm; it hissed again as it caught Anthony's arm as he lay on the ground.

With a tremendous effort, Sarah got to her feet and stood, swaying for a moment on the gleaming cobbles. She too had struck her head on the ground, though it was not this blow, not a concussion that made her stand like this and sway. The man in his drunkenness fell once more against the sandstone, away from her as she stood reeling. Her arm was throbbing from the lash of the belt; blood was trickling from her hand: she looked at it, wiped it across the front of her coat. She was disembodied: she was light with – shock, with something; she rocked on her heels. On the ground beside her, Anthony rolled over and then got to his feet. Blood was trickling here too, trickling from his temple and down his cheek and onto his collar.

He said, 'Sarah,' – and the drunken man lunged once more. She watched, rocking, floating, the scene in front of her, but now it was silent; the volume gone, the noise turned off. Her father was drawing his leather belt: it was singing shrilly as he whipped it through the air; and in the next room, behind the door Cassie was crying. But no, it wasn't her father: and she watched as Anthony's fist slammed into the man's cheek, as he fell, as Anthony kicked him in the stomach, kicked him hard, again and again. The man lay on the ground, unmoving now – and Sarah moved, she was gone, blindly through the prurient crowd that had collected to watch. Within a few seconds, she had stumbled underneath the dark arch of the city gate and was walking, running up Shipquay Street. The noise of the world had returned now: excited voices on the square behind her and, in the black sky, the drone of a plane dropping, coming in to land.

*

Anthony had the better of him now, but still – better to make sure. He took the man's head in his two hands, brought it sharply down on the cobbles. There was a clear crack – and now someone at last lunged forward, caught his shoulders.

'You don't want to kill him, so you don't,' said the man, a Derry man at his elbow. 'Do you? You've done your worst: it'll have to be the hospital for him as it is. Come on now,' the man went on, solicitously, ignoring for the present the figure prostrate on the ground, 'come on, you've done your worst.'

Anthony looked around. 'Where is she?' For Sarah was gone. She was there a minute ago, but now gone; now nowhere in sight. 'Where did she go?'

The man pointed towards Shipquay Gate. 'That way. But you need to get your face seen to.' From the crowd, voices joined in with eagerness; this man had proved his worth. 'You do. Your face is all blood, so it is.' But he ignored them, ran across the square. She was gone.

ELEVEN

Patrick was a dead weight. He was weighing himself down. He knew how a cat behaves when she is reluctant to be moved: she turns herself into a lead weight, a dead weight.

Which was the way to do it. No point making it easy.

'You're not making it easy for us,' said the nurse, 'are you?' She was panting slightly, although she was young and strong, and he was neither now. He was twig-thin. They wanted to turn him, to check his back, his buttocks, his calves for evidence of bed sores. 'It's for your own good, you know,' reproved the nurse. 'We're not just doing this for the sake of it.'

He kept his silence, his eyes closed. They tugged and pulled.

'All clear here,' one of them said at last. 'Terrific.'

'Terrific,' the other echoed. 'That's right.'

The sheets were crisp and fresh now, and his body checked over as though it was an Ordnance Survey map. The women were on their way out of the door. Tea was on its way in.

The season had turned, in the course of these – these two weeks or three weeks or whatever it was. From his window now – for there were no more genteel little rambles across to the window and back; everything had to be deduced from the bed – Patrick could see the trees beginning to crisp, to yellow; the occasionally blue sky was paler, its fitful summer vibrancy gone for this year. Of course the bell continued to toll, unchanging, in the school belfry across the way: but he knew without looking that the boys entering and leaving the school gates were beginning to wear coats and anoraks. Time was up.

'Did you hear about –' one of the nurses said as the door opened and closed with a sigh. Did you hear about – but they were gone now, out of earshot; and only the sentence remained, suspended there in the air. Time was shifting too much, backwards and forwards: slipping now back into a hateful past and now forward into this painful, truncated present. Now it was happening again: voices rang and shoes squeaked and trolleys rumbled in the present: he closed his eyes, and footsteps clipped and cutlery clinked and tinkled in the past. Did you hear about? There was nothing else to do: and his mind settled on the sentence, set to work worrying at it as though it was a bone. Gnawing, turning it over and over. Did you hear about? Did you? Did you hear about?

Patrick's mind settled on himself. Did you hear about? – when did you? What was the context? The questions jabbed and stabbed: this was a court of law. *When* did you hear about? – are you certain? Did you have suspicions before that? What, none? And he shook and shook his head. No suspicions. Misgivings? – yes, plenty of them, his mind dwelling on his brother-in-law: but of course that could be put down to his own spite, his own small-mindedness.

Suspicions, no.

And now his mind settled on his sister. How had Margaret kept her composure, even for a moment? In his mind's eye he saw the scene: the Formica-topped cafe table, and his hands warm and snug around a mug of coffee, and Margaret's hands snug around her cup. And now their mother appearing at the door of the cafe, and starting – actually, visibly giving a start – as she saw them: and then moving towards them: the morning turning, now, in a new direction.

'Did you hear about the mother of that girl who went missing?'

Yes. Margaret had heard, by then, about the mother of that girl who went missing. Lying in his blue bed, Patrick closed his eyes. She had heard. Robert had told her, that very morning.

*

'You didn't hear the news about that woman,' Sarah said, and glanced around the cafe. 'The mother of that girl who went missing: you remember, they found her at Inch Levels.'

His mother wasn't asking. She was telling: she looked – not avid, the way that people tend to look avid when they have shocking news to impart, when there was news of a scandal or tragedy: they wanted to be first in, like some town crier of old. His mother wanted to be the first with the news for sure, but she didn't look avid.

There was something about her today, something different. She had seemed as composed as ever, but now he noticed – yes, in fact she lacked that customary cool. Was that it? He watched her from his usual distance – what was it? A shaking? The feeling was wrong: she seemed to be – vibrating in some way. The air was already vibrant with noise: one of the girls behind the counter sorting knives and forks and spoons into their places, with scant regard for her customers' aural comfort. But his mother was vibrating at her own register: had she been a sherry glass, he thought, you'd almost say she was about to shatter.

He watched her, from afar. He shouldn't judge: he knew this, but he did anyway.

'She drowned herself,' Sarah went on – and yes, she sounded a little different too; her voice thinner, more tremulous.

'Walked into the sea,' she said, 'yesterday afternoon.' She rearranged her long, purplish scarf more snugly around her throat. 'Just walked into the sea.'

This was October: a month, already, since Margaret's gluttonous birthday dinner and now their father was fading, failing in front of their eyes. Clutching one of his canes a little more tightly, walking for shorter distances; his skin paling, thinning. Martin wasn't fighting it, either: 'Let it be,' he said, when someone – not generally Sarah – hung over him, fussing. 'Let it be.' Not much to be done about it, and he knew it: they all knew it, even before the doctors reported. A series of new strokes, after a long respite: little strokes; and a bigger one could come at any time. 'They're a little like earthquakes,' one of these doctors told them, confidingly. 'You find yourself waiting for the big one to strike.' As if that was a consolation. They'd just have to watch, he went on, and wait and be on hand, OK?

Patrick nodded; and 'OK,' Margaret agreed. Though it didn't seem like much of a prescription, she said later. 'You'd think they'd train them in how to use language. An earthquake? – I mean, it's hardly a useful analogy.' But Patrick didn't agree. 'Useful enough,' he said. After all, they *were* hanging around waiting, weren't they?

The waitress had finished rattling cutlery now, and was moving on to glasses, cups and saucers.

'It was on the radio,' Sarah said, 'this morning.'

Margaret was cupping her coffee now in the palm of her hand, looking out of the window at the street. The distant hills were bluer and the sky paler and the cherry trees in the Diamond were beginning to sport bare limbs rather than foliage; their long yellow leaves littered the pavements. A few hundred yards away, cordon tape fluttered in the wind; a police Landrover squatted. Patrick saw this; he looked away.

Sarah said, 'Did *you* hear about this?'

Margaret put her coffee cup down carefully. She shook her head. Patrick, tucked into the banquette beside her, cupping his coffee in the way that Margaret had cupped hers, glanced at her – just an instant's glance – but said nothing. Sarah continued talking in that same tense, highly strung manner; and Patrick watched her: his instincts now up and buzzing, raring to go to work, a tiny point of chill in his heart. Covering some tracks – some unknown tracks – instantly, without a thought.

Margaret needed to be protected.

'Never recovered,' Sarah said, 'according to the neighbours. They had people watching out for her: but you know, when people want to go, they just make up their mind and go.' She paused for a moment. 'So she walked down to the foreshore and just walked into the water, and –' Now she stopped and there was a beat of silence. 'And the sea took her and that was that.' She sipped her coffee. 'Poor soul.'

Patrick watched and watched. This autumn morning had already taken a different, unexpected shape. And now the shape was changing again.

Because his Saturday mornings tended to have a familiar pattern. He liked to be in town early to do a little shopping, and be gone before the crowds arrived. His father's illness was beginning to prise apart his routine, but his Saturday mornings had thus far remained sacrosanct. Nobody else figured. Early meant avoiding his students, who would be storming through the Saturday afternoon crowds in their civvies. 'Alright, sir?' the older boys would sometimes hail him, jauntily, on the rare occasions their paths crossed in the supermarket, at the pictures. Sometimes – though more frequently, they lowered their eyes or looked at him as though at an animal on the loose from a zoo.

Early was always better.

But this morning, Margaret telephoned at cockcrow, suggesting a meeting, sounding tense and strained. 'Just a coffee,' she almost pleaded, beating against the solid metal walls of his Saturday morning. 'It won't take long.' And so they met in a cafe off the Diamond and settled themselves in a booth by the window, milky coffees before them.

Margaret looked – dreadful, he thought. Her hair needed a wash, for one thing. He observed her more closely: her pale skin, her tired, shadowed eyes. 'I need to tell you something,' she said, lowering her voice so that she could hardly be heard over the Saturday morning hum. She paused: he waited. At last she said, 'Did you hear about the mother of that girl? The girl who went missing? – they found her at Inch Levels.'

'The mother, yes: something about it.'

'It was on the news this morning,' she murmured and he nodded.

And then, their mother appeared, framed for a moment in the doorway. A collision. What was she doing here? This place, this time, wasn't part of her routine.

He watched her look around, and see them, and start, and pause for a moment. But there was no turning away – not from her own children; even his mother's strangeness did not scale such heights – and instead he watched as she made her way between the tables towards them. 'God, please no,' Margaret murmured and closed her eyes. 'I don't need this.'

And now she was in front of them, surveying their coffees – and their clothes, most likely, and their hair. Their demeanour and their posture. 'Straighten up!' she liked to tell him when he was younger. 'Pull your shoulders back!' And now a memory flashed into Patrick's mind, there in his blue bed, memories

245

lying upon memories as he stretched flat: he is trying a pair of trousers on for size in a little shop, a little boy, long ago – a cramped fitting room and a curtain that does not quite cover the entrance. Yellow fluorescent strip lighting that shines around the edge of the curtain – and now the curtain is suddenly whipped across. The metal hooks glint and squeak in their channel. There stands his mother; he cringes in front of her in his shirt and his little yellow underpants, there in full view of the shop. 'I thought I'd thrown out those pants,' she says. 'Didn't I throw them out? We'll do it when we get home.' The assistant cranes her neck to see the underpants. 'Get a move on now, Patrick. We haven't got all day.' The curtain is pulled across again, noisily.

There stood Sarah; and the waitress, stacking glasses now, just behind her. 'What are you doing here?' Patrick asked, perfectly unceremoniously.

Sarah shed her dark coat, exposing another layer: a long woollen cardigan, in lilac. This she kept on. And a purple scarf, wound around her throat. 'I just felt like a cup of coffee,' she told him. 'Just a notion.' She sat down and now they looked at each other.

He fetched her coffee, in the end.

But what was the news Margaret had wanted to impart?

And his mother in such a strange mood – and the conversation so strange too. So very strange. At last, though, she stirred and seemed to gather herself into the present.

'And what about Robert?' she asked. This was not a usual question: usually the attitude was that Robert didn't exist unless he was incontrovertibly there, flesh and blood and impossible to ignore in front of them. And yet it was a usual question too: or rather, it had the feeling of it. It was one of Sarah's usual questions: as a boxer might punch the underside of a jaw with a gloved fist, so Sarah liked to identify and isolate a weak spot too. She usually deployed the jab to take her mind off a given problem: Patrick had come to understand this over the years. What current problem might be preoccupying her this morning? – he had no idea; only that she had one, only that it was almost visibly there in this cafe, at this table, with her.

Hence the jab.

Margaret shrugged. 'What about him?'

'Well, how is he?'

'He's OK,' Margaret said, expressionless.

'Is he busy?' Robert had a job now, for the first time in a little while. He worked as a landscaper of other people's gardens.

A labourer, Sarah described him.

'Busy enough.'

He leeched off his wife, Sarah liked to say. 'A leech,' she liked to say. 'Couldn't even pay for his own wedding.'

'Making money?' she asked now.

'For Christ's sake, would you leave off?'

Margaret was paler than ever now: and suddenly it occurred to Patrick that she might be pregnant again. Was that the news? Was it welcome? – or maybe it was unwelcome: did she want to go to England? – was that it?

But now their mother was launching into a new phase, holding forth across the table's white plastic expanses. Talked about – what? The evil eye. What? The air was thickening as she spoke. As she went on and on and on. Patrick felt himself assaulted by strangeness. What was wrong with her today? Why go on and on like this – right now? She had moved on from the dead child's mother, from Robert, from Margaret – and that was a relief, true enough, small mercies and all that – but what was she talking about and why?

What was wrong with everyone?

But this was the question of his life.

The cafe was filling up now, gearing for the lunchtime rush; the assistants were bringing out the hefty fare of this place: dishes of bronze sausage rolls, shining with grease, and trays of yellow chips, orange fillets of breaded fish and green, plump marrowfat peas. Their table, their comfortable banquettes would soon be needed; hungry shoppers were arriving in their turn in the doorway, sweeping the cafe with narrowed eyes, fixing on their emptying, cooling coffee cups. And yet they sat on, the three of them. It must, thought Patrick, have looked like fellowship, like family felicity – but it was not. It certainly was not. For his mother was behaving so strangely; and Margaret was silent. No, more than this: she had absented herself completely. It was her time-honoured coping mechanism: and he couldn't blame her for that.

*

I can't stand this, Margaret said.

To herself, she said it. She was scarcely capable – no, that wasn't it; she was actually incapable, of saying a word aloud. At this point, anyway. She needed to pull herself together.

What was her mother *doing* here? What was she doing *here*? – of all places, here, appearing like that in the doorway?

'The coffee's fine,' she said. 'No, nothing for me.'

Patrick slipped off to the counter. She looked at her mother, seated there opposite, her arms tightly folded across the front of a long, warm-looking cardigan. She geared herself up to speak at last. She said, 'What brings you to town?'

Sarah said again that she just fancied a change.

'And how's Daddy?'

Her mother shrugged a one-shouldered shrug. Their father, she seemed to say, hardly deserved a two-shouldered one, did he? 'I left him in bed.'

Silence settled, then, until Patrick returned with coffee and a scone. Sarah stirred a little sugar into her coffee, she buttered her scone, she looked up.

'You didn't hear the news about that woman,' she said. 'The mother of that girl who went missing.'

There was a moment, and Margaret shook her head. No. That woman, who had walked into Lough Foyle and drowned herself at twilight. Their mother talked on for a little while, her voice fading in and out. She talked about the woman. She talked about her little girl: who could forget it? 'That was the night of your birthday,' she said.

I can't stand it, Margaret thought.

The cafe was filling. Margaret thought about making a move, about bundling herself into her coat, braving the

October chill. But now her mother was off on a new tack: so strange a tack that Margaret was almost distracted, for a moment, from her own concerns. Almost.

These would have to remain unsaid, if only for a few more minutes. Her windpipe felt constricted, with – grief, of course, and a creeping sense of horror and fear. Her life, surely, was over.

*

It had to happen just there, on that part of the coast, Sarah thought. She almost laughed: it just had to. She could picture it, of course: she knew it from childhood; she had gone paddling there, just there beside the pier where the best rock pools were to be found, poking in the deepest, coldest pools for crabs. 'Mind yourself,' her mother called, 'go carefully.' And her father pushed a stick into the water and – right there! a crab emerged from the deep and took hold of the stick with its pincered claws. 'There now! But we'll just let it go, Sarah, will we? No point taking it home,' he said and she shook her head and her father shook the stick and the crab scuttled away, back into the seaweed and shadows.

And later, at the beginning of the war, she and Cassie had gone down to the end of the pier, to watch the grey warships sailing by – so close you could almost touch them – easing through the narrow mouth of Lough Foyle, and then sailing south to the docks at Derry. Sometimes the sailors waved. Sometimes the little pilot boat puttered out from the pier with apples and pears, with green stuff. 'Sure, we'll make a bit of money out of them, Cassie,' the pilot said to them. 'We have too many apples, and they don't have enough. No harm.' He threw a green apple at Cassie, gently. 'Catch!' and she caught, deftly, and smiled. 'No harm,' the pilot said again.

No harm.

Contaminated now, for her. That place, that town and its past, over and over again, contaminated.

And now here was this woman, choosing a shore that was already pregnant with death.

At least she hadn't walked out to Shell Beach. Not to the beach itself: it seemed instead that she had clambered through those rocks that bristled, jagged and pitted with pools and oily with seaweed, just to the left of the pier. The tide was in, though, and that must have helped: in spite of the rocks, it probably hadn't been all that difficult. Sarah imagined her setting out, in failing light, moving along purposefully.

And yes: it was a relief, a blessing that the poor woman hadn't trotted out to Shell Beach, which after all was not a half-mile further along the coast; and much easier to access.

She had done Sarah a favour, there.

So she told herself. How sick I sound, she thought. Making it all about me. But she was wound up by this: of course with good reason; of course she disliked that coastline, disliked any mention of it; kept her distance from it; had never taken her children there; Kinnagoe was as close as they had ever come, and that was too close. She hated the remembrances, the dreadful reminder.

She sipped her coffee.

'What are you doing here?' Patrick asked here – but impossible to put into words: what? That she had felt her past snapping at her heels? That she felt the walls closing in on her at home? That she needed to move, she needed some movement, to escape the past that was snapping, snapping? Explosions and deaths. And so she had left Martin in bed and jumped into the car and into town – only to find, not space, but her children. But she could not form these thoughts into words: there were embargoes on every avenue, every sentence. She could hardly imagine the words; and speaking them was out of the question.

'I just felt like a cup of coffee,' she said. 'Just a notion.'

Just a notion – and looked at the two of them across the expanse of plastic table. Which was of course not broad enough, for any of them.

Then she spoke again: said something that surprised her just as much as it surprised her children.

'Sometimes I think I have the evil eye,' said Sarah, and in instant discomfiture she picked up her coffee cup and swirled around the dense, sugary remnant of coffee inside, first in one direction and then in the other.

They looked at her. 'What?' said Patrick – and indeed, it was almost as if another person had spoken, an invisible fourth person seated there at the table, putting in their spoke with dreadful unexpectedness. And yes, Sarah was as startled, almost, as everyone else.

'Nothing. Nothing.' Forget that. She was holding onto the edge of the white plastic table with her fingertips. There were rings marking the table surface, indelible marks, ancient cups of coffee. That was the trouble with such surfaces: they seemed to be wipe-clean and low-maintenance and all the rest of it; but they were in fact fairly unforgiving. She could have told them. Those rings would still be there come Doomsday.

'No,' Margaret said now. She leaned forward. 'What did you mean, the evil eye?'

Sarah said abruptly, 'I see a shop, I look in the window, and –' And yes, it had been this that propelled her out of the house this morning: a need to escape her surroundings, at least, even if she was unable to escape herself. And perhaps it was this propelling her words forward now. She was aware that she was behaving in a way that was – unexpected, to say the least; she was aware that they were staring at her.

She had been drowsing off last night, safe and warm and snug in bed, when another bomb had exploded, its sound wave travelling down the river and colliding with the walls and windows of the house. As it had done countless times before. Well, not countless: countless was an exaggeration; but a great many times. It was abnormal and it was normal, all at the same time. Martin woke momentarily and then slid off again into sleep. She might have done the same: these blasts were routine; there was no need to break one's stride in the face of them. They were nothing remarkable.

But not this time: and not simply because of the memory that the sound invariably brought: the coastal footpath at home, the gust of noise, the gulls that she watched being forced straight upwards by the force of the explosion: straight into the air before turning and wheeling north and south in the freezing winter air. No: she had had a premonition, this time: she sensed which building, which business, which shop had just been pulverised.

So: the evil eye?

Was that the explanation for all these events over the years?

What nonsense: of course not.

And yet.

'I knew which shop it was, as soon as I heard the explosion last night.' She gestured out of the window and down Shipquay Street, where the white cordon lines flapped in the cold breeze and police Landrovers squatted nervously and half of what had once been a building lay spread across the road. She almost expected to glimpse a mannequin, its blonde wig all askew, lying on the ground in a provocative pose, legs spread – but no, no mannequins. Just rubble and bricks and shattered glass.

Her children looked. Until this moment, they had tried to ignore the whole scene.

Margaret said, 'The evil eye?'

'It was Toner's shop,' Sarah said, 'and I passed it yesterday afternoon and looked in the window and I remember thinking how nice the displays looked. They'd really made an effort, I thought. And now today,' and she stopped and took a yet tighter hold of her coffee cup, 'it's blown to kingdom come. And that isn't the first time that something like this has happened.' The second, the third time, she thought: I could name each shop. Is it any wonder, then, that I'm thinking along these lines?

'So I'm wondering if I'm carrying some kind of curse around with me. I see the shop this morning, bombed out, and I wasn't a bit surprised.'

Did this explain Anthony, too? Of course not. *What nonsense*, she thought again.

Patrick said coolly, 'But you don't have the evil eye. There isn't any such thing.'

Now Sarah drew herself up a little. 'I said that it makes me *feel* as though I have. As though I have the evil eye.' She was being misunderstood deliberately. Margaret made as though to speak, but Sarah went on, speaking rapidly now as though she absolutely could not bear another interruption. 'It isn't the first time a thing like this has happened. That's all I'm saying.' She paused for a breath; Patrick was gazing out of the window. 'It makes me think.'

'Think what?'

Sarah paused again. 'That maybe bad luck follows me.'

Her son and daughter looked at her now. Neither said anything, and after a moment she watched Patrick resume his study of the window, the view of cordon tape and leaves and bomb damage.

Sarah knew that the tenor of this conversation was utterly new. And again now, a moment came – and again it went; a branch in the road was noted, ignored. 'Your father,' Sarah said now, 'he'll be wondering where I am.' But she stayed where she was as other instincts took over: to fend people off, to keep them at the end of a cattle prod. To probe their weaknesses, the better to protect herself – and to protect them from her.

She had said too much.

'And what about Robert?' she said – and was duly rewarded, for Margaret flinched. It was all too easy to make the girl flinch; Patrick, really, was a much tougher nut to crack.

Well, and he took after her, didn't he? – her own shell was like a Brazil nut. You'd have to get right in there with heavy-duty metal, with muscle and force of will; and even then, there were no guarantees that the shell would crack even a little. The metal might break first. The only person who had managed to get inside had been Cassie; and Cassie was gone now. Long gone: and even Cassie hadn't always been successful. Sarah remembered now that evening, long ago now, when she tapped on Margaret's bedroom door and sat on Margaret's bed – eager, desperate to unburden herself, to shed a burden that in her rational mind she knew she ought not even to be carrying.

And instead, had asked Margaret about her upcoming exams.

I don't like Physics, but even that's going along, you know, well enough too.

Cowardice. She remembered the misty rain and the streetlamp and the sound of the television drifting the length of the house. There were moments when it was possible, when the option was given to you to turn off onto another road, to begin another journey. I suppose that these possibilities become fewer and fewer, she thought, the older you get; eventually, they stop coming; they stop completely. She would put it down to God shrugging in irritation and impatience – if she believed in God.

As it was, she put it down to nothing, or to herself. I'm too set in my ways, she thought, now. Set fast.

*

Margaret and Patrick were on foot. 'Will I give you a lift?' their mother said – but no: Margaret scotched that idea immediately. There was no need for a lift, for the weather, though chilly, was still dry; they would walk. 'Are you sure?' Sarah said, already poised to go. They were sure. They parted on the corner of the Diamond: Sarah glanced once more along Shipquay Street at the cordon, the Landrovers, the scattered remains of the building. 'See you, then,' Sarah said and they nodded – the Jacksons knew they did not kiss – and she was off, trotting away briskly along Ferryquay Street, eddied and spun by passing shoppers on the narrow pavement, giving as good as she got, passing out of sight.

Now, a brief silence. To Patrick, a moment of consideration: it seemed to him that he should take a moment to brace.

Later, he would imagine that a presentiment came out of the crowds of shoppers: squeezing out of the gap, perhaps, that his mother had left as she had retreated. A shadow, bearing down on them. Though even this was hardly the case: had he not felt this premonition earlier, early this morning, with the sound of the ringing phone? He had. They were coming thick and fast now, these shadows slipping out of corners. And now, standing there on the street corner, he was aware of taking a deep breath, and holding it in his lungs for a second. Bracing himself, and then turning and seeing Margaret's face, chalk-white and turned up towards him.

'Let's go somewhere to talk,' she said.

'What did you want to talk about?' he said, still braced; and she took his arm and they set off walking.

'I don't know,' Margaret said.

He was aware of her clutching arm: their family did not hold or embrace, any more than they kissed. This clutch was uncomfortable; again, he felt a shadow behind him, shadows at either side.

'I don't know,' she said. They were walking south now, along Bishop Street, away from the cordon and the flashing lights, the rifles and bullet-proof vests that dredged up unwanted, ugly memories – but aimlessly just the same. There was no end in sight – but now, he was aware of her taking a deep breath too, and holding it; and now she pointed along narrow, shadowed Palace Street. 'Shall we go down there and onto the city walls?' she said. 'Let's do that.' He nodded and they crossed the road and turned onto Palace Street and here, with neat terraced houses on one side and a high brick wall on the other and already bare branches overhead, she seemed to breathe normally again. They turned the corner and the lane widened: they passed the churchyard now and stepped up onto the ramparts. Margaret's face was paler than ever. 'I need to sit down,' she said.

It was dramatic up here, for the whole city opened up: the cathedral on its hill and the long terraces of houses, and spires and the sweep of the river; and then the distant hills like blue whales, with cloud shadows moving smoothly and silently along their dark slopes. Closer at hand, late roses were still blooming in the pretty churchyard behind them; and the avenue of sycamores, that had been planted perhaps a century ago on the walls themselves, were shedding yellow leaves. But the views were closed off by high metal security fences: ahead and to left and right; they could walk only a hundred yards or so along the ramparts before being turned back; and the wide views were obscured and barred. Yes, it was dramatic – but maybe not in the best way, he thought; and it was not really a place to go walking.

Again he said, 'What did you want to talk about?'

Margaret glanced: there were benches placed at intervals along the avenue of sycamores; and she gestured at one. 'I need to sit down,' she said, and made her way over, and sat.

'What did you want to talk about?'

She replied, 'My head is light.' Well, he could understand that, he thought: their mother's sudden strange appearance, strange mood and strange language – it had all been enough to turn anyone's head light.

'Adrenalin, and caffeine,' Margaret said, as though beginning to compose a shopping list. 'And the cafe.' For a moment, she said nothing: he began to think that whatever this news was, he was not going to hear it – not today; and quite possibly not ever. But then she said, 'You know those cop shows. Those American cop shows. Kojak and all.'

He nodded.

'They go, like, "Zip it!"' She sat forward on the bench. '"Zip

259

it, man! or I'll zip it for you!" And "Or I'll zip *you*!" And next thing they're lying dead.'

Patrick nodded again.

'Robert,' she said. 'He told me to zip it. Last night. He told me to keep my mouth shut, or I'd wreck everything.'

Another pause, this one hanging on. He watched Margaret's profile as she looked out through the metal bars of the security fence at the distant hills, her eyes moving in time with the silent shadows of the clouds moving across blue slopes.

'Mouth shut about what?'

Margaret shook her head – but then she began to tell him.

'The child who went missing – Christine Casey, the night of my birthday dinner.' She took a breath. 'And then, last night, I told Robert I was leaving him.' And a short, snorting, desperate laugh. 'And he said I can't, and then he told me why.'

*

The previous evening, Robert had moved around the house unplugging lamps and flicking switches: now only one light burned in the hall, outside the children's bedroom; the living room, where she sat on the sofa and he sat in the deep armchair, was in gloom. Now he said, 'And no, you can't leave me.'

Margaret had intended to be kind, circumspect: not to describe the suffocation of her life, the corridors that ended in a blank wall, the days and months of her life running away like sand in an hourglass, with nothing to show for it. She did not love him, she felt nothing for him, really – this was no marriage.

He listened, composedly. No sign of his temper. No sign of anger, of despair – of anything, really. He listened from the depths of the armchair, the tips of his fingers pressed together in front of him. She could just make out his shape, there in the darkness: he seemed calm, dreadfully composed.

'I need to stay here, the girls will need some sense of a stable environment, their things about them. But you can take all the time you need to find another place.'

He sat, looking at his fingers.

'Look: can't we have a light on?'

He looked at her now through the darkness, then shook his head a little.

'No.'

She opened her mouth to speak again: but now he held up a hand to silence her, shook his head again.

'And no, you can't leave me.'

She caught the glint of his eye in the darkness. 'Why? Why can't I?' She laughed, a little uneasily as he shrugged. A short silence.

'You can't, because if you do, I'll pull the plug on the girls' lives.' Another shrug. 'Do you want me to tell you how I can do that?'

Margaret stared at him.

'It'll be easy,' he added. 'The easiest thing in the world. If you stay with me, though,' he added, as though offering her a most beguiling choice, 'I won't have to.'

'What did you do?'

Now Robert sat up, turned in the gloom: the glint left his eyes, which were dark now, and his outline was dark against the thicker surrounding darkness.

'Inch Levels,' he said. 'You can imagine the rest.' And then, in the same reasonable, almost jaunty tones, 'But if you stay with me, I won't have to go to the police, I won't have to blow the whistle on myself, I won't have to do that to the girls.' He pressed his fingertips together again. 'Stay with me, and we'll carry on; and nobody need ever know; and our girls can get on with their lives.'

Margaret sat very still. She didn't ask the natural question, not yet: *why* he had done it; why, in the first place. She was instead chilled by the familiarity of the story, by her sense that this story was horrible – was horrible beyond description – and yet was not wholly unexpected. She had married – badly, though of course she had not known quite how badly, had not known the extent of his periods of silence, his flashes of temper, his black fits, his deep and profound introspection. But she had known she was marrying him on the rebound: not from another man, but from her family, from her mother, and with a sense of desperation.

And six years and two children later, she realised the extent of her mistake.

But now, in this instant, she saw that a trap had been sprung – that leaving Robert was indeed impossible. Because it was true: she could not after all leave her husband, not if it meant that her children's lives would be blighted by the facts attached to their father. Of course, she thought in this instant, they'll be blighted in another way: they'll be blighted by living in the midst of an unhappy marriage – but I'll find ways to compensate for that. Won't I? Clarinet lessons – her thoughts in a tumbling rush – and checks, and balances: and there is time, only a few years, really, not many years before the two girls fly the nest. I can manage until then. Yes, she thought: surely I can.

'You're shaking,' Robert said coolly. 'I can feel it, even from here. You need to pull yourself together.'

'I'm chilled.'

'Chilled. I'm the one who should be chilled, Margaret. Pull yourself together.'

This was brutal – but worst was the familiarity of this story: as though she knew it already, as though she had come across it long ago, in some story, or book or magazine; or had intuited it at some deep, cellular level.

As though – yes, she had imagined that something like this might happen, at some point. It wasn't so very surprising.

She almost physically moved away from this thought. And now she asked the question.

'Why?'

No, she thought: I don't want to know the why. The why is too much for me. I don't want to know about the why; I don't want to understand something like this.

In any case, she knew Robert too well to expect an answer. And of course she knew herself even better. Yes: she would make her bed. She would change her mind, make her decision:

she was prepared to weather anything now, rather than admit these facts into the light, to the gaze of her children.

She was prepared to weather anything.

Up to and including the death of a child?

Yes, even that. And he knew it.

'It wasn't intentional,' he said. 'Have we a deal?' His voice was dead and cold in the darkness.

She nodded – but he was looking again at his fingertips and did not see the movement.

'Margaret. Have we a deal?'

She had to say the word.

'Yes.'

'Yes?'

'Yes,' she said. 'Yes. A deal.'

And there was more too: more Margaret was prepared to do. She was prepared to spread her net. She was prepared to yank her brother into this situation.

Yes, this too. Because here was Patrick sitting on the bench under the sycamore trees on the grey city walls of Derry. Saturday morning now, and here she was, telling him her story.

Silence when she had finished. Margaret watched him, there on the bench under the sycamore trees. She was good at watching. She had watched Robert, earlier, watching her have breakfast. She had watched her children shovelling cornflakes, watched them put on coats and scarves and go out to the garden. She'd taken her time with her own breakfast: a cup of tea and then another cup, and perhaps she'd have another slice of toast and honey? – and so on and on. 'Have you anything else to say?' Robert said at last. But – no: she shook her head. She had nothing to say; at any rate, not at the moment. The deal was sealed.

And at last she moved, leaving the table just as the sun reached the side of the kitchen window and began to shine onto the table. The edge of a square of pure light: Patrick, when he was younger and they had just moved into their new house, had liked to move things – knives, pens, the edge of a newspaper, anything with a side – across the tabletop, sliding it across in time with the sliding of the sun shining in from the skylight above. 'A straight line, look!' he exclaimed. Cassie would look, would praise. She, the superior elder sister, would scoff – 'so what? big deal!' – when in reality she envied his focus, his concentration. She thought about him as she slipped out of the kitchen and away from her husband: Patrick, whom she was going to draw into this ghastly affair. And she watched him as they settled themselves around the table in the cafe – until their mother appeared so unexpectedly and joined them.

What would happen now? Well, time would tell, of course: but she was fairly certain that nothing would happen. Nothing to upset the steady tenor of their lives. She would not leave Robert; she would certainly not turn him in; her brother would not, either. Nothing would happen. They would carry on; they would put all this behind them.

And so, in time, would the remnant of the other family, of the Casey family in their bungalow on the hill overlooking Lough Foyle. Already she had acknowledged the limits of what she was prepared to do. She would tell her brother; and that would have to be an end to that. She would get it off her chest, and move on. They would all move on.

And even this fresh news, this news of the death of the girl's mother, that newly minted news: it changed nothing, not in its essentials. Everyone would press on.

TWELVE

As Margaret spoke, Patrick remembered her birthday meal. Her feast. The windows rippling, visibly buckling as the wall of sound collided with the house – not that that had put them off. They had eaten like – like pigs, he remembered, like pigs that night: like pigs eating their own kind. They made their way through pork fillet and platters of potatoes, and lemon meringue pie and birthday cake; they stuffed themselves. Martin opened a bottle or two of red, with his usual care and reverence: 'Smell that,' he said. 'What would you say? Blackcurrant, would you say?' Patrick said nothing to that – not a thing; there was nothing left to say, the barrel scraped clean – but Margaret laughed. 'Blackcurrant, Daddy!' she said. 'You spend all that money on a bottle of wine,' she said, 'and then you say it reminds you of Ribena!'

A little laughter: Margaret tittered at her own joke; and their dad laughed at himself; and even their mum smiled a little, a very little, as she forked the pork from pan to platter, carefully, piece by piece by piece. The mandarin orange segments pressed into the cream on the side of the birthday cake, Patrick remembered, and gleaming prettily in the lamplight.

Robert, though. He didn't smile. Patrick remembered that, now. He didn't smile and he had even less to say that night than was customary. He just sat there and said nothing. Cleared his plate, though: ate every last thing.

Margaret talked on.

And now Patrick saw in his mind the previous day's sun, setting in a cold sky: and the woman stepping out on her final walk. How had she moved? Slowly, tentatively, with indecision? Or with something like confidence, telling herself that if this was to be her final act, she had better perform it with panache?

No. He could hardly imagine the latter, really.

No, he saw her as a somnambulist: setting out from the house, closing the front door behind her, and heading down the hill and out towards the rocks. Chances were that nobody else was even around: a chilly October evening and not much to be seen on the pier or down by the water; the sun setting behind her, shining red onto the black cliffs of Benevenagh on the far side of the lough. And the shock of the icy water on her calves, on her knees; her coat beginning to float up around her waist, her movement hampered, slowing; the iron resolve in taking another step and another, until contact with the sea floor was lost. Had she stones in her clothes, dragging her down? – plucked from her garden or the side of the road, weighed judiciously in the palm of her hand before being transferred to her coat pockets? And that cold white current that flowed silently just offshore taking her, then, and depositing her a little later a couple of miles down the coast.

Easy to accomplish. And how straightforward to imagine. He could see it all.

He had heard about it, early that morning. A short report on the radio: and then he had a few minutes to fritter away while waiting for Margaret; and he had spent it away in the kitchen department at Austin's – and there he had heard more thoughts on the matter. 'It was selfish of her,' opined one woman, speaking to her friend between the rows of food mixers, 'to leave her two other girls like that. Selfish of her, really.'

The other woman demurred, mildly. 'People that would do a thing like that: they're not in their right mind, are they? So you can't call them selfish.'

'Well, and what will those girls do now?' said the first woman. 'And what about their poor father? Sure, I know she couldn't have been in her right mind, of course I know that,' she went on, looking around at the gleaming appliances, 'but still. She could have caught herself in time, is what I think. Now,' she went on, 'I fancy a Kenwood, myself. In red, would you say?'

'I like the silver.'

But the first woman shook her head decisively. 'Silver, no. Not the silver. Think of the dirty hand marks showing up. Red.'

Now Patrick sat on the bench, and said nothing.

So yes: perhaps there had been a premonition. That's what his dream had been, of course. Of course. That was it: of course he had never talked to anyone about this; what would he say? *My dream*, he would say: *let me tell you about my dream, the dream I have over and over. Let me tell you about that.* This was his own private dream – but of course nobody would ever want to know anyway; nobody ever wanted to hear about other people's dreams.

So there it was: the plants severed at the roots. A premonition. And – information that nobody would have wanted; information that was useless to anyone, that was pointless.

And nothing else: only the whirl and gyre of his own head, into which nobody would ever think to look. They would ask him about history, if he was lucky: about policies and war and personages: that was all. If they bothered to ask, bothered to enquire, then – but the real facts and truths and history – yes, the real history – nobody would ask. They would come close: *did you hear about? Did you? Did you hear about? Terrible, isn't it?*

And at a same time, an uprush of sick pleasure. Gladness, that at last Robert had shown his colours. Hadn't they always been apparent?

He had Robert, now.

And he felt himself flush, felt Margaret's eyes on him.

And then what? Well, who could say? And then what? And then what? What was he supposed to do with this information? A few sycamore leaves drifted down, falling splayed and crisp on the cobbled surface before him. Margaret sat silently – but he turned now.

'Why did you tell me?'

To tell me what to do.

That was what he expected Margaret to say. Why else would she confide in him, tell such a terrible story?

She must need his advice, his guidance; she must need him to formulate a plan for the future.

So he felt sick again – a wave of nausea that ran through his body like electricity – when she shrugged, when she said, 'Confession box? I want to get it off my chest.'

Was that it? Was that the point of this – recitation? Because it amounted to nothing more than a recitation – a story, held comfortably at a remove – if reality was not to be allowed to intrude.

To ensnare him, then: was the truth of it. She had ensnared him. She wanted to involve him in this hellish history, but she didn't want to do anything more. She wanted to talk it over with him – and that was it; and then to get on with life. 'What? Not to make some plan? Not to do the right thing?'

His mouth was dry and his lips felt stretched and dry too, as though they might crack at any moment. The weight of unwanted information. What would he do now?

'This is the right thing.' He opened his mouth, but she carried on. 'Nothing. We do nothing. We carry on.'

Patrick sat, looking straight ahead, at the terraced streets and cathedral spire and the blue hills beyond. Then he turned to her.

'Hardly.' A pause, and then, 'To carry on regardless? And you mentioned absolution? Don't you need restitution for that? Isn't that what we were always taught?'

He meant it cuttingly, but Margaret was uncut. She laughed – a most incongruous sound in this context. Yellow sycamore leaves scudded along the cobbles in front of her, and she said, 'You're not joining up the dots. I'll be staying with him, won't I? Isn't that restitution?' Strands of hair were blowing in the wind and she tucked them neatly behind her ear. 'The most complete kind?'

Already she had it worked out. So Patrick thought, so it seemed. Repent at leisure, was to be her mantra: for the decisions made, the objectives followed through, the choices clung to, over years and in the face of all the evidence in the world. She would see it through. He watched her, feeling himself filled with spite and hate. And feeling degraded and soiled; and betrayed, at being pulled into something that had nothing to do with him.

'Forgive, and carry on? Is that it?'

Margaret looked at him. 'I never said *forgive*. I won't forgive him, and I won't forgive myself. *Carry on*, I said.' Her feet scuffed at the yellow leaves. 'And after all, this family doesn't make a habit of forgiving. You've never forgiven me for marrying him, have you? Our father has never forgiven our mother for being the sort of woman she is; and *she* has never forgiven *him* for marrying her, for being so weak. So, don't you think there's plenty of experience out there? I have it all at the tip of my fingers.'

Patrick said carefully, 'So year after year, for the rest of your life, this is the way you'll live?'

But he hardly listened to her reply – for in the midst of all this, something was being ignored, was being skirted with deftness and efficiency. She might live the rest of her life in this way: yes. Focused so squarely on her own penitential ways? Yes. Ignoring the howls at the door, the fist thumping the table, the need for justice, for vengeance? The child who would never return home, the life snuffed out, the second life taken away, the family that must rearrange itself – somehow – around this gaping hole?

No. Nobody could ever do that.

But Margaret was watching him, was reading his mind. 'People do it all the time,' she said. 'They make a deal with themselves, and they live with it. Robert will never hurt anyone again,' she said, 'and I'll make sure of it. The only hurt will come to Robert himself, and to me. Nobody else. That's the deal.'

Patrick thought: but what about me?

'I shouldn't have phoned you this morning.'

This was a concession – but Margaret's tone was cool.

'I'm sorry about that. I shouldn't have; I panicked, for a moment. I should have left you out of it.'

But it was too late now. Patrick too saw years and years ahead. Loyalty, binding his tongue. Unwanted knowledge carried like a stone. The drag of it, year by year. Complicity, and the silence and isolation, the degradation – of the soul, of the heart – that it brings. His mind had been settled – so virtuous! – on the woman who had walked into the sea the previous evening. Of course his mind dwelt on it, on this catalytic moment: now, amid the darkness and confusion, he could see the woman's family, the scene silent and terribly clear as though he were standing there, viewing the internal spaces of the house as through a transparent glass screen. But now, there he was, allowing these thoughts to waver away from the dead child, her mother, her family. Moving his thoughts like pieces on the draughts board, deliberately onto new terrain. To check, to block, to overcome.

He was no better than anyone else in this scenario.

'Too late now,' he said.

*

'It wasn't intentional. Have we a deal?'

A silence, and now Robert looked up.

'Margaret. Have we a deal?'

'Yes.'

'Yes?'

'Yes. Yes. A deal.'

Because Robert had seen what was coming. She seemed to have some notion that he could not read her, that he had lived these years with her without learning a thing about her. The set of her jaw, the set of her shoulders: they told a story; and so he had got ahead, had moved round the house, turning off lamps, leaving just the one burning. The girls were asleep, the scene set – and better for it to be played out in the darkness. That way, he had a little protection from the expressions tracking across her face: the relief as she said her piece, and the change when he said his.

'Inch Levels,' he said. 'You can imagine the rest.' He breathed. 'But if you stay with me, I won't have to go to the police, I won't have to blow the whistle on myself, I won't have to do that to the girls. Stay with me,' he said, 'and we'll carry on; and nobody need ever know; and our girls can get on with their lives.'

Hardly – and he felt it himself. It was hardly likely: he was buying himself a little time; that was all. There was not much of it left: he couldn't carry on much longer. But that, he could see now, that was all he was after, really: the time and the dignity to do this at his own pace. He deserved neither of these, and he knew this too: time and dignity were, after all, exactly what he had failed to offer the little girl. But he would keep his face; he would do it at his own time.

The next morning, she escaped from the house.

Which meant that soon, Patrick would know too. This was disagreeable, but was a price worth paying. It was permissible; Patrick could do nothing, would do nothing to shake his sister's life. Robert still retained control. He would relinquish it at a time of *his* choosing.

He took his daughters to netball, he returned home, he filled the kettle, he switched on the radio for the news. And heard that the child's mother was dead: that she had drowned herself the previous evening at twilight.

*

A couple of hours to himself, to walk. Now he looked up at the green copper onion dome of the church that rose like a mosque a few hundred yards away to the left. He could sit there.

The traffic was picking up: people didn't really walk in this town unless they had no choice in the matter, and walking the length of the unpicturesque Strand Road in particular seemed to invite attention. The inmates of car after car looked and glanced and stared and stared again as they glided past, noticing: probably, his gait, his pallor. His guilt? – perhaps that, too. He entered the church grounds: nowhere to sit, here – no inviting wooden bench, worn and smooth with use, nothing like that – the church steps would have to do. He hoped a priest would not appear in the church grounds: bad timing if one did, sniffing out the rank, malodorous scent of a sinner, and making tracks to save his soul before the Devil got there first. Well, Robert thought: I'll take my chances with that one.

He sat, then, heavily on the granite steps that led up to the main doors. He could feel the chill of the stone almost at once begin to strike through the seat of his trousers. He thought about Margaret, about the radio news of the previous night, about the little girl. This was deadly serious. Now he had told the story to someone else; now, perhaps, the clock was ticking.

And then what? And then what?

'Bless me, Father,' said Robert, 'for I have sinned.' A pause, then, 'I can't remember, ah, how long it's been since my last Confession.'

This was a bad idea; and the priest's tetchy response from the shadows on the far side of the grille, seemed to confirm the fact.

'Well, you must have some idea, son. Is it – what? Days, weeks, months?' A pause. 'Years?'

Now Robert paused. 'Years.'

Yes. This was a bad idea.

'Years,' the priest sighed. 'Well, go on then.'

How long since he had examined the inside of a confessional? He sat silently in the warm darkness. Outside – not close enough to be overheard, so long as he kept his voice down, but close enough – the coughs and sighs and cleared throats of sinners waiting patiently in a queue. Well, they might be waiting some time.

'Go on, son,' the tetchy priest repeated.

Something – he hadn't examined what it was, not yet – had pushed him through the heavy wooden doors. He had walked the length of the nave: the confessional in use was – wouldn't you know – against the back wall of the west chancel: miles and miles, it seemed, to walk, the hard soles of his shoes clack-clack-clacking all the while on the stone floor. The little lines of confessants took him in, before shifting a little further along the smooth pew: placing him, probably, with unerring ease in the local firmament. And now here he was in the shadows of the confessional, in a place that had formed none of his calculations half-an-hour before. And the priest was silent: realising a trifle late, maybe, that he had a task on his hands.

A long silence.

'The thing is, Father –'

Another silence, and now the priest broke it, delicately this time.

'Tell me what you've done, son.'

'That girl, Father. The Casey girl, from up the road.'

Robert was whispering. This knowledge: it came in waves. How could it be, when his head was screwed on and his brain was functioning and when there was nothing, nothing obvious, wrong with him: with all this, he thought, how can I just keep on moving through my days, doing my work and eating my meals and sleeping at night, and all as if nothing was wrong?

How could it be that this knowledge can be shoved aside, for the most part, as if it never existed at all?

It was as if his life was being presented on a screen: and that he was watching it, as just one more member of the audience.

This was how he had managed to get through his conversation with Margaret the previous night: yes, by playing his trump card; and then by taking a mental step back, by allowing the scene to play out, almost as if he was not even involved with it.

This was the way it had been for him, ever since that afternoon in the middle of September – what, more than a month ago now. He sat in the close darkness: I've watched a month slipping past, he thought, as if nothing much had happened in my life. Only sometimes did this – whatever it was, this screen, this barrier, like the grille between his face and that of the priest – only sometimes did it seem to break, or vanish before his eyes; only sometimes did reality flow in. Like now, he thought: this morning, with another death to reckon with, too.

He leaned his forehead against the grille. He thought – for a moment of the girl's mother, that woman who had walked into the sea the previous evening; and then of his wife. Margaret's face, shadowy in the darkness the previous evening. *I'm leaving you*, she'd said. And then of her mother: of Sarah, harsh and hard and filled with secrets. Whose approval would have meant something to him: but that had never been given.

And it was then: only when he thought of Sarah; then, only then, did the tears come, silently.

'Say what you came to say, son,' the priest said, almost inaudibly; there were, after all, ears wagging not two feet away. And Robert did.

It was me, Father. I killed her. It was me.

'It was me.'

On the far side of the grille, the priest sighed again. 'Go on,' he said. 'Say what you came to say.'

*

A calm September day. Clearing skies, at last, after a morning of drenching rain; and the hedges dripping; water lay in potholes and flowed in the ditches as he drove. There would be a frost tonight: he could taste the cool air, the coming tang of early ice. It was his wife's birthday: an ordeal of a family meal awaited him.

The road home took him across the upland and down again, then home by the coast road. He hadn't planned to be here at all: a late call from a potential client deep in the countryside, who wanted her garden turned around and wanted a few ideas, a price. 'You go,' said the boss man, 'and quote low; don't scare her off.' And he had, though suspecting that in fact she wanted only some ideas, and not really a price at all, much less a job done by the firm. Enough to put anyone in a grim mood; and the sight of the clearing sky lifted his mood only a notch. He hated being the prey of the tight-fisted and calculating, and that's what this afternoon was really about.

And yes: dinner with his in-laws tonight. A birthday dinner, for Margaret's birthday. They had insisted. 'We can do something ourselves, later,' Margaret said – though the truth was that they seldom went out, just the two of them. They preferred the bolstering of company; they both did.

Tonight, Patrick would be there, a sneer barely hidden. *Dark as sherry, they said, with the iron content. You could draw the water right here. Set you up for the day.* The sentence slid into his mind, uttered long ago on a sultry evening in Hampstead. The whole occasion got up to humiliate, to put him in his place.

And the mother-in-law. 'A labourer, is it? Well, it takes all sorts.'

Yes. As a family, they knew how to put people in their place.

Robert turned off the road – itself a country road, a minor road that dived downhill from this point, finally emerging in the main square of the town there below. Not that there was likely to be a traffic jam – but he knew another way, marginally faster, that would bring him out on the coast road on the near side, the Derry side, of the town, that would shave a minute or two off his journey home. He swung onto the lane, then, that branched off here. To his left, now, the sea: Lough Foyle spreading flat and wide and blue at the bottom of the hill, and the town pier and the town itself, climbing its hill. The clearing sky above, and the setting sun shining on the black cliffs on the far side of the water; a glint of gold, a waxing moon, a tang of frost in the air. Then the hedges rose up and cut out the view, climbing above his head to form a sort of tunnel: green and dripping and dark.

There was a girl ahead of him: a young girl on her bicycle. On the way home, presumably, from school. He slowed.

*

There seemed to be less coughing outside now, less sighing, less rustling of plastic shopping bags and occasional hollow thumping, as of patellae against church furniture. Most of them, the true believers, presumably knew a heavy-duty sinner when they saw one: maybe they began to think about upping sticks and heading home as soon as the heavily varnished confessional door closed behind him with its little, satisfied click, maybe they weren't ready to hang around the slightly chilly church for what remained of their Saturday.

Or maybe they were all ears, who knew?

Robert had paused in his story now – to draw breath, to arrange his thoughts, the narrative to come. The priest hadn't moved: for a startled moment, he wondered if his companion had fallen asleep – but no, hardly. They must get training, he thought, to stop such things happening.

'And what happened then?' the priest murmured. Possibly this was the most engaging Confession he'd heard for ages – though, given that this was Derry, probably not.

And then what? And then what?

*

He pulls over. Finds himself pulling over.

A world of difference between the two – so which one was it?

The light is – cut out. A dark, muddy green, through those damned hedges. They need cutting right back: so who's the farmer around here? He needs a hiding, whoever he is. And the girl is too slow on her bike and is cycling, not in a straight line or anything like it, but rather swerving in one direction and then the other, the wheels swinging from one hedge, one ditch, to the other. At first – for the wind in her ears surely cancels out any other noise – she doesn't hear his van approaching from behind; in fact, he is practically upon her. And then he sounds his horn: cruelly, for there is no need;

he is in no especial hurry to get home, God knows, given the evening that looms ahead of him; and truth to tell, shouldn't be driving on this narrow lane in any case; he should be on the main road. He sounds his horn – and the predictable happens: the girl swerves again, but sharply this time, uncontrollably; and both she and the bike end up in the ditch.

He stops the van, gets out, intends to indulge his foul mood in a mouthful of ugly words – but she is up already and pushing her dark, straggly hair away from her face. 'That wasn't fair,' she says. There is no heat in her words, no cheek, no lip of any kind: only the truth, delivered fairly, even politely.

*

'Haven't you ever lost your temper?' he murmured, in the darkness of the confessional.

The priest said nothing.

*

He says, 'What's not fair?'

'That,' she says, and she points at her bike, its front wheel still turning in the ditch. 'What you did. It wasn't fair.' She pushes her hair away. 'You might have hurt me.'

And it is more, suddenly, than he can take. He reaches for her, for both her shoulders, intending to teach her a lesson, to give her the kind of shake that she won't forget. This is what he will remember, as his life turns silently on a pivot:

the girl's own silence as she tries to struggle free, to push his hands from her shoulders. She struggles but there is no scream, no call that anyone in the nearby fields might hear. Robert remembers these moments as silent: he plays them in his head, over and over, in silence. She struggles for a moment, but of course she is no match in strength for a grown, angry man. Not at first. He gives her the intended kind of shake, but – perhaps collecting what might hurt a grown man – she tries to run her fingernails down his face, to scratch him, to make him let go. She misses – but this is enough to unleash all the frustration and anger of his day, of his life: and he thrusts her back now, with force, with furious force; and she falls back and strikes her head violently against the tarred surface of this silent, green-roofed lane.

And there it is. There she is, as the front wheel of her bicycle spins lazily in the ditch. No sound, no movement now – only the green, hazy light and the acrid smell of hawthorn leaves glinting minutely in the fading light.

*

'And what happened then?'

Robert paused, moistened his mouth.

'Father, you know what happened then.'

The priest replied, with a touch of asperity even at this ghastly moment, 'Indeed I do not.' Less of your lip, was what he appeared to mean. Priests, as Robert well knew, tended not to lose sight of the importance of status, regardless of whatever else happened to be going on at a given moment.

On the other hand, it was true: the priest did not in fact know what happened then.

*

No time, no time. The lane might seldom be used, but that didn't mean that someone, anyone, might not drive or cycle or saunter past at any minute. No time to waste, and the thing to be done clear: within a minute, the back of the van is standing open and the girl – who after all weighs very little – deposited inside, and the door closed again. And that's all there is to it. He hasn't even had to waste time checking that she is indeed dead: his instincts are clear enough about the difference between life and death.

That's all there is to it. That, and presence of mind. Robert knows that certain precautions have always to be taken: and so he pulls the sleeves of his sweater over his hands before he picks the child up. No need for fingerprints. And within another minute, the lane is deserted again, and only the bicycle, lying in the ditch, is proof that anything at all has happened on this cool afternoon.

Robert drives, then, south along the coast road: the tide is well out, and the flats are exposed, with a wading bird or two busily pecking at the rich mud. Close to the city, he indicates and turns right and up, steeply up the hill again, passing a lonely church, and then onto the hilltops once more. They are purple with heather at this time of year, and greying with the fading grass: behind him the broad, glassy surface of Lough Foyle narrows to the river, and now in front of him Lough Swilly stretches sinuously north and south, silver in the evening light; and there he is, driving across the narrow neck of land pinched between. There is Inch Island directly ahead now, and the flatlands of Inch Levels: he knows where he is bound. Calmly, quite calmly, all the while. He knows – he knew from the moment the back of the girl's head hit the surface of the road; so odd, the way in which the mind works – where he's going, to a lonely, secret place: he knows when to turn off the main road and into the hills; when to turn again and then again, until at last he reaches the lonely car park in the shadow of the sea wall, there in the middle of these flatlands.

And of course nobody there.

No-one here. A bird calls in the distance, a high, piercing cry which echoes in the clear, cooling air; and the hum of the machinery in the pumping station; the glint of still water held back by the sea wall; the rush of a swan's wings overhead. Again he pulls his sleeves over his treacherous hands and then – with effort; the girl's body seems strangely less light now, more than a lead weight – gathers it together, half-lifting and half-pulling it from the van, and then lugging, carrying it along the straight track towards the water's edge. A lead weight; and better simply to deposit his load into the water and leave, to get out of there as quickly as possible.

At length, then, he comes to the water's edge. Until this moment, he tells himself that this has been an accident, a moment of anger gone wrong: nothing – so he has told himself in the course of his short drive across country – he could have done about it, not really. Until this moment.

For now, as he reaches the water, he feels a movement, a beat of life. A flicker of an eyelid.

*

A silence of excruciating moments in the dark confessional; the priest's shape motionless behind the grille. At last: 'And then what?'

Except that this time the priest knew what happened next: it had been all over the news at the time. No wonder, therefore, that Robert had a strong impression, the strongest, that now the priest really, truly, didn't want to hear another word.

Well, too bad for him.

And in fact, the description took very few words, very little time: a few sentences to set out how he put her down on the shingle by the water, on her back, and then pushed her into the water, holding her legs on the grass, watching her head dip below the surface. No struggle: the girl was still almost concussed; her arms hardly moved, hardly worked; before long, it was over and done, at which point he gave her another push, her whole body slipping into the water with barely a ripple. The description of a drowning, accomplished quickly and quietly, as the sun set behind the ruinous silhouette of Inch Castle on the far side of the water.

There is nothing for it. He has to do this. He's in too deep. In too deep, is what Robert actually thinks, not considering the, in the circumstances, inappropriate turn of phrase. 'In too deep,' he thinks: he has to press on, he has to close his eyes and carry, carry on. Sure, hasn't he, already hasn't he, done enough to get into – well, something, into serious trouble? Into prison or something? That's just by injuring this child, who's probably going to die anyway. Then hasn't he made it worse? – hugely, unimaginably worse? – by bundling her into his car, thinking she's dead already? – and then haring across the countryside with her right there in the boot? And all with the intention of heaving her into the water. In the distance, a swan honks, another answers.

And so he stands looking at the water, breathing the cold air; and he knows that, at this moment, when it comes down to it, it makes sense to do this. It makes sense to finish the job he had started – what, forty minutes ago? An hour ago? It actually makes sense to do this, to heave her into the water and then get the hell out of there. He'd thought she was dead: if he hadn't thought this, he would have brought her to hospital, or called for help, or something. Now it's too late, for all concerned.

He watches as her face slides below the surface of the water. He keeps a firm hold of her legs. She doesn't move, much: only the fingers of one hand open slowly and then slowly close; and her dark hair fans out around her head like a cloud. And then, when he is quite sure, quite safe, he gives her legs a push and her body slides neatly into the water; and there is an end to it. The swan calls again, a flat, grunting honk that travels across the surface of the water; and now he is pounding along the path to the car park and he is in the car again and the car is on the main road, and he is home.

Margaret tuts, on his return. 'We'll be late. Seven o'clock, we said.'

He has a bath and dresses again, and they are ready to go. They will dine off the fat of the land, he knows: his mother-in-law, with all the list of faults, is a handy cook. He is starving.

The following morning, he discovered the name of the child. Christine.

*

'What have you done since, son?' the priest asked, shadowy in the shadowy confessional.

To buy a moment, Robert said, 'What do you mean, Father?'

The priest merely repeated himself. 'What have you done since?'

Silence in the church now. Yes: the last sinners must've become fed up with kicking their toes against pew legs, must have gone home.

Robert said, 'I haven't done anything.'

Which was a form of truth. How could he account for the slow close-down of his mind in the month since? He moved through the days easily enough, he even transacted business, did his job, ate and drank and got on with things.

He threatened his wife with an impossible future. But in the middle of all this, his mind had begun closing down.

'I haven't done anything.'

'And now, the mother.'

And now, the mother. He hadn't done anything: and now he had another death on his conscience.

The priest stirred, sat upright. The seal of the confessional was absolute, he murmured through the grille, that was understood: but with the sacrament came acknowledgement and restitution. Something else must now happen, before absolution was possible.

'Can you absolve me now?' But Robert knew the answer to that one already, even before he saw the priest's head shake slowly in the darkness.

'In time, son, I hope. I trust, in time. But first –'

But first. Yes.

But first, he had to step out of the confessional and listen as the door behind him closed with a smooth click, its insides by no means buoyed up with sins forgiven and absolution gained.

No, that wasn't it. First he had to wind up this particular session.

'Oh my God,' he began, murmuring in the close darkness, 'I am heartily sorry for having offended you –' Then he stopped: the priest was moving, wriggling, shifting behind his damn grille, holding out the palm of his hand.

'Not yet,' he said. 'No act of contrition yet.' Robert sat still: surely every Confession ended with an act of contrition? – and he remembered learning this old-fashioned one, laboriously and long ago now. *Because you are the chief good and worthy of all love, and everything that is sinful is displeasing unto you.* Where had he found that from? – it really had been years since his last Confession. *I am resolved with the help of Thy holy grace never more to offend you, and to amend my life. Amen.* He knew all the words, was the point, and he wanted to finish the thing properly.

But no.

'Not yet,' the priest repeated, a little less stern now. 'Later. When you have done what is necessary.' Then this can be wound up, he seemed to say. No point gabbling an act of contrition in advance of all that. Wind it all up, and then we'll see. He still seemed stern, but not especially shaken – or rather, he had recovered his clerical poise rather rapidly, which just went to show that he probably did hear some incredible stuff sitting there in the confessional. It was probably all in a day's work for him.

Then Robert left, his business unfinished behind him, and the confessional door clicked and he was at the back of the church and through the double doors.

What had just happened?

In a way, nothing had happened. History was rushing on, and this morning's news meant that it would reach its conclusion sooner than expected. And he remained in control, for now. As for absolution: that would never come, and he knew that too.

THIRTEEN

The door to the ward opened – and Sarah was glad enough of it: conversation was sparse, laboured; Patrick was in no mood for chitter-chatter. His eyes were closed, his grunted answers insufficient to keep any conversation rolling along. And Sarah was insufficient herself: she was insufficient to the situation. I should just go, she thought – and was about to act, to grasp her pink scarf, the handles of her bag, when the door opened and Margaret walked in.

Patrick opened his eyes, saw her.

'Oh good,' Patrick said. 'Today just gets better and better,' and he closed his eyes again.

Margaret came further into the room.

'Quite the crowd,' Patrick said. 'I'm blessed.'

'Don't start up, Patrick,' Margaret said.

Now he opened his eyes again.

'No intention of starting up,' he said. 'This is what I'm going to do. I'm going to lie here and leave you both to it.'

Which he did. He closed his eyes. The two women looked

at the window, at the flowers, at the man in the bed. A silence fell.

They had made their beds.

*

The Guildhall was utterly dark. The blackout meant that no lights shone behind its four-faced clock, no lights gleamed from its long windows; and the great oak doors were closed and locked. As she waited for the bus in the deep winter gloom, Sarah looked up at the building, a deeper black against the darkness, and closed her eyes.

She had got up very early. Anthony would be at her quarters very early: she was due in the mess hall; she must be well ahead of everyone. She got up in the deep winter darkness and made her way downhill and back into the city. The first bus departed and the sun eventually rose to show a world glittering white with frost.

She was going home. No, not home: she was going to the only place that she could think of, that might receive her – in spite of everything. There were no other choices, now.

And what happened next? – she knew: she had plenty of time, in the years that followed, to put the story together. She was gone – but not without leaving a trace. She was gone, and had left nothing behind: but it needed no intelligence agent to work out where she was bound. There was only one place where she might now go: home; and Anthony would follow her there, therefore, driving out of Derry and north along the road that hugged the western shore of Lough Foyle.

Later – years later, and over and over again – in her mind's eye, she traced the journey. The tide was well out, exposing the seaweed-laced mud flats: a freezing morning; but just the same there were lone figures out on the mud, bending, digging into the cold, salty mud for cockles. She had seen them from the windows of the bus; most likely they had still been there when he followed a couple of hours later. Yes: he had driven north along the shore of the flat, shining lough, the skies seeming to enlarge as he drove north, and now the town came into view for the first time, with its white buildings and slate roofs climbing up from the sea, its little pier flanked by a rocky foreshore, its green waterside park, its handful of large, handsome Victorian houses hidden in the trees beyond.

She saw it all through his eyes. She had plenty of time.

*

Anthony parked his jeep in the square, got out, took his bearings. Of course he was accustomed to being an object of attention in Derry: in spite of the swarms in the streets of service personnel from every corner of the world, the townsfolk there were unsparing in their glances, their up-and-down scrutiny of everyone in a uniform. In this little seaside town, however, the watch seemed redoubled: whereas in Derry, the raking look was delivered in passing, in a well-practiced instant, in this town people seemed to dissect him in long stare after long stare.

No wonder she had got the hell out of the place.

He stopped one such staring person: an older woman, dark-clad and not, it seemed, willing to stop for anything. 'I'm looking for the McLaughlin house,' he said hurriedly, before she was past him and away.

She turned. 'Now which McLaughlin would that be?'

'I don't know.' He wanted to avoid her name, if possible: but she was prising the information from him simply by standing there. 'They have a farm.'

'Farm,' she repeated, slowing, turning, taking him in, noting the fresh wound on his cheek. Their breath smoked in the air. 'Sarah, is it?'

'Sarah, yes, that's right.'

'I thought that's what it was.' She directed him through the town: a half-mile or so, then left at a pair of white-washed gateposts. A long lane and then the house at the end of it. 'If she's there. She was away, is what I heard.'

'I think she's back,' Anthony told her.

'Who knows?' the woman said. 'Who knows? – with that one.' Then she was gone.

The white-washed gateposts were easily found, and the long lane running downhill between dense hawthorn hedges – and the house too, white-washed too and low, with a densely smoking chimney; and fields beyond, furred with frost. The deeply shadowed yard was overlaid with frost too: and while the whitewash was fresh and the door painted a bright glossy green, the whole place felt sad. It was not merely his imagination that, rushing ahead of itself, made it so –

but rather the air, he thought, and the situation, the tell-tale rushes growing in the fields. Yes, sad, and lonely, and that – as his mother back in Winnipeg liked to say, with a brisk rasp together of her hands – really was that.

He stood for a few moments in the tidy yard, feeling the sadness, snuffing the turf smoke that rose in the icy air, and then the back door opened and a young woman emerged, lugging a bucket of laundry. She was well enough dressed, short and a little too stout, a slightly crossed eye – but sweet of face as she turned and saw him and a hoarse voice when she spoke.

'She's inside.'

No explanation of his presence seemed necessary.

'Do you want her?'

He returned her slight smile, and, now seeming emboldened, she stepped from the doorway and into the yard.

'She should go with you, I think,' she said, 'but I'm afraid that she won't.'

This confused him. 'Do you mean you know she won't?' Now she was frowning slightly. 'Or do you mean –'

'I'm afraid she won't,' the girl said again. 'I mean, I'm afraid she won't, is what I mean.' The slightest emphasis on the *afraid*; clearer now.

'Well,' he said, 'I can maybe persuade her.'

But she shook her head. 'I'm afraid she won't.' And looking at her more closely, he could see that this was the literal truth, that this stout, odd-looking girl was afraid. 'But go in,' she added and pointed at the door. 'Go in, and try.' He flashed what he hoped was a reassuring smile, and moved towards the door. On the step, he glanced back. She hadn't moved, though now she was plucking the skin on her arm. There were tears standing in her eyes.

He pushed the door and went inside.

*

Cassie's underarms were clammy. She stood on the step, feeling their dampness, feeling beads of sweat run coldly down her arms, smelling her smell. A smell of fear: she was frightened, had been frightened since the frosty early morning when Sarah came home again. And Sarah was frightened too, and not able to talk. I can't talk to you, Cassie, she said, so don't talk to me. But I don't want to talk to her, Cassie thought: I didn't want to talk to her then, this morning, and I don't want to talk to her now. Leave me alone, Sarah said to me. Just leave me alone. And I wanted to say, leave me alone too. I don't want you here now.

Not now. Cassie brushed the tears from her eyes, and then fell again to kneading the skin on her arm. The back door closed behind him, shutting her out here in the frozen yard. He might, she thought: he might take her away, I want him to take her away. I'm afraid he won't; I'm afraid of what will happen if he doesn't. In her insides, deep in her belly, a deep animal howl was building; a terrible knot of pain and fear growing. And another knot in her throat, taking her breath, taking her voice, painfully lodged there in her gullet. Help me, she thought, I want someone to help me. But nobody was there to help – and she even looked around the yard, a distracted look, a miserable look – only this man, she thought, and he is too late and not strong enough. Not enough.

The scene earlier this morning: it was terrifying. Earlier this morning, the sun barely up behind bare trees and a white frost on the grass, when Sarah walked through the yard and into the house: distressed, defeated. And Brendan went – berserk. Cassie backed into the corner, upsetting the turf scuttle, the poker: a clatter that was fearful, but that was not even attended to. Too many other things going on to think about an overturned turf scuttle: bellows and shoves and the copper bowl dislodged from the dresser onto the flags; the flash of Brendan's belt; and screams that gave way, eventually, to tears.

And now, this man in an army jeep, arriving too late.

Help me, Cassie, she said. Help me. That was afterwards. Brendan was first, she thought; and the copper bowl, with a bruise now on its lip. I know who brought the bowl here to the house in the first place, as a bride, years ago, years before I ever arrived. And now it's damaged: and I have to do something with it before Brendan comes back and sees it again. But I have to do something with it, I have to, but I don't know how.

The back door was closed and the yard was quiet, except for a hen or two, and the rooster waving his wattles; and Cassie stood in the middle of it, in tears once more. They were talking, inside, but she knew it was too late.

It was too late. Surely Anthony felt it, in the air; and surely he saw it, in the red marks on her wrist where had father had held her. Sarah caught her reflection in the dim, spotted looking glass on the wall: it was set, it was frozen, there was no expression at all. Even in the midst of this – of the thick, congealed air in the room, dense as porridge – surely he noticed this: how the muscles in her face hardly moved. Shuttered, a sealed window.

But no. He could hardly *see* her at all. The room, with its dresser, a wooden table and chairs, a smoking fire at one end – was only dimly lit. There were too few windows in this house, there were patches of darkness in every room – and so perhaps it was too dim to see her face, to see anything. Perhaps we should go outside, she thought, into the sunshine – and she felt startled at this faint thought, this pulse of hope.

Perhaps he could see her face, perhaps he could see the change in her expression – for the first thing he said was, 'Can I see around?' Not a demand for an explanation, not a note of complaint. Perhaps he thought there were rooms in this house where you could actually see the hand in front of your face.

Sarah said, 'No.'

'Let me see around.'

'There isn't anything to see,' she said, 'and I don't want to show you anyway.'

He said, 'So that was Cassie I met outside.'

'Yes,' and there was a pause.

'I don't know what happened last night,' he said at last.

Now he dragged a chair across the flagged floor – a fearful clatter, and her eyes flickered to the window – and sat down. He sat there, solidly. Not going anywhere.

'Where's your father?'

'At the barns.' Sarah remained standing: she had scarcely moved a muscle since he arrived, except to glance towards the window now and again. Then, after the silence had continued for a few more reverberating moments, she spoke.

'You'd better go. He'll be back.'

'I'm not going.'

She paused, then seemed to gather her strength and said again, 'You'd better.'

He said, 'Why?' More abruptly than his usual manner, to be sure, perhaps his patience was wearing thin.

'Because you'd better.' She glanced again at the window. 'Because he'll be back soon and –'

'And he won't want to see me.'

'Not you,' she told him. 'Anyone in uniform. Anyone at all.'

He paused.

'And because he did this,' she said. She held out her wrist. 'And other things here,' and she pointed at her legs, 'with his belt.'

He stared at her.

'So you'd better go.'

'Or I'd better have a word with him,' Anthony said; and she shook her head violently at this, and moved rapidly across the room.

'No. That would be worst of all. You'd better go.'

'Is that what you want?'

She paused now, but only for a moment. 'Yes,' she said. 'I want you to go too.'

'And that's all?'

She shook her head slightly. That was all. But she was aware of the din in her head. She had heard the town band tuning up several times over the years, in preparation for a Christmas or Easter or summer concert in the Temperance Hall – and this noise in her head was like that noise: discordant, appalling, deafening.

It had been like this all morning – all the previous night, in her quarters at the hospital, lying in her narrow bed and looking up at the curved, damp metal ceiling of the hut; listening to the other girls arrive home in the early hours, whispering and laughing in the darkness, finally falling asleep. She had lain awake the whole of the night, unable to sleep because of that terrible din in her head; before getting up in the darkness and catching the first bus heading north, heading for – home, she should say. But not home: she was here only because there was nowhere else to go.

She had walked as slowly as she could up the lane. In springtime, these familiar hawthorn hedges were white and heavy with blossom, these banks were a haze of bluebells: now, in freezing December, the hedges were a different white, hoary with frost; and the banks frosted too, and muddy-brown in sheltered crevices where the chill could not reach. The low winter sun was rising as she turned the last corner: it was just clipping the roof of the house and shining cold into the near corner of the yard. She paused on the step, girding herself, then turned the handle and walked into the kitchen. And there the scene was laid: her father bent, setting the fire; Cassie at the range, busy with porridge.

This was the same scene that she remembered, in which she had participated, morning by morning, year by year since Cassie came to live with them. The only difference had been in the light, in the fall of sunshine on the ground, on the white walls of the yard outside, varying minutely as month had followed month. In May and June and July, these white walls were splashed with a glowing white from the sun, high then in the sky; now, in December, the sunshine barely touched that far corner, before sinking again behind the roof. The inside of the house – this dusky, smoky kitchen – never saw the sunshine.

Brendan turned from the hearth: and she saw at once that he was furious: raging, she thought, raging and furious; as though a threshold suddenly had been crossed or a dam broken. She watched him standing there, his eyes gleaming with rage and immediately she was fighting the impulse to run.

'What are you doing here?'

Worse, much worse than she expected. It flashed through her mind to use this welcome as an excuse, to seize her opportunity and take to her heels out of the place. But go where? – and now Brendan was striding across and taking her by the wrist and bringing, dragging her into the centre of the dark room.

'We're surprised to see you here, aren't we, Cassie? We haven't heard a peep out of you these weeks and now here you appear…' He paused for breath: Cassie had her back pressed to the range; she looked petrified. 'Bold as brass,' Brendan went on, 'and healthy as a trout too, from the look of things. What's been keeping you healthy as a trout, eh? The British army paying you and feeding you and putting a roof over your head, is it?' His grip tightened, bulging eyes uncomfortably close to her own. 'No shame, have you? And coming back now to flaunt it in our faces? Why didn't you just stay away for good? No shame. Your mammy'll spinning in her grave at having such a daughter.' His breath was hot on her cheeks. A pause and then, 'Cooking and so on for them, I hear you are. Well, you didn't do much of that for us, did you? That's a new talent for you, isn't it?'

'I came to see you, to see how you were doing,' Sarah said at last. Then, in a rush, 'No, that's not it. That's not why I came.'

'Needed time off from the Army, is it?'

Her lip trembled. She shook her head. 'No, that's not it.' Impossible to say what it was. What was she doing here, when it all began here?

Cassie hadn't moved – but now, though still pressed against the range, she said, 'Will I make some tea?'

Sarah nodded. Yes, some tea, but before she could say anything, her father released his terrible grip and as he pushed her away from him she flung her hands out – and caught her mother's copper bowl that stood poised on the shelf. It fell to the flagged floor and rolled away.

A dent showed on the lip of the bowl.

There was a silence. Brendan was staring at the bowl, at the dent.

'Now look what you did.'

'I didn't –'

'Look what you did,' Brendan repeated, still gazing at the floor, the bowl.

Cassie said again, 'Will I make some tea?'

But Brendan was taking off his belt. In a familiar way: deliberate and purposeful and very slow. 'I'll give you tea,' he said.

When he had finished beating her – on her back and her legs – and when Cassie's screams had died away into whimpering, he put his belt back on, again in a familiar and deliberate way and left the house.

'Tea!' he said as he was going. 'Give her some tea now, if she wants it.' And Cassie brought tea – and yes, she and Sarah drank: standing, of course, for Sarah's pulsing stripes would not allow her to sit. Cassie picked the copper bowl from the floor and set it in its place. Then, she gathered the washing into the basket: Sarah stood in the heat of the range and watched Cassie go out into the yard with the laundry; and then watched as Cassie turned and stood stock-still in the middle of the yard. And now there was Anthony, framed in the window; and that din rang louder in her head, as though someone was raising the volume notch by notch.

It seemed that there was a choice to be made, once and for all.

'I'll tell you what I'll do,' Anthony said. 'I'll go down to that pretty park by the water, and I'll wait for you there. I'll wait for one hour, no more. And if you don't come, I'll leave.' He looked at her. 'And that's the deal.'

She looked at him.

'That's the deal, Sarah,' he said again. And after a moment, 'And something else too. You weren't loved here, in this house: or not by everyone.' He looked at her red, swollen wrist. 'That's plain enough. But you're making a mistake if you think that because of this, you can never be loved anywhere else. That's a mistake, Sarah,' he said and now he got up from the chair. 'There's plenty of love to go around,' he said, 'and you need to remember that: and there's still time.'

Without another word now, he left the kitchen: the door closed behind him and she saw him nod to Cassie and go to his jeep. He was gone.

She waited until the sound of his jeep vanished into the distance, and then she went out into the yard to where Cassie was standing: there, on the frosted triangle of yard where, at this time of the year, the sun never reached. She must surely be freezing, standing there for so long in that chilly, deeply shadowed yard, and her hands damp besides. But she showed little sign of it if she was: her nose was perhaps a little more red and the rest of her face a little more white than usual; her hand, when Sarah took it in her own, was cold. But she wasn't shivering and her teeth weren't chattering: she remained still and motionless.

'Will you not come into the warm?' Sarah said. Cassie

shook her head. 'But you can't stand out here all day,' Sarah said, 'can you? Come into the warm, Cassie.' But she shook her head; Sarah clicked her tongue in exasperation and turned to go. Do as you please, she thought but did not say; instead, a few beats of silence, broken only by the crunch of her feet on the frost-covered ground. Do as you please. You'll catch your death out here, but do as you please.

Then Cassie spoke.

'You should have gone with him.'

Sarah paused, looked back, shrugged.

'I couldn't.'

'You should have,' Cassie said. 'You should have gone back with him.'

Sarah shook her head again. 'I couldn't.'

'It's what you should have done,' Cassie said.

The same sentence, again and again: Sarah's hands flew up in frustration, her temper broke suddenly.

'I couldn't,' she screamed. 'I couldn't, I couldn't, it was a mistake, don't you see that?'

But Cassie only said, again, 'It's what you should have done.' She seemed to gather herself. 'You can begin again. You can begin again. Can't you?'

'And what will you do?'

Cassie's clear, light laugh. 'Follow you, maybe. But I'll look after Brendan, first.'

Brendan?

'He gave me a home. I'll stay with him, until it's all over.'

'And then what?'

But now Cassie had said all she could say. That was plain: and in the face of this, Sarah walked across the frost and into the house, leaving Cassie and the tub of wet laundry standing in the middle of the yard. Sarah wanted to shout, to bawl back through the open door: *and then what? And then what?* But she knew Cassie: knew she had said her piece, would say no more; and besides, there had been enough raised voices this morning. Brendan might come pounding across the frozen fields if there were any more, and then there would be hell to pay.

For a while, she moved around the dark kitchen, from table to sideboard to table again; the fire was dying in the grate; the room was growing cold. She expected Cassie to appear at the door, but no figure appeared framed in it. At last, Sarah moved in exasperation to close the door, to keep the heat in; but before she did – before she gave it a good, satisfying slam – she peered out into the icy yard. She expected to see – what did she expect to see? Not Cassie standing in the same chill corner: for even Cassie could not continue to stand in the one spot for ever. What, then? Perhaps Cassie engaged in some chore: sweeping the place out, or something. But no: the yard was empty, except for the laundry. There was nobody in sight, not a soul.

After a moment, she realised something else: that the din in her head was gone. That silence had taken its place – that the past was in the past, yes; and that the future was a clean, empty space – and that surely twenty minutes must have passed, twenty-five, perhaps, since Anthony left.

And quickly now, she caught her coat from its hook and her bag from the ground, and left the house and began pounding up the lane. Towards the white gate posts, towards the town, towards the sea.

*

At the corner of the lane, Cassie stopped, looked left, looked right, looked straight ahead, looked right again. Danger could come from any direction, but right was the real danger, what Father Lynch would call the True Danger, though he was talking about sin: right was the sharp corner, and right was the town too, and the shops and the Green leading down to the sea. Right was – too many people, too much noise; she felt tight and dry-mouthed there in the town, in the shops, doing what needed doing. It had become a little easier, maybe, with practice: with Sarah away, she had had to do the shopping, do what needed to be done; she was used, now, to people saying *hello, Cassie*, and *that's a nice day, Cassie* and staring at her, taking her right in. She was used to it, but that didn't mean she liked it. Her mouth was dry now, as she turned right and bent around the corner, and towards town.

The road, never busy, was empty this morning: the hedges on the other side were white with frost; and the road itself glittered under the cold sun. The icy air stung and her mind stung too: I'm not properly dressed, she thought, I'm not warmly dressed. I'm a holy show, she thought, and they'll all be looking at me and looking at me even more now. But

I have to go. She knew she had to go, she had to see if she could find him.

This had come upon her, in the second after Sarah had marched into the house, leaving the door open wide behind her, letting the heat leak and flow out of the house. She stood for a moment, watching the black rectangle of the doorway – and then moved quickly: out of the yard and up the frosty lane. This was a thing she had never before done: what? to leave the farm, the house, her work in the middle of the day? and all driven by – but driven by what? Driven by something she could not have expressed, even if Sarah sat her down hard in a chair and grasped her shoulders and said *tell me, tell me!* She couldn't have told her. She only knew what she had to do, which was to go after that man, Anthony, and beg him to come back. What would she say? – even supposing he had paused in the town, even supposing she could by some fluke catch him and speak to him. That was all; that was all she knew.

No: not all. There was more than this: I have to, I have to find him, she thought, walking, swinging along the icy road. The first houses were coming into view now, the blue sheet of the icy sea to the left, the distant cliff face on the far shore shining under the winter sun. I have to, I have to; Cassie, you have to. Her hands were fists, balled into her pockets. I have to, she thought, and if I don't find him, it will be too late. She thought of a ball of wool unravelling, rolling away into a shadowy corner. I have to find him: that was all she thought as she half-walked, half-ran down the incline of the road and into the town square.

And there he was: his jeep parked by the stone wall that marked the edge of the Green, by the flight of old stone steps that descended into the Green and so down to the shingled foreshore. She ran down the steps and onto the pinched winter grass – and there was Anthony himself, sitting on a stone bench and looking down at the sea. There he was; and Cassie stopped and looked and drew a breath. Here was a chance to say what she wanted to say, and she took it.

'This is her chance,' she said, 'to get away from here, from Brendan, to begin again – and I'm afraid of what will happen if she doesn't.'

And that was it. That was all. That was what she wanted to say.

That was what she was afraid of: a hole, shadowy and terribly deep, that was opening up in front of Sarah, in front of all of them, if she didn't get away. *She has to get away,* cried the voice in her head. 'This is her chance to get away,' she repeated, and then it seemed as though she ran out of words, suddenly, all of a sudden. She had nothing else to say.

He cleared his throat.

I will howl, she thought, like a dog. Like a dog on a bad, wet day, when he wants to get inside, when he sits and howls at the door, like their farm dogs. He won't, he isn't listening; if I howl like a dog he might listen.

But she couldn't howl, not like a dog or like any animal. Her throat was caught.

And then he spoke.

'I can help Sarah,' he said, 'if she wants to come away.

If she wants to stay at home, then she can stay at home.' He shrugged, 'and if she wants to come with me, then she can do that too.' He looked at his wristwatch and said, 'And she has about thirty minutes to decide. Thirty minutes. Can I call you Cassie?'

She nodded.

'Well, we have time to kill, Cassie. Let's take a little walk in this park, and you can show me what there is to see.'

He was trying to be kind; and she smiled a little.

'Those steps,' she pointed, 'and we'll be at the water. We can walk for a few minutes by the water. To Shell Beach and back.'

'Shell Beach,' he repeated. 'That's pretty. A few minutes, you say?'

She nodded.

'Let's do that, then.'

They descended carefully the further flight of stone steps that led down to the sea. Her shoes crunched on the frost; the frost furred the grass on either side of the path; the water ahead was smooth, like a sheet. And blue, she thought, as blue as – as anything could be. Bluer than the sky, bluer than – than my hands; and she looked at her blue-tinged, icy hands. Bluer than anything; and now they reached the foot of the steps and turned left, taking the footpath along the shore. We'll walk, she thought, and Sarah's angry face and tears rose into her blue face. We'll walk a while, and then we'll turn and there will be Sarah, waiting for us.

A little gang of six or seven boys were on the path: they were kicking a football ahead of them; they pushed ahead, heading for the beach too; they disappeared around a turn. Otherwise, all was calm and silent: nobody else was about on this chilly morning; the only other moving creatures the gulls, white with black throats and black eyes and black wing tips and the tips of their beaks red like blood, hanging and wheeling over the water or perched motionless on the rocks. She remembered again the oystercatchers that walked so fast – so fast! she thought, by the edge of the water, their little feet, their little legs, they moved so fast I couldn't even see them. She laughed, almost, at the thought. Her spirits were rising now. We'll walk to the beach and then we'll walk back and Sarah will be there.

But at Shell Beach, a shallow crescent between tall jagged piers of rock, they stopped. The football lay abandoned on the fine sand: and the boys had formed a little curving line ten feet or so from the object on the sand. There were gulls here too, many of them poised motionless on each rocky pier: motionless, but now these creatures turned their heads, their red-tipped beaks in unison, their black, bead-like eyes watching with avidity as Cassie and Anthony stood there, arrested on the path; before turning in unison again to watch the curving line of boys on the sand.

And now in a moment, Anthony swore and jumped from the path down to the sand, bellowing a warning as he crunched across the shells. But already two or three of the boys were moving towards the object, which was glossy black and very large – three, four feet across, three, four feet high – and set with black spikes. An ugly thing – and she knew what it was.

One final frozen moment of watching the scene there on the sand below her: the gulls silent, intent, greedy; and Anthony pounding across the fine white shells; and the boys turning and scattering – but not all of them, for now one stretched out a hand to touch these vicious spikes. And now Cassie ducked behind one of the tall piers of black rock, just as the world seemed to erupt around her.

As the sea mine exploded, the black-eyed gulls rose into the air as one and flew north into open ocean, south into the lough, east towards the far shore. On the little beach, a wide crater yawned where the sea mine had lain on the sand; the strand was empty now of life.

*

Sarah ran down the stone steps and onto the grass. The sun was shining now brilliantly on the sea, and she raised a hand to shade her eyes. She had seen them from the road, walking slowly north along the coastal path towards the beach: she was on time, she had a stitch in her side and her bag jiggled in her hand – but she was on time. She was leaving Cassie, she was making Cassie explain to her father, later – but she was on time.

She reached the coastal path herself, now, and turned north. They were only a minute away, two minutes away – and now as she turned a corner, the force of the explosion lifted her off her feet. She fell heavily back on the grass and lay for a moment, dazed and shocked – but already she knew what

314

it was. She knew the dull thump and report of torpedoes exploding out to sea, she was accustomed to going down to the shore in the days that followed, accustomed to the sight of what they saw there: a foreshore littered with bodies, bloated, nibbled, their humanity barely in evidence.

But this sound was different, closer, more violent: this was no secure cataclysm at sea. This would affect them all. She staggered to her feet, she dragged herself on along the path, she turned another corner. There was Cassie, on hands and knees at the foot of the black rocks. There was the beach and the crater. Nobody else in sight. Nobody else alive.

*

Sarah built up the dying fire into a decent blaze: soon, the chilly kitchen would warm up nicely. The short December day was already over, the furry frost was returning to the yard, Cassie in bed on the doctor's instruction, Brendan in his room with the door closed. Sarah sat down now at the table. The backs of her legs pulsed and stung. She hardly knew what she had to do, although she understood that she had little time in which to do it: the word had gone out; and soon a neighbour or two would be calling on them. But in her mind's eye, the town fell upon them in force; she saw rivers of people filing out from the town and descending the lane and filling the yard and encompassing the house, all in silence. She had scant time, but for the moment she sat and looked at the fire.

She had always been responsible for Cassie: she knew that, had always known it. Cassie could run a house, that was true. She could mend and bake and keep a place ticking over – very nicely indeed. But always she needed looking after, in a million other ways to do with people. Always, always; and Sarah had always known it. Always, until recently. Always, until the world had muscled into her own life, and left her with no time and certainly no compassion or patience for anyone else and for Cassie least of all.

She was sitting very upright, and her hands were grasping her knees. On the shelf, the copper bowl glowed in the firelight, its new dent a shadow on its lip. Help me with this, she said aloud to the empty kitchen. She said it to the kitchen, not to any actual person – Brendan, her mother, being all long gone. She looked at the pair of family photographs, dim on the wall in the far corner of the dim room. Help me with this – silently now. There was no longer any help to be had. Help, she knew, would have to come from within.

It made sense, now, that the kitchen was so dim. She felt as though she had to feel her way to some kind of conclusion, something that would make sense. That would form some solid shape in this bleak light. Perhaps not the right shape, perhaps not a form that would be of any great use in the months and years to come – but something that she could take hold of, that she could carry with her, that would give form and weight and substance to what remained of her life.

That would protect her.

Because yes: there was nobody else – not even God who,

she realised with a sort of dull surprise, had not been around for some time now. She thought: I didn't notice that. I didn't even know.

This, then, was the job she had, the task she had been set, had set herself: to protect her life. To protect herself, come what may. She did not yet know, sitting there in that dark room, how she would go about this; on whom she might conceivably call to help her in this task; what consequences might flow as a result. But at this moment, none of this mattered. What mattered was salting away her emotions, salting away her weakness.

Arming herself for her life.

It was like this with her memories of – of violence (for even here she flinched at the prospect of naming) and of betrayal by Brendan: by the person she had a right to look to for succour, to love. Salt away her weakness, so that it could be retrieved, examined again as necessary – later, much later, when its potency was gone. Then she could look at it again – and remember again why protection must be the key to her life.

And arm herself too, armour herself so that she could never hurt anyone again.

For this is what had happened today. Anthony, who had liked her too much and who had been prepared to come and bring her away: Anthony was dead now. And this was her responsibility, was it not? Yes: it was her responsibility; and she knew she must make certain that she could never create such a situation again.

So she reasoned. Arm myself, armour myself – and nobody

else need ever get hurt again. Had she protected herself in the course of these last months – so she reasoned – nobody *would* have got hurt.

And she would dedicate these efforts to Cassie. After this, Sarah thought, my hands at least will be clean. Because she was clear about this: that what had nearly happened to Cassie too – it too had come about as a direct result of Sarah's own actions. She was clear about this; she was flinty when it came to her own culpability. Cassie did not take walks, by the sea or anywhere else; it was not something she ever did. So the fact that she was walking this morning – by the sea, on the beach – could be traced back and back. Back and back, Sarah thought: not only back to this morning but further and further back: on and on, and always involving me. She would protect herself from now on, and in doing so, she would protect those around her.

This was the resolution she made. This was the deal into which she entered, drawing now on the dense, reddish silence of the room for strength. There were additional advantages: by salting the past away in such a fashion, she need never look at it again unless there was good cause to do so. She need not drag it around behind her for the rest of her life. Distinct advantages, yes: she could see this, she could think clearly even at such a terrible time. She could cast off anything she needed to cast off – such as (she was honest enough to admit) the feelings of self-importance that seemed to arise, in spite of the efforts of her best self to damp them down. Self-importance? – well yes: because when the neighbours began to arrive, to enquire after Cassie, and bring the names of the dead, to drink tea and eat brack, it would be the grief of those bereaved, as well as the thrilling nature of the day's event on which they would want to dwell. That was where Sarah would come in – since Brendan hardly fitted the bill.

So yes: once this was over, she could salt away – right away – these feelings too. She could consign them to the darkness, where with a bit of luck she need never remember them again. She flushed with shame at these thoughts, though – and here she sat upright once again – at least they were honest ones.

She looked again across the room. Then, slowly, she stepped across the room, reached up, unhooked the second photograph from its large brass sickle-shaped hook driven into the wall and lifted it down, holding it by its length of rough twine. There they were, the three of them, the polished black mahogany chair. There was Cassie, looking into the distance. She slipped across the room once more and into their bedroom, where Cassie lay sleeping in the big bed. The room was stocked with Cassie's few possessions – the blanket in red and green plaid laid across the bottom of the bed, the solid trunk that she had brought with her from the Home, the St Brigid's Cross woven from rushes and pinned onto the wall. Sarah glanced at the sleeping figure in the bed: and now she glanced again at Cassie, and stole from the bedroom and returned to the main room. She took a cloth and dusted the photograph – its glass, its plain silver frame – until it shone, and replaced it on the wall beside its twin. Her grandparents, the boy who became her father, gazed at her: their faces, their chins tilted upwards. She looked back and then sat down in the silence. The coals hissed, settled in the hearth with a tiny sigh.

A matter of minutes later, the white lamps of the first visiting neighbours came bobbing down the lane.

FOURTEEN

Margaret was sitting with her back to the light. Her features Patrick could not make out; the edges of her silhouette, when he closed his eyelids and looked through his lashes, smeared and melded into a corona of yellow and white.

It must be midday or thereabouts: the sun was shining into the room, onto the waxy floor, the blue coverlet and those glossy yellowish walls. 'Shall I pull the curtains?' she'd said, and he had shaken his head and she sat and settled herself. And now here she was, backed and lit and obscured by the sun.

And his vision was going, besides. This was a stage, they had told him: the next stage. *The next stage* sounded as though a further stage might eventually be reached: a joyful stage, over Jordan, involving the return of his vision.

But no: hardly.

He knew better. His vision was going and was not coming back: Margaret would be blurred, regardless of where she sat.

'Move your chair a little,' he said.

She did this, angling the chair so that the sun now fell at an oblique. Now he could make out her face a little better: dark eyes and dark shadows and pale skin.

It had been the usual pattern, these last few weeks. He had kept her away, at arm's length – even while he longed for her to be there, the only visitor he ever wanted to see among armies of the eager unwanted, pressing their noses against the little porthole window, misting the glass with their breath, bustling about offering dreadful sympathy. His mother had visited yesterday. He had sent her away. 'Go away,' he said – and she went. With relief, he'd thought.

No: he wanted to see only his sister; and wanted only to shove her away.

The sunlight slipped, hard and white, between his eyelashes. Now the sand in the hourglass was running out.

He moistened his lips a little, moved a little in the bed. 'I thought I had all the time in the world,' he said. 'I thought I had time, that we all had time.'

Margaret nodded.

'This really stinks,' he said.

'I know.'

'I thought I had time to try to put things right. I didn't know I'd run out of time.' His voice grew feeble with these last words and he sank back into his pillows.

A nurse clipped in. 'Everything alright?'

Margaret nodded. 'Fine,' she said, 'thank you.'

'Tea'll be coming around in a few minutes,' the nurse said and smiled.

'Lovely,' Margaret said. 'Thanks.' The nurse left; and Margaret turned towards the blue bed once more.

They had spoken only once more about what happened to Christine Casey and her mother. A year or so later, a year or so ago: another chilly October day, and in Margaret's over-furnished living room, this time, rather than in some clattering cafe with ears wagging and eyes on the watch. Knowledge in this period had sat like a stone in his stomach. He felt weighed by this knowledge: its presence contaminated his days, his profession, his relationships. He saw how he was responding to its presence: by cultivating even more a sense of dryness, a desiccated air, that kept them at arm's length and that kept him safe.

And with the rest of the world, too: dry and papery, like autumn leaves. It had never been likely that he would meet someone, that he would have the chance to reconfigure his life to allow in heat and fluidity. The scales, already weighed against him, now seemed to topple over. No chance: the very idea seemed absurd; and now it was too late.

Because this is how it is with secrets. So he realised now. They stay intact – it is an easy matter to keep a secret, in spite of what people say: but the price is a deformation of the soul; and eventually, the secret will create a hollow which the soul had once inhabited. So Patrick told himself: he noted this in no time at all. Noted the change: and saw that there was no help for it.

This is how it would be.

This was the price that must be paid for protecting his sister.

There might have been time to set things right – but no: his story would not evolve in this way. It would barely evolve at all.

And the strange thing, he thought, was how naturally it came to him. It was as though he had been in training for such a scenario, his whole life long. As though the skills were there already, taught and honed and ready to be deployed. He knew how to keep the world around him at a distance, how to cultivate this tough, lacquered veneer, how to do what was necessary to maintain this situation.

Ironically, Margaret was less adept – and he was there, perched on her unyielding and over-contoured sofa on that October Saturday, because he had observed this lack of adeptness for himself. He drove to her house – a Sixties bungalow with steeply pitched roof, overgrown hedging, overgrown back garden – and parked on her quiet street. This had once been part of a far-flung suburb, but it was now well inside the city limits; he could hear the steady hum of Saturday traffic on the new road nearby. He rang the bell and Margaret admitted him and directed him, not to the kitchen, but to her good front room, with its excess of furniture.

Such seriousness, now, was part of the deal – though they did at least drink their tea from everyday mugs, and not from her good china. That would have been too much.

She had aged in the course of the last year. Perhaps Robert had aged too, but perhaps not: it was difficult to tell, what with his rangy frame and prominent bones. And besides, Patrick did not care to study this brother-in-law of his, did not care to look at him at all if he could help it.

He no longer cared to look at Margaret all that much either – but this was crucial. An untrained observer might have thought she looked better these days: her hair was shorter and lighter of shade; and she was lighter of frame too, trim and neat. 'I'd hardly recognise you these days,' he said, 'you look so changed.'

Margaret shrugged at that. 'I am changed.'

He kept his gaze on her. Lighter hair and a lighter frame – but less substantial, to his eye, already; more hollow. To his eye – yes, a replica of the being who eyed him, hollowed-out, in the bathroom mirror each morning. On the other hand, the colour of her hair suited her, and he could imagine people saying so: and why care about anything else?

'So,' she went on, tucking herself into a wide, spreading armchair, 'what brings you here?'

He had stopped calling in, though she refrained from making this point. He appreciated that.

'I wondered how you were,' he said. 'Last time I saw you, I didn't think you looked yourself.'

This was it, wasn't it? Margaret had ceased to look herself.

But she laughed at that. 'I don't think any of us do, really – do we? But there it is. And at least we're still alive, aren't we? How we look is neither here nor there, really: not in the face of the basic facts.' She paused for a moment. 'Is that why you're here? – to say that I look a little different?'

He shook his head.

'No,' she went on. 'You're here to make sure that I'm OK in the head. That the deal I struck with myself still holds. Yes:

325

well, it does.' She ran a hand over the velvet arm of her chair. 'I'm sorry I involved you: it was wrong of me, completely wrong. But,' paused – though not from delicacy, he thought; there was a touch of brutality, instead, 'you would have figured it out yourself, in the end. You would have winkled it out of me, wouldn't you?'

Brutal, yes – but Patrick nodded. Because it was true: he would have. He had worked this out himself, already; and in the face of it, he had less reason for these jangling feelings of bitterness and resentment. He felt these sensations, though, just the same. They were lodged, immoveable, they were going nowhere.

'So you don't need to worry about anyone blowing the whistle,' Margaret added. 'That won't happen.'

The sofa was terribly unyielding.

'What will happen instead?'

She shrugged – and now she looked at him, and he read again a terrible bleakness in her eyes.

'Nothing,' she said. 'We carry on living. Isn't that what we've always done?'

It was true. How many times had she pulled his head back into the air, into the light? How many times had she made sure that he carried on living?

And now look at us.

And that was that conversation.

Not so long ago, Patrick thought now, as he lay in his blue hospital bed. Not so long; and not long to go. For me. He watched his sister through virtually closed eyelids. And it's true: we've carried on living.

Although in my case, no. He smiled slightly and closed his eyes. No, not me. I've carried on dying.

'Do something for me.'

She stiffened a little. 'What?'

'Something difficult,' he said.

'Oh – Patrick –'

'– but not impossible.'

Margaret relaxed a little. 'Go on.'

'Just – make a little effort with her, that's all.' No need to name names. 'She is the way she is: and besides, you might need each other in the future.' Margaret stirred uneasily at that – well, he could see why, pregnant with potential meaning as those few little words were – and Patrick went on, speaking as clearly, as lucidly as the drugs and his dry mouth permitted. 'I mean, it'll just be the two of you left. You might need one another, that's all.'

From the expression on Margaret's face, it would seem that she rather doubted it. But still – circumstances being what they were, as Patrick well knew, she nodded, she agreed, she promised.

And when she left, Patrick waited a couple of minutes and then pressed the little red button on the end of the flex that would summon a nurse. When one arrived, with gratifying speed, he said, 'I need to speak to someone in the police.' She looked a little – startled, he noted, though 'instantly engaged' might be a better way of describing it. Well, let her look whatever way she wanted to look. 'Can you do that for me?'

When she left, bustling and squeaking out of the room, Patrick sank a little further into his pillows. Yes: this was right. The sands were running fast now in the hourglass – and besides, there was really no other decision he could make.

*

Five months later, late March of the following year – and Margaret and Sarah went walking again at Inch Levels. The winter just past had been damp and mild, with hardly a frost: and now the fields were beginning to respond to the sun again, and the hedgerows, tentatively, to swell and green. The ditches were brimming and the geese were already gone. The trial was scheduled for May, though of course it was understood that the verdict was already a foregone conclusion. Robert had gone mildly: his relief had been tangible.

The two women might have turned right, following the little river upstream through sparse woodland to the bridge and back: a short walk, avoiding the shingle beaches, the lough, the gaunt, ruined castle outlined on its little promontory. They might have: and in fact, there was a short pause as they stood there in the car park, a short pause as Margaret grasped her courage. A firm hold: white knuckles, she thought; and if the set of her mother's shoulders was anything to go by, she was feeling the same. And nobody, surely, would blame us if we turned right.

They turned left.

They walked slowly along the gravel track. Calm, white

skies and calm green fields. This is a good thing we're doing, Margaret thought: the right thing, a healthy thing.

But there was a self-consciousness to their walk. It showed in their gait, in their hands shoved into pockets, in a pattern of lifetimes that could not be overcome so easily, not just like that. Not easy, she thought: damn, it never will be easy. We're feeling our way, that's all. Trying to square up, she had thought, looking at herself in the bathroom mirror: and it'll take as long as it takes. And Patrick was right: it's just the two of us, now.

And there the sea wall ended, and the natural contours of the land took over, gathering themselves into the hills to the west; and there was the lough, the place where Christine Casey had been set on the ground and then pushed, shoved into the shallow water. A single posy of yellow daffodils, some muddy footprints: that was all, now. They hadn't brought flowers themselves: they hadn't brought anything except themselves – though this, surely, was the point. Wasn't it? – Margaret had thought that morning, considering herself in the bathroom mirror. Yes, it was: flowers, or any other offering, would have been – a shield, brandished, a defence of some kind.

Better to come naked, better to come as themselves.

'Do you remember coming here?' Sarah said, looking out at the water. 'A long time ago now? What, coming up on twenty years?'

'I remember.'

'Your brother was here, and Cassie.'

'I remember.'

'My head was full.'

Margaret paused and then said, 'None of it was your fault.'

'I know that, in my head. But,' and now Sarah breathed in deeply, a long and noisy breath through her nostrils, 'my heart tells me something else. It tells me that a lot of things have been my fault. So –'

'So –'

'So, be patient with me.'

Margaret said nothing.

'Please, be patient,' her mother repeated, and Margaret nodded.

'We might walk on,' she said, 'a bit further; make a longer walk of it.'

Sarah smiled a little. 'A longer walk,' she said, 'let's do that.'

So they struck out along the shingle, the two of them. The sky was lightening a little now, Margaret noticed: the disc of the sun was showing white, sailing behind thinning white clouds; and their shadows were falling away behind them as they walked.

AUTHOR'S NOTE

The scene in this novel in which a sea mine explodes on 'Shell Beach', is drawn directly from Irish wartime history. On 10 May 1943, a sea mine was observed by local people floating in shallow waters off Ballymanus beach, on Donegal's west coast. A crowd had gathered on the beach when the mine exploded, killing nineteen men and boys.

Although such an event could not be hidden – the blast killed a large proportion of the townland's male population; and it was heard across half the county – the Ballymanus disaster has never, for a variety of reasons, entered the popular consciousness in the way it ought to have done. Sixty years passed before an official memorial was established on the dunes above the beach.

The absorbing *Tubáiste Bhaile Mhánais* (directed by Keith O'Grady and produced by Westway Films in 2011 for BBC Northern Ireland) tells the story of the Ballymanus explosion. The film is recommended to readers with an interest in a secluded history.

ACKNOWLEDGEMENTS

I acknowledge with gratitude a Literature Bursary from An Chomhairle Ealaíon/The Arts Council of Ireland, which enabled the completion of this novel. Thanks are also due to the staffs of the National Library of Ireland; the Library of Trinity College Dublin; the Irish Studies Reading Room of Dublin City Libraries; the Museum and Heritage Service of Derry City Council; and the Central Library, Derry; and to the Director and staff of the Tyrone Guthrie Centre at Annaghmakerrig.

Impressions of historical Hampstead are borrowed from Penelope Fitzgerald's essay 'Well Walk', in *A House of Air* (Harper Perennial, 2003).

I'm grateful to Lucy Collins of University College Dublin for vital and generous comments at a critical moment; to Sarah Bannan, Stephen Faloon, Marie Gethins, Martina Kelly, Anne Mary Luttrell, Ruth McDonnell, Eina McHugh, Gary McKeone, John McManus, Niamh McManus, Caitríona O'Reilly, and Catherine Toal; and to Marja Almqvist, Bernie

Furlong, Eileen Kavanagh, Kathleen Murray, and Suzie Perry, for constructive and necessary feedback.

Thanks also to Maurice Walsh; to the splendid team at Head of Zeus, especially Georgina Blackwell, Richard Milbank, and in particular my editor Neil Belton; and to Véronique Baxter at David Higham Associates.

Love and thanks to my family: especially to my parents, Maureen and Charles Hegarty, and my aunt, Anne Farren, for sharing with me their childhood impressions of a distant Derry and Inishowen; and above all to my partner John Lovett, for encouraging this book over the line.

Neil Hegarty, 2016